STAND
OFF

Books by Andrew Smith

WINGER

STAND-OFF

STAND OFF

ANDREW SMITH

PENGUIN BOOKS

PENGUIN BOOKS

UK | USA | Canada | Ireland | Australia
India | New Zealand | South Africa

Penguin Books is part of the Penguin Random House group of companies
whose addresses can be found at global.penguinrandomhouse.com.

puffinbooks.com

First published in the USA by Simon & Schuster BFYR 2015
Published in Great Britain by Penguin Books 2015
001

Text copyright © Andrew Smith, 2015
Book design by Lucy Ruth Cummins
Illustrations copyright © Simon & Schuster, Inc., 2015

The moral right of the author and illustrator has been asserted

Set in Adobe Garamond Pro

A CIP catalogue record for this book is available from the British Library

ISBN: 978-0-141-35477-4

www.greenpenguin.co.uk

Printed and bound in Great Britain by Clays Ltd, St Ives plc

To my friend and editor, David Gale

ACKNOWLEDGMENTS

THERE ARE A MILLION THINGS THAT almost caused *Winger* to never happen, which naturally would have prevented *Stand-Off* from ever reaching the hands of readers as well. Fuck you, million things.

When *Winger* and I found a home at Simon & Schuster, Ryan Dean West and I had an awful lot of growing up to do. I still don't know if I look at myself as a "real writer," but I'm getting closer to that place, with much gratitude to all the people who have patiently supported and believed in my work along the way.

And as far as patience and kindness are concerned, you'd be hard pressed to find a man with a larger capacity for these qualities than David Gale, my editor, to whom I dedicate this book. Thank you, David.

Simon & Schuster's offices are in one of those monstrously big Manhattan skyscrapers. It would take hundreds of pages to list all the people there who worked on Ryan Dean West's team, but I am so grateful to every one of you. The first time I met Justin Chanda, just after he'd read *Winger*, he took me aside and told me how much he loved the book. That encouragement had such an impact on me, but it still didn't make me quite feel like a "real writer." Thank you, Justin. Lucy Ruth Cummins, who has designed all my covers at Simon &

Schuster, is such a bright, glowing soul with an amazing power to give off smiles no matter what kind of mood you're in. Thank you, Lucy, for just being you. And Liz Kossnar put so much work into *Stand-Off* for us, despite having to exercise her patience due to how slow I was in finally turning it in.

But I had a lot of fun writing it. I'm going to miss all that private time I got to spend with Ryan Dean West, Nico, and Sam Abernathy, whom I now have to set free and allow to go off on their own.

I also need to thank all the readers who fell in love with *Winger*. Talk about patience! It was a long haul between *Winger* and *Stand-Off*, and you managed to hang in there. I hope this is an adequate payoff for your efforts.

As always, great thanks to my friend and agent Michael Bourret. I know I don't bother you as much as I should, but I'm really working on being more clingy and high-maintenance. Hopefully, uncontrollable weeping will occur.

And finally, I could never do any of this if my wife Jocelyn, son Trevin, and daughter Chiara ever refused to put up with me. I sometimes marvel at their tolerance, and I love them very much.

amicus certus in re incerta temporum cernitur

the abernathy

PROLOGUE

EVERYONE KEPT TELLING ME, "YOU need to draw again, Ryan Dean. You need to draw. . . ."

So I did.

I started drawing again in the summer before Annie and I went back to Pine Mountain for our senior year. The problem is, I'm pretty sure I didn't draw what everyone expected.

Let me explain.

Annie Altman, the most beautiful and together girl on the planet, an undeniable five out of five Swiss Army knives on the Ryan Dean West If-You-Could-Only-Have-One-Thing-When-You're-Stranded-with-Nothing-Not-Even-Your-Clothes-on-a-Deserted-Island-What-Would-It-Be Scale, happened to be on an island with me, but it wasn't deserted, so decency laws required us at the very least to have our swimsuits on. And I didn't have a Swiss Army knife either, which would have come in handy because neither one of us remembered to put any utensils in our picnic basket, so we had to eat my mom's potato salad with our fingers, which—*ugh!*—I thought was kind of sexy when our fingers touched in the cold mayonnaisey mush. But at least I had Annie, and we both had our swimsuits, and it was August, on one of those rare crystal-clear windless afternoons in Boston Harbor.

We spent the day at the beach on Spectacle Island, lying next to each other on a blanket in the sand. Naturally, I couldn't help but think about how there was only one thin article of clothing on my body; and how Annie and I were so close, our hands and feet touched, and I could feel her electricity sending sparks right up through me.

But I couldn't help thinking about a lot of other things too: about going back to Pine Mountain in a week, about how tough last year had been on me, and about the likely impossibility of me surviving my senior year there.

Annie put her hand on my belly and rubbed.

"You have to know how crazy that makes me, Annie."

"I do?"

"In about five seconds, I don't think I'll be held legally responsible for my actions."

Annie laughed. "Calm down, Ryan Dean. I was only trying to get the potato salad smell off my fingers."

"Oh. Nice. Ryan Dean West, fifteen-year-old human napkin."

Annie lived on Bainbridge Island, in Washington. It meant a lot that her parents trusted us enough to let her come to Boston to spend the last whole week of summer vacation with me before we had to report back to Pine Mountain Academy. But it wasn't like anything was going to happen, right? Annie was seventeen, and so beautiful. And I was just a fifteen-year-old napkin-boy who couldn't shake the feeling that something terrible was going to come out of nowhere and ruin everything for me again and again.

Drawing, for me, was like Pine Mountain Academy: I wanted to go back to it, and I also didn't want to go back.

CHAPTER ONE

OKAY. YOU KNOW HOW WHEN YOU'RE a senior in high school, and you officially know absolutely everything about everything and no one can tell you different, but on the other hand, at the same time, you're dumber than a poorly translated instruction manual for a spoon?

Yeah. That was pretty much me, all at the same time, the only fifteen-year-old boy to ever be in twelfth grade at Pine Mountain Academy.

When you're a senior, you're supposed to walk around with your chest out and your shoulders back because it's like you own the place, right? I didn't feel that way. In fact, from the first day I got back to Pine Mountain, I was quietly considering flunking out of all my classes so I wouldn't have to move on with my life and be a sixteen-year-old grown-up.

What a bunch of bullshit that would undoubtedly be.

And, speaking of bullshit, the day I came back to Pine Mountain Academy to check in and register, I learned that I would be rooming—in a double-single room no less—with some random kid I didn't even know. It had somehow failed to sink in to my soiled-napkin brain that my last year's roommates, Chas Becker and Kevin Cantrell, had graduated from Pine Mountain and moved on to the fertile breeding grounds of adulthood, leaving me roommateless, condemned to a single-size room with two beds in it, and matched up with Joe Randomkid, whom I'd already pictured as some bloated, tobacco-chewing, overalls-wearing midwesterner who was missing half a finger from a lawn-mowing or wheat-threshing accident and owned a vast collection of '70s porn mags (since we weren't allowed to access the Internet at PM and look at real porn like most teenagers do).

Not that I look at porn, like most *normal* teenagers. I'm not like that.

But nine-and-a-half-fingered Joe Randomkid would be exactly like that, I decided.

So by the time I turned the key on my all-new, 130-square-foot boys' dorm prison cell with two twin beds, two coffin-size closets, and matching elementary-school-kid-style desks with identical 40-watt desk lamps, I already deeply hated Joe Randomkid and, at the same time, had no idea in the world who he was.

Even before I fully opened the door on our bottom-floor-which-is-usually-only-reserved-for-freshmen dorm room, I had pretty much everything about Joe Randomkid all figured out.

Joe Randomkid Ruins Twelfth Grade: A Play by Ryan Dean West

SCENE: *A very small ground-floor room in the boys' dorm at Pine Mountain Academy, a prestigious prep school for future deviants and white-collar criminals, located in the Cascades of Oregon.* JOE RANDOMKID, *a chubby and pale redhead from Nebraska with a stalk of straw pinched between his lips, is lying with his hands behind his head, dressed in overalls (with no shirt underneath the bib) and work boots, on one of the two prison-size twin beds, as* RYAN DEAN WEST, *a skinny, Bostonian, rugby-playing fifteen-year-old upperclassman, enters the room from the outer hallway.*

JOE RANDOMKID: Howdy! The name's Joe. Joe Randomkid. I'm from Nebraska, and my pa's a hog farmer. We have, I reckon, close to twenty-two-hundred hogs on the farm, give or take a few depending on how hungry me and my brothers are. I have ten brothers! And no sisters! Can you imagine that? Ten of them! Their names are Billy, Wayne, Charlie, Alvin, Edmund, Donny, Timothy, Michael, Eugene, and Barry, and then there's me, Joe. How come I ain't ever seen you around? Are you a new kid? I been here every year since ninth grade, but you look like you're just a kid who can't possibly be old enough to be in twelfth grade. What sport do you play? Me? I'm on the bowling team. Got a two-oh-four average, which is number one in the state in Nebraska and Oregon for twelfth-grade boys. I bet being all skinny like that, you're on swim team or maybe gymnastics. Or do you cheer? Are you one of those *boy cheerleaders*? I don't think there's nothing wrong with that at all. Cheerleading's probably more of a sport than NASCAR is anyhow. Who's your favorite driver, by the way?

Are you one of them ones who get to pick up the girls and spin them around over your head like that? If I ever did that, I couldn't help but look up their skirts, am I right? Or do you not like girls and stuff? 'Cause if you don't, that's okay too. I realize it takes all kinds. All kinds. And maybe you're from California, after all.

RYAN DEAN WEST: (*Ryan Dean West walks across the room and looks out the window.*) Now I know why they put me on the ground floor.

The End

Mom and Dad had helped me move in this time. It was weird. All the other times they'd dropped me off at Pine Mountain, it was like they couldn't possibly leave fast enough.

Dad carried in my two plastic totes. One of them contained all my clothes and boy stuff—you know, deodorant and the razor Dad sent me last fall that was still as unnecessary as ever—and the other had school supplies, some brand new bedsheets, and a microwave oven, which I had no idea why they'd insisted I bring along. I lugged in the big canvas duffel bag filled with all my rugby gear that was soon to be packed away in my locker over at the sports complex.

I wanted to play rugby again almost as much as I wanted to see Annie, whom I hadn't seen since she left Boston for Seattle five days before.

And—*ugh!*—Mom cried when she put my new sheets on the exceedingly gross, slept-on-countless-times-before, yellowing boys' dorm twin-size fucking mattress, and I just stood there, helplessly giving my dad a *what-the-fuck* look. He shrugged.

At home in Boston, I had a big bed. I'm not sure where my Boston bed fit in on the hierarchy of royalty—you know, queens and kings and such—but it was easily twice as big as a twin, if this thing even *was* an actual twin. It was probably a preemie or something—the afterbirth of a twin. So we'd had to stop at a department store in this little town called Bannock, which is about twenty minutes from Pine Mountain, to get some sheets, and the only ones they had that would fit my dorm bed following the incoming rush of PM brats were pink flannel and decorated with a winged unicorn who, according to the inscription beneath her glinting hooves, was named *Princess Snugglewarm*.

Yeah. It was going to be a great year, wasn't it?

"Why are you crying, Mom? Don't worry about the unicorns. We can hide them beneath the blanket. I checked. It only has Princess Snugglewarm on one side, so we can flip it over so it only looks a little gay," I said.

Mom sniffled. "Oh, Ryan Dean. It's not that, baby. There's only so many more times left in our lives when I'll be able to put sheets on your bed and tuck you in."

This coming from the woman who wept when she bought me a box of condoms because she actually thought Annie and I were having sex—like that was ever going to happen—when I was fourteen.

It was hopeless.

And not only do horses with big fucking spikes coming out of their heads scare me, but I hate flannel sheets besides.

CHAPTER TWO

JOE RANDOMKID TURNED OUT TO BE
named Sam Abernathy.

It had to be a fake name. Nobody in the world could possibly be
named *Sam Abernathy*.

I realized that every time I'd been dropped off for the start of
school at Pine Mountain Academy, there came the predictable and
awful dread of wanting my parents to just get the hell out of there so
I could mope for a while in the quiet of my mold-and-disinfectant-
smelling room. And each time, I'd wonder why in the name of hell I
was here to begin with, and convince myself that I was not going to
be able to make it through an entire school year on my own, alone.

That's what I was doing: lying on my little pink bed in my
ID-photo school tie, button-down shirt, and creased slacks, moping
and frightening myself with visions of a dreadful future here, when
Sam Abernathy—well, to be honest, it was Sam and the entire fucking Abernathy clan—knocked on my dorm room's door.

And who knocks, anyway? You don't knock on the door to your
own dorm room. It wasn't like they didn't give Sam Abernathy a key
to Princess Snugglewarm's 130-square-foot empire.

So, thinking it was someone else, and not my new roommate, Joe
Randomkid, I ignored the knock and resumed my pout session.

Thirty seconds later: *knock knock knock!*

For just a minute, I thought that maybe it was Annie. But there was no way Annie Altman would ever break a rule like no-girls-allowed-in-the-boys'-dorm at Pine Mountain Academy, even if it would have been a highly combustible five out of five propane tanks in a campfire on the Ryan Dean West Scale of Hot Things You Are Never Supposed to Do.

Ugh! I wanted to go home already, and I wanted Annie, too. And I felt like such a pathetic loser for forgetting to register my dorm preference and ending up in a ground-floor double with someone who undoubtedly was a match in every degree to my colossal loserdom.

Knock knock knock!

"Go away."

Through the door came a very soft voice that could easily have belonged to one of Princess Snugglewarm's loyal subjects—maybe a royal eunuch or something.

"Uh. But I'm supposed to live here."

"Then why the fuck are you knocking?"

Okay. To be honest, I didn't say "fuck." I never cuss out loud. Well, I can't say *never*, but, really, it's like *almost never*. And it didn't happen that day before the start of school as I lay on my less-than-twin-size Princess Snugglewarm bed, pouting and listening to Joe Randomkid, a.k.a. Sam Abernathy, timidly and patiently knocking on his own goddamned front door.

Click. Squeak. Creak.

The door cracked open, just about two inches. I saw a flash of a Pine Mountain necktie and an eyeball. It was human, I'm pretty sure. Then the door closed again, and I heard this:

TIMID VOICE IN THE HALLWAY: He . . . he's in bed.

MAN'S VOICE IN THE HALLWAY: Maybe we should wait out here for a while.

WOMAN'S VOICE IN THE HALLWAY: What's he doing?

TIMID VOICE IN THE HALLWAY: I don't know. I didn't really look. All I know is he's in bed.

LITTLE BOY'S VOICE IN THE HALLWAY: Is he naked?

LITTLE GIRL'S VOICE IN THE HALLWAY: Eww. Boys are so gross.

WOMAN'S VOICE IN THE HALLWAY: Maybe letting Sam room with a twelfth-grader, even if he *is* only fifteen, wasn't such a good idea after all, Dave.

MAN'S VOICE IN THE HALLWAY: Honey, why don't you take Evie out to the car? The boys and I can wait here till Sam's roommate wakes up or puts some clothes on or whatever.

And, at precisely that moment, I was wondering if I could figure out a way to turn a microwave oven into a bomb.

You can do that, right? If anyone would know how to turn a microwave oven into an explosive, it would be my friend Seanie Flaherty, assuming he was still my friend after the separation of summer vacation, and after the fights I'd gotten into last year with

JP Tureau, who was Seanie's roommate and my decidedly ex-friend.

I pulled the door open.

"I'm not naked, and I wasn't asleep, and it's your room, so I'm assuming you probably possess your very own key, which is why you will never be allowed to knock again."

I'll admit I was a little edgy, and the Abernathy clan looked as though I'd slapped each one of them across the face with a dead cod or something. They were all so nice looking, like if they had wings, you would swear you were looking at a family of angels: father, mother, two angelic, big-eyed, blond-headed sons, one of whom was dressed in a perfect Pine Mountain boy's uniform, and a little daughter who looked like the poster child for all things pure and scented of baby powder.

Mr. Abernathy, being the brave cod-slapped angel that he was, forced a contrived smile at me and said, "Sam, this must be your roommate, Ryan."

To be honest, I didn't know where to begin. Initially, I wanted to launch into a scolding tirade about my name *not being goddamned Ryan*, that it was Ryan Dean and I hated it when people took it upon themselves to assume the appropriateness of an abbreviation, but I was momentarily overcome by the realization that Sam Abernathy—Joe Randomkid—was only twelve years old.

And he was going to be my roommate this year.

Princess Snugglewarm, save me!

CHAPTER THREE

I FOUND OUT THAT THE IDEA BEHIND pairing me up for the year with Sam Abernathy came from the headmaster himself, Mr. Lavoie, and the school psychologist, Mrs. Dvorak. The Abernathy Tabernacle Choir was concerned about having their supergenius kid start Pine Mountain at the tender age of twelve, so Mr. Lavoie and Mrs. Dvorak thought it would be a perfect plan to room the boy up with the only other person in the history of Pine Mountain Academy who'd ever done such a ridiculous thing: a really nice, comic-drawing, supersmart, rugby-player boy from Boston named Ryan Dean West, who was a senior, and only fifteen years old.

Ryan Dean West could show little Sam the ropes, Headmaster Lavoie promised!

Ugh.

I felt like I'd been signed up against my will on one of those creepy online dating sites and I had no power to refuse my suitor.

And, by the way, did I look that small when I was a twelve-year-old freshman here?

Sam Abernathy could have fit in my pocket.

No wonder Annie felt sorry for me back then. They might just as well have left Sam Abernathy in a diaper inside a wicker basket on my doorstep. Or a cigar box.

I did *not* want to do this.

My quiet pouting turned to silent rage after all the Abernathys crowded into our tiny princessdom and began setting up Sam's closet and desk and making his bed and folding his little outfits. I decided I wasn't going to say a word to them, not even when Sam Abernathy's four-year-old brother, Dylan (which, by the way, is an annoyingly perfect name for a little kid who looks like one of the babies—take your pick—in Raphael's *The Madonna of the Goldfinch*) climbed up on my bed—*my bed!*—and sat down beside me and asked me if I wanted to make a fort with my blanket.

Ignoring a four-year-old is as good as granting full consent.

"Princess Snugglewarm!" Dylan gurgled as he tugged away the top layer of my fucking bed.

Everything in the room went deathly silent.

All ten Abernathy eyes fixed on me with congruent expressions of wonder and acceptance.

I was one with all things Abernathy.

"Oh, you boys are going to be such good friends!" Mrs. Abernathy cooed as she unfolded and spread out Sam Abernathy's Super Mario Bros. sheets.

I made a mental note to myself that as soon as I got back from Headmaster Lavoie's office to petition for an impossible-to-get dorm assignment change, I was going to hunt down Seanie Flaherty and ask him if he knew how to make a microwave oven explode.

So I left without saying anything, certain that when I came back I'd find an elaborate live-action camping diorama set up on the floor between our beds, complete with campfire-singing Abernathys, toasted s'mores, and swarms of lightning bugs and mosquitos.

Okay. Well, you know how when you're storming over to some important person's office in order to voice an outraged yet well-deserved complaint peppered with the adverb-adjective double combo of "completely unacceptable" and then as you get closer and closer to that important person's office you begin to realize that (1) you're actually afraid of that important person—in this case, Headmaster Lavoie—and (2) you don't really know how to pronounce his last name because you've only ever seen it written on official letters from his office of importance, and nobody ever says his name out loud, which makes you think he could quite possibly be some unearthly manifestation of the Dark Lord, and (3) your armpits are sweating a lot (hello, being fifteen years old!) and you have really bad B.O., so you start walking slower and slower and then just about the time the administration offices come into view and you're halfway around the goddamned lake you suddenly realize there could be nothing in the world worse than starting off the year—no, negative year, since the year hadn't officially begun—by getting into a complaint match with someone who frightens you *and* whose name you can't pronounce, so you decide to give up and turn your stinky sweaty self back in the direction you came from?

Yeah.

That.

So I stopped and I thought about all the terrible things that had happened to me last year, and tried to erase the nagging premonition that I was fooling myself if I didn't think this year was going to be even worse. I took a deep breath.

I sat down on a bench and faced out across the lake to the spot in the woods where O-Hall, the "bad kids" dorm they put me in last year, sat abandoned and shut down.

Why did I come back?

I put my face in my hands.

I decided a long time ago that I was never going to cry again. Never. So I just sat there, trying to zone out, seeing if I couldn't just fall asleep, so maybe I would wake up and find out that everything had been a dream and I was fourteen still, or even thirteen again, so things wouldn't be as bleak as they were now in Ryan Dean West's fifteen-year-old nightmare.

"Dude. Winger? Ryan Dean?"

I snapped my head up and turned around. Sean Russell Flaherty and Jean-Paul Tureau had been standing there on the walk, watching me. They must have just come out of the registration lines in the admin building.

I got up. I really didn't want Seanie and JP to think I was still feeling sorry for myself.

"Holy crap!" Seanie said. "Dude. You're, like, taller than me."

He was right. Growing is something about which you don't have any say-so when you're a teenage boy, and my body had stretched out another three inches of vertical over the summer.

"Maybe he'll go out for basketball this year," JP, always glum, always digging at me, added.

That's all right, JP, I thought.

"Actually, I'm considering going out for number fifteen," I said, and smiled.

Fifteen in rugby is fullback, which was JP's position. I wasn't crazy enough to want to ever be fullback, which is the worst position on the field besides hooker, which isn't what you think, okay? But if JP wanted to start the year off hurling shitballs at me, he was going to get them right back.

JP extracted an insincere laugh and stuck out his hand. It's a rugby thing—we all shook hands. We had to. Rules persist on and off the field when you play rugby at PM. That was all there was to it.

So maybe I'd misjudged JP's intent. Maybe we actually could be friends again.

Seanie grabbed my biceps and rubbed.

"Damn, Ryan Dean, you're hot. If JP wasn't the jealous type, I'd put my tongue in your mouth right now."

That was Seanie Flaherty, in all his creepy deadpan weirdness. He never changed.

"You two still rooming together?" I asked.

We started walking back along the lake in the direction of the boys' dorm, Seanie, as always, between me and JP.

Seanie said, "Yeah. Who are you with this year?"

"You wouldn't believe it. I'm in a ground-floor double single. With a freshman named Sam Abernathy."

"You're fucking kidding me," Seanie said.

I shook my head. "And the kid's *twelve years old*."

"No shit?"

JP chuckled. "Ryan Dean West the Second. That's a roommate match made in heaven. I hope you're prepared to deal with all the Calculus homework, the kid's separation-anxiety nightmares, and him pissing the bed."

To be honest, it wasn't Sam Abernathy's nightmares I was worried about.

And where did dumbass JP ever learn a concept like *separation anxiety*?

CHAPTER FOUR

I SAID A QUICK GOOD-BYE TO SEANIE and JP in front of the registration office and let them go back to their two-room suite on the top floor of the boys' dorm.

Telling them that I wanted to wait around for Annie to come through was an opportunity for me to get one last nothing-he-could-do-about-it dig at JP, who'd tried to hook up with Annie last year. But he lost. To me. And losing out in a competition for the most amazing girl at Pine Mountain Academy to another boy who's two years younger was something JP Tureau's ego still could not accept.

In fact, I'm sure JP had somehow convinced himself that Annie had a deep-rooted psychiatric illness that made her unable to accurately process reality, or maybe he attributed it to her having some bullshit issues with *separation anxiety*.

Whatever it was, JP Tureau was going to have an awfully long year of being forced to put up with seeing me and Annie Altman together.

I felt like this tremendous weight had been lifted from my chest—although my armpits were still dripping like twin condenser coils on a moonshine still—when Annie Altman, gleaming her perfect eyes and that beautiful smile, came out of the registration office, waving her papers at me like she was maybe afraid I wouldn't notice her.

But it was Annie, and I couldn't possibly notice anything else.

Well, except I noticed how goddamned sweaty I was in every spot on my body that had hair on it and that was also located south of my hairless chin.

We have this thing—Annie and I—where we'll just look at each other for a while before either of us says anything. We never planned this routine, but I think we both understood that we didn't need to nervously rush into saying just *anything*, like so many other uptight couples do. Because sometimes words can wreck all the other things that actually go on between us in those beautiful, rich, and silent moments.

It didn't matter that Annie was probably thinking about what she was going to wear to the Pine Mountain homecoming dance, focusing on some messed-up or crooked patch of hair on my head, or silently extending a conversation we had four months ago because there was some point she still needed to make (and why do girls do this?) that would probably result in a random outburst of a contextually anchorless exclamation like "because you'd never have enough electricity to do that, Ryan Dean," and I'd be all, like, *what the fuck are you even talking about?* Except I wouldn't actually say "fuck"; and I was probably—okay, I'll admit it, *not* probably, I *was*—thinking about how fun it would be to talk Annie Altman into swimming naked with me in the creek below Buzzard's Roost, the place up the mountain we run to every year on the day before school starts, which meant we could be there and out of our clothes and in the icy water naked together within an hour if we hurried. But, yeah, none of that mattered, because I was here, and so was Annie.

I inhaled through my nose and tried to catch a hint of Annie's perfume, but I only smelled fifteen-year-old boy, which made me gag just a little bit.

"I missed you so much when you left Boston," I said.

Annie knitted her fingers through mine and we walked along the lake.

"Sorry if I smell like an airplane toilet mixed with B.O., Annie. It's really hot today." (And I had been on a plane pretty much all day. Also, thinking about swimming naked in the creek with Annie definitely kicked up the moisture output.)

Annie laughed. She looked around quickly. I knew what that meant. We got a one-second kiss in. Kids at Pine Mountain are not allowed to kiss each other in broad daylight. Well, actually, kids at Pine Mountain are not allowed to kiss at all.

It's a pretty uptight school, considering all those no-kissing, no-girls-in-boys'-dorm-rooms, and no-cellphone rules and such.

"I think you smell like home," Annie said.

Sweat. Sweat. Sweat.

I licked my lips. "In that case, I'm sorry your house smells like gross boy smell."

"Maybe we have time to tear off each other's clothes and have sex before dinner," Annie said.

Okay. I'll be honest. Annie actually said "go for a run" in the part where my brain wanted to hear her say "tear off each other's clothes and have sex."

I wish my brain would stop doing that. One of these days, Annie was going to actually ask if I wanted to "tear off each other's clothes and have sex" and then I'd dash away and grab my running shoes, because that's pretty much exactly how much of a loser I have always been.

But settling for just the go-for-a-run part of Annie's proposition was exactly what smelly, sweaty, mopey, jet-lagged kid who wanted to go skinny-dipping needed before dinner. Besides, I couldn't wait to see if everything was still the same—all our running trails, the meeting place we called Stonehenge that we'd made in the woods, and, well, how much water was in the creek, and if it was warm enough for swimming.

I guess it's an unreasonable expectation, isn't it? Everything changes, constantly. I learned that lesson the hard way.

"I met my roommate," I said.

Annie asked, "Is he a rugby guy?"

That was funny. I had to laugh.

Sam Abernathy wasn't big enough to be the ball.

"Actually, I came down here intending to petition the headmaster—how do you say his name?—to switch my dorm assignment, but then I chickened out."

"Yeah. How *do* you say his name?" Annie asked.

"Sam Abernathy," I answered.

"Your roommate?"

I nodded.

"I never heard of him. Is he a new kid?"

"Brand new," I said. "Newer than new. He's a freshman."

"Why would they put you with a freshman?"

"It's worse than that. He's not *just* a freshman. He's a freshman who's twelve years old."

Annie got this wide-eyed look of understanding. She nodded and said, "Oh . . ."

"Yeah. Oh. Right? It's not fair. They can't expect me to help the kid out. He can survive on his own, just like I did."

"You survived on your own?" Annie said.

I never would have made it through ninth grade if it hadn't been for Annie's friendship. Not tenth or eleventh, either, for that matter.

We stopped at the T in the path, where it branched off into "boy" direction and "girl" direction to safely segregate the dorms with wide banks of shrubs we called the DGZ, the De-Genderized Zone.

"Well, it's my senior year. I don't want a little-kid roommate. I want to have fun. It's not fair."

"Wow. Just listen to you, Ryan Dean."

I felt my naked ears turn red.

"Oh. Sorry."

"It will be good for both of you, Ryan Dean," Annie said. "You remember what it was like when you first started here, don't you? You were so scared."

"I've blanked it from my memory," I said.

"Well, that poor boy. I can't wait to meet him. I bet he's adorable."

Ugh.

Annie Altman had a powerful mommy drive, I thought.

"I'll draw you a Sam Abernathy comic," I offered.

"Good. It's about time you showed me something again."

"That's a very perverted thing for you to say, Annie. Maybe you should wait till we get up to the creek."

Annie laughed and pushed me away from her and said, "Meet me back here in ten minutes, okay, West?"

So.

I almost felt the urge to knock on *my own* door when I got back to our dorm room, but Sam Abernathy was definitely *not* going to make knocking on doors become *a thing* that would define our relationship from day one forward.

I took a deep breath and braced myself for the ungodly things I might see on the other side of my door: a congregation of Abernathys singing hymns over an autoharp, or maybe they'd finally gone home to wherever their gene pool had settled and I was about to walk in on a twelve-year-old boy doing something really awkward and embarrassing like twelve-year-old boys tend to do if you leave them alone for long enough, which is probably about forty-five seconds, but I wouldn't know anything about that, considering I'd already erased all twelve-year-old memories from my head.

The Abernathy population inside my dorm room had been reduced to one.

At least someone had bothered to make my bed after the four-year-old exposed my unicorns.

Sam Abernathy, all properly angelic in his Pine Mountain Academy tie and blazer, sat on the edge of his bed and stared across the floor to what I could only estimate was the little black gap beneath my bed. Maybe he was afraid of monsters hiding under there, or the other things you get scared of when you should still be in elementary school.

"Hi," Sam Abernathy said.

"Hello."

I unknotted my tie and pulled off my sweaty shirt and tossed them onto my bed.

Unlike O-Hall, where boys had to keep things perfectly neat at all times, here in the regular dorms guys were allowed to be as sloppy as their roommates could stand. And since it was clear to me from the moment I set eyes on Sam Abernathy that he was not going to have a say in the matter, I'd already pretty much decided to mess this place up beyond recognition as quickly as possible.

While I was gone, Sam Abernathy had also taken it upon himself to raise the blinds and open our window, which made living on the ground floor like some kind of ongoing performance art for all the kids walking around the campus. I glared at the Abernathy and pulled down the blinds.

I kicked my shoes into the monster gap beneath my bed and slipped off my Pine Mountain boy's uniform trousers.

"Are you just going to take off your clothes right here? Right in front of me, Ryan?" Sam asked. The kid's cheeks looked like strawberry ice cream.

I balled up my pants and tossed them on the floor at the foot of my pink bed. So far, the mess was looking pretty . . . um . . . messy, or something. I let out a dramatic sigh and faced the kid, putting my hands on my hips and sticking out my chest, so I'd look authoritarian, which is kind of hard to pull off when you're just standing there in nothing but socks and briefs.

"Look," I said. "Two things: First, my name is *not* Ryan. My name is Ryan Dean. Not Ryan. I hate it when people call me Ryan, so don't do it."

"Oh. Sorry. Ryan Dean."

Sam Abernathy squirmed a little. His bed squeaked. Maybe Sam farted. It sounded like a chew toy for a puppy, which is exactly how I would imagine a little kid like Sam Abernathy's farts would sound.

"And second," I said, "this is a dorm room. It did not come equipped with separate changing facilities. If you haven't noticed yet, the doorknob inside our bathroom pokes you in the back when you stand up to pee. Get used to it. I'm gross. You're gross. And there's no room here. Living in a dorm room the size of my closet back home with another guy is goddamned disgustingly gross."

Okay, I'll admit I did not say "goddamned" to Sam Abernathy. A word like that from an angry naked guy could break a kid as innocent as Sam Abernathy.

Sam Abernathy didn't say anything. He just sat on his bed in front of a pile of textbooks and school papers, staring at me.

God! He had actually already started reading the textbooks for his classes.

I hopped from foot to foot and dropped my socks and then my underwear onto the floor. I got into my running shorts and tank top, then slipped my bare feet into my trail-runner shoes and headed for the door. As I shut it behind me, Sam Abernathy said something, but I wasn't paying attention to him.

I did glance back for a second, though, just to catch a glimpse of the mess I'd left behind.

I felt virile and godlike—and angry, too—like a senior should.

CHAPTER FIVE

BUT THEN THERE WAS THIS. ALWAYS THIS.

CHAPTER SIX

ANNIE AND I WENT ON OUR USUAL Buzzard's Roost run that afternoon. I kept trying to notice if things were different now, but everything around Pine Mountain seemed to have been stuck in a sort of suspended animation since last year. Annie and I kissed at the top of the mountain. The day was clear enough that we could see the ocean.

And I wasn't joking when I asked Annie if she wanted to go swimming naked in the creek with me, but when she didn't answer I took it as a sort of challenge. So I told her, "Okay, Annie. I am not joking. You and me. Naked swimming is totally going to happen one day before we graduate out of this place."

And later at dinner, Annie wasn't joking about the comic I'd drawn either.

Annie had a serious, but very hot, about-to-scold-me look in her eyes.

"Were you really this mean to him?"

I'd given her my "Meet My Roommate: Sam Abernathy" comic as we sat in the crowded and buzzing cafeteria for dinner together. It was the first time I'd shown Annie one of my drawings since my friend Joey died the year before.

I wagged a french fry at her like a potato finger of correction. "I wasn't *that* mean to him. Just *sort of* mean."

"Sort of?"

"Yeah. Like, not too much. Kind of like a you-don't-want-to-cuddle-with-a-smelly-cat mean. That's all."

Annie avoided making eye contact. That's what she did when she was disappointed. I instantly felt like shit.

She said, "You, of all people, should be ashamed of yourself, Ryan Dean."

The bite of fry I just swallowed seemed to balloon to the size of a porpoise in my throat.

"I . . ."

"And what's *this*?"

Annie put her fingertip on the dark figure I'd drawn clawing his way into our room through the open window.

"Oh. Him? He's Nate. Just someone I draw now," I lied.

It was a lie, because Nate wasn't *just someone I drew*. I couldn't get away from him. He was everywhere, and he made himself appear in everything I drew or daydreamed about. It was inevitable that Nate—the *Next Accidental Terrible Experience*—would catch me again and again.

Wasn't it?

Annie shook her head. Her hair danced. It was hot, the way she could do that. Then she stared at me and I could see her eyes getting wetter. Annie folded my comic and slipped it into her bag. Neither of us said anything.

When we finished eating and put away our trays and stuff, Annie took me by the hand and walked me over to the freshmen's side of the cafeteria.

She said, "I want you to introduce me to your roommate."

"Sam Abernathy?"

"Yes. Sam Abernathy."

"Well, he might be hard to find. He's really small. We might have to get down on our hands and knees."

"Stop being mean," Annie said.

I was confused. I didn't think I was being mean.

As we threaded our way through the tables of ninth graders, all these sets of little eyes fixed warily on us, as though they expected some major and humiliating act of hazing to initiate them into Pine Mountain.

Now I knew how sharks felt when they cruised through massive schools of mackerel.

But Sam Abernathy wasn't among the fry.

It wasn't like I was keeping tabs on the kid, anyway. He could easily have come, eaten, and gone without ever being noticed.

"The Abernathy fish stick is not here," I said. "He's probably asleep inside his Poké ball or something."

"Oh, stop it, Ryan Dean," Annie said. But she was smiling, too.

We walked slowly back toward the De-Genderized Zone between the dorms. I was so tired, but I didn't want to say good night to Annie and then have to be alone, far from home, in a room with a stranger. Because I'd never really been alone since Joey died. I always had people I knew—my friends—to stay with. Now it was as though everything was new, changed, and I didn't really want things to be like that.

And why does that last night of summer, on the day before school starts, always have to be so goddamned depressing?

We stopped at the T in the walk.

"You think something bad's going to happen, don't you?" Annie said.

I shrugged.

"Do you want to talk about it?"

"I guess we are," I said.

"I mean talk to *somebody* about it. Maybe my mom."

I kind of lit up at the thought of visiting Annie's house again. Her mom was a psychologist, and she'd helped me out more than I can say after Joey died. But I didn't want to talk about it anymore.

And I could feel Nate watching me, hidden in the dark thorny hedge that separated the dorms. I felt dizzy and sick, like I was about to fall off the ledge of a skyscraper, worried that something bad was going to happen to Annie.

I leaned close to her—so close, our bodies touched, and I

thought about duct-taping Sam Abernathy inside a desk drawer and sneaking Annie into my dorm room so we could mess up Princess Snugglewarm together.

I shook my head. "I don't need to talk to anyone, Annie. I'll stop drawing that guy if it bothers you. I just . . . I . . ."

And when I put my lips to hers, a flashlight beam splashed onto our faces.

"Hey! That's enough of that, you two!"

It was Mr. Bream, the resident counselor who lived on the ground floor of the boys' dorm.

"Are you trying to start off the school year with a PDA write-up and a call home to Mommy and Daddy?"

Annie and I backed apart.

I cleared my throat and squeaked, "I'm sorry, Annie."

Mr. Bream turned off the flashlight and stepped up to us.

"Ryan Dean West? Is that you?"

Mr. Bream combed his mustache with his index finger. He always did the same thing when he was angry: two strokes on each side, then a final swipe on the right.

"Yes, sir," I confessed.

"Did I read the housing assignments correctly? That you're on floor one with a freshman roommate?" Mr. Bream asked.

I gave Annie a pained look, like I'd just been kicked in the balls, which is a look I have had quite a bit of experience with.

I sighed. "Yes."

"Did you get in trouble again?"

I shook my head. "I honestly don't know why they did this to me."

Mr. Bream combed his mustache again. Five times. Then he pointed his flashlight at the center of my chest. "I don't agree with putting a senior on floor one, so you just better know I'm keeping an eye on you."

"Yes, sir."

"All right. Well, you two can say good night and run along."

And Mr. Bream just stood there watching me and Annie.

Annie said, "See you in class tomorrow."

"Yeah," I said. "I'd better run along, Annie."

CHAPTER SEVEN

IT WAS NINE O'CLOCK.

What twelfth-grade boy on the planet goes to bed at nine o'clock at night?

Ryan Dean West does, that's who.

I grudgingly dragged my feet back to Unit 113, which was my new home away from anywhere I cared about; and one that came equipped with a built-in Sam Abernathy. I thought about going upstairs and hanging out at Seanie and JP's, maybe watching some television with them, but I didn't really feel like they'd want me around. I could only hope that the Abernathy larva was such a bigger loser than me that he'd already be fast asleep, so I wouldn't have to talk to him or listen to him or look at him or anything else with him for that matter.

No such luck.

When I got back to my—*ugh!*—*our* room, the Abernathy was awake, sitting up under the covers in his Super Mario bed with the lights off and the television on. Also, I might add, once again our window, and the door to our pint-size bathroom (*our!*) were both fully open—and didn't Sam Abernathy know about the dark guy who'd been standing outside the window all day watching me?

It was freezing cold.

I didn't bring a television to Pine Mountain. I had a microwave oven. To me, watching the illuminated countdown of LED numbers when you're zapping instant mac and cheese was just about as thrilling as looking at most television programs. The Abernathy had taken it upon himself to bring a notebook-paper-size flatscreen TV, which he placed on top of our one and only book/microwave oven shelf located along the wall at the foot of my Princess Snugglewarm child-size-extra-small bed. The Abernathy had to sit up in his bed to watch his TV due to the desks forming a kind of Maginot Line of defenses between Princess Snugglewarm and the Mario Bros.

It was 130 square feet of hell, except that it was freezing cold.

The other thing I noticed right away, besides the open goddamned window and the icicles that were forming on the sill—and Sam Abernathy's pleading puppy-dog eyes staring at me as soon as I got through the door—was that, apparently, the Abernathy had taken it upon himself to very neatly fold and hang all the clothes I'd strewn around the Ryan Dean West half of our divided state. That was gross. I did not want the Abernathy to ever touch my socks and underwear.

Did I mention it was cold?

Seriously, my breath fogged the moment I entered my (*our*) room.

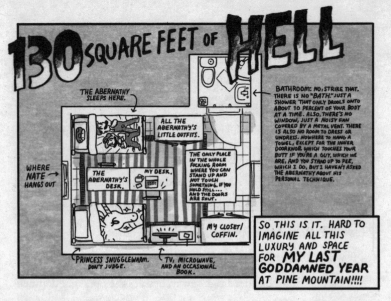

"Hi, Ryan Dean."

Okay. Let me make this clear right now: Sam Abernathy was the kind of kid that human beings instantly like. He was as cute as a laundry hamper filled with beagle puppies and cotton balls, and he was just so goddamned nice all the time.

But what did I care about that? I'd already decided I was not going to like or be nice to Sam Abernathy, and that, as far as I was concerned, was that.

I stood inside the door, shifting my eyes from Sam Abernathy to the television (he was actually watching a cooking show), to the open window, to the bathroom door that I practically tripped over, and then back to the Abernathy without saying anything to him.

So Sam picked up the pleasantries on his own.

"Do you want to watch TV with me, Ryan Dean?"

I took a deep breath. I gave the airsacs in my lungs frostbite.

If I could give a score to the degree to which I wanted to use a choice swear word at that point, it would easily be a five out of five skinny-dipping sessions with Annie Altman on the Ryan Dean West Scale of Things That Ryan Dean West Had to Deny Himself the Pleasure of Doing.

Because I am responsible, and also mature and in control. After all, I'm fifteen and a senior, right?

So I said to him, "I do not cuss, Abernathy. I want that to be known up front."

Sam Abernathy lit up like a six-month-old Christmas tree on the surface of the sun.

"I don't cuss either, Ryan Dean!" he gurgled.

Okay. I'll admit that I sometimes take liberties with the truth, like when I drew my Sam Abernathy comic for Annie. But the kid actually *was* wearing pajamas. Not the kind with built-in feet, but still . . . Sam Abernathy's pajamas had soccer balls on them. Actual soccer balls. And he was wearing the pajama top, too. No boy in high school wears pajamas, much less full-set pajamas with soccer balls on them.

I sighed a swirling cloud of angry fog.

"What I mean to say, Abernathy, is this: It is thirty-five insert-appropriate-swear-word-here degrees Fahrenheit outside, and you have the insert-appropriate-swear-word-here window open."

Then I dramatically stormed across the room, which, architecturally speaking, was not suited for dramas involving flailing teenagers storming and such, so I ended up bashing my right shin into my desk chair, which then caused a domino-type chain reaction involving gravity, a fifteen-year-old storming senior, and both of our desks.

"Oh my gosh!" Sam Abernathy, who was probably having an internal dialogue about the swear-worthiness of exclamations that included the word "gosh," said, "Are you okay, Ryan Dean?"

And the level of niceness and concern in the Abernathy's voice was so infuriating, I thought I might actually burst into flames. I sprang to my foot (my left one, because my right one may have actually been severed, it hurt so bad) and grabbed my desk chair in both hands and started to lift it.

Thankfully, I controlled myself before raising the chair even half an inch. Any higher than that, and I would certainly have snapped and thrown the thing out the goddamned window, or possibly—probably—at Sam Abernathy's face.

Another deep breath.

"Sam," I said, my voice quaking, "it . . . it's just really cold in here. Sam. Abernathy."

And I hobbled over to the open window. Did he actually remove the screen, too? There was no screen. I'll admit that it kind of creeped me out, going to the window, because you know how when it's dark outside you can imagine all these terrible and horrifying things that aren't really there. They aren't really there, are they?

"You took the screen off?"

He didn't need to confess. I could clearly see the screen lying on the ground right next to where the footprints of the monster were.

Sam didn't say anything. He just grunted softly, like he was being stabbed or something, when I slid the window shut and latched it. Then I limped around the debris field between our beds and shut the bathroom door, and Sam Abernathy whimpered again.

In the flickering light of a television program about reducing a sauce and pan-seared something, I stripped out of my shoes and clothes, threw them on my upended miniature desk, examined the purple mark on my right shin, and slid into bed. Okay, two things: First, our dorm room looked like a bomb had gone off, which made me feel strangely satisfied, and second, there was something to be said for flannel Princess Snugglewarm sheets, considering that I was going to bed inside a fucking meat locker.

"Is it okay if I watch TV?" Sam's little voice drifted across the wreckage.

I rolled over and faced the wall. I was so not-tired, and I was convinced I would lie there for hours seething at the Abernathy.

I waved a dismissive hand in the icy air between us.

"As long as you promise not to talk to me."

The silence—well, with the exception of something about roasting

Brussels sprouts with cherries—lasted for a whopping fifteen seconds.

"Don't you have any pj's?"

I sighed. Fog. "This is high school. Grow up."

"Oh. So, in high school boys don't wear pajamas, and you also don't brush your teeth before going to bed?"

The only person I had ever punched in my life was JP Tureau. Sam Abernathy was pretty small, and, like I said, he was cute enough to be his own Internet meme, but I can't begin to express how much I wanted to punch the kid at that moment. And Mom would be so mad at me if she knew I skipped brushing my teeth.

I storm-limped across the room to the cabinet-size bathroom, which didn't have a bath—unless you were the size of an Abernathy, in which case the sink would do.

Brush. Spit. Rinse. Spit. Back to bed.

Thank you, Sam Abernathy, for being my dental hygiene conscience.

The program had moved on to something about making a roux. I had morbid thoughts of cooking the baby marsupial from *Winnie the Pooh*.

"I have microwave popcorn."

NOOOO!!!!!

I said nothing.

Thirty seconds of silence, during which time my blood pressure elevated to Himalayan altitudes.

"Would it be okay if I used your microwave oven, Ryan Dean?"

But I endured.

I lay there, refusing to speak to the Abernathy, listening to the psychedelic mix tape of microwave corn explosions layered over an explanation of Moroccan carrot ribbons with black lentils, steeling myself for what was undoubtedly going to be the longest night of my life.

You know how when you're lying there, thinking about methods you might use for falsifying your own disappearance and assuming a new identity, and you're trying to *not* pay attention to the other person in the room who is responsible for your disappearance fantasy, so it is inevitably all you do—pay attention to *that one thing* that is giving you a severe fight or flight crisis? Yeah. That.

So Sam Abernathy and his soccer ball pajamas stood *on my half of the empire* (Yeah . . . I'm like that: his half/my half. Deal with it.) and his little face lit up in pulses of golden light as his bag of microwave fucking popcorn spun around and around, just inches from my bare feet, which I had to stick over the end of my child-size goddamned bed.

"That looks like it hurts," Sam Abernathy, obviously ogling my naked right shin, told me.

That was creepy.

I curled up into a fetal position beneath my unicorns so the Abernathy would stop examining me.

Then he scampered back over to his bed and sat there in the glow of the Cooking Channel and played a dental symphony that sounded like a beaver clearing a forest while Sam Abernathy ate his popcorn.

Okay. So, you know that moment when you're just at the balancing point between consciousness (agony and awareness of the proximity of a masticating Abernathy) and sleep (pure unaware bliss), and you're just about to fall, fall, fall . . .

"I have really bad claustrophobia."

What the holy hell?

I jerked back to the land of consciousness as Sam Abernathy padded across the room and cracked our door open a few inches, which allowed a shaft of the most-annoying-possible glaring incandescent hallway lightbulb light into our room.

"What?"

"Really, really bad claustrophobia, Ryan Dean. That's why I had the bathroom door and window open, and why I took the screen off. In case you were wondering."

I was not wondering.

Why did he make me wonder?

Chomp chomp.

And the television said, "The worst crime you could possibly commit with a scallop is overcooking it."

Great.

Just fucking great.

CHAPTER EIGHT

I'LL ADMIT IT: I DO NOT LIKE TO GET out of bed once I'm in it.

But I didn't need an alarm clock on that first day of twelfth grade. Who needs an alarm clock when you're stuck in a refrigerator-size room with Sam Abernathy, and all night long you've had to try to sleep with your front door wide open while people—guys—pass by in the hallway and offer commentary like "Why are these assholes sleeping with their door open?" and "Hey, do you smell popcorn?"

So I got up before sunrise. And I shut our door so I could undress and take a shower. I even shaved. I didn't need to shave, there was just some keen sense of satisfaction I got from leaving my razor and shaving cream sitting out in the same bath—no, shower—shower room Sam Abernathy was going to use. And you couldn't bring a change of clothes inside the shower room either, unless you wanted your school things to get soaked, not that there was enough space to actually get dressed in there to begin with.

When I came out, naked and wrapped in a towel, Sam Abernathy had reopened our window.

We were ultimately going to have to negotiate a claustrophobia treaty, but I wasn't in the mood for talking to Sam Abernathy while I was freezing and naked and trying to get ready for school with an open ground-floor window through which any passerby could watch the naked-Ryan-Dean-West-and-his-unstable-roommate show.

Also, the Abernathy had straightened out our desks and picked up and folded my clothes again too. I concluded he was likely a claustrophobe with a neatness obsession. Ryan Dean West, child fucking psychologist. With just a sprinkle of pyromania and perhaps a shoe perversion, Sam Abernathy could potentially be the most insane twelve-year-old on the planet.

I closed our window and lowered the blinds.

"I need to get dressed," I explained. "And it's cold. And that's exactly eight words more than I intended to say to you this month."

Sam Abernathy sat on his Mario Bros. bed in his soccer pajamas. He'd laid out his perfect little Pine Mountain first-day-of-school boy outfit neatly beside him.

"I need to pee," Sam Abernathy said.

"So?"

I put on my socks and underwear.

"I also need to take a shower."

"Again. So?"

And I realized my shirt and school pants looked pretty nice the way Sam had folded them.

"Well, I can't be inside the bathroom with the door closed. I would stop breathing, and nobody here would know they need to call an ambulance or start CPR. But if I leave the bathroom door open, then I won't be able to pee or take a shower because you'll be in here watching me."

I thought about doing CPR on the Abernathy.

No.

The kid was squirming and his eyes were watering.

What boy doesn't know that look painfully well?

"It's not a bathroom," I pointed out.

I tried to calculate how long I could take getting dressed so that the Abernathy's bladder would explode, and if all this could happen in time for me to meet Annie and my friends for breakfast and still make it to my first class on time.

"Dude. Trust me. I am *not* going to watch you pee or take a shower."

Sam Abernathy rocked back and forth slightly, his knees clenched tightly together.

And I kept telling myself, *I am not going to be nice to him, I am not going to be nice to him.*

Then the Abernathy looked at me with his gigantic Internet-meme, basket-full-of-puppies eyes and said, "Please?" Which, when you think about it, could be a perfect meme.

At which time, my inner mantra evolved to *I am not going to strangle him, I am not going to strangle him.*

I grabbed my backpack and schedule, and, shirt unbuttoned and hanging out, I threw my untied tie over one shoulder and my Pine Mountain sweater over the other and stormed—without tripping once!—out of our (*my*) fucking dorm room.

CHAPTER NINE

"IT HASN'T BEEN TWENTY-FOUR hours, and I just can't take him anymore."

I was sitting in the dining hall before class with Annie, JP, Seanie, and Annie's roommate, Isabel, whom I still found to be wildly hot. Also, there was something dramatically different about Isabel, but I couldn't exactly put my finger on it. So I concluded it had to be one thing: Isabel had lost her virginity over the summer.

What else could it possibly be?

She had this all-knowing, goddesslike, and voluptuous look in her simmering black eyes. I had to find out. She would tell Annie, right? Because girls do that, right? Just like guys, right? I need to know these things. I had to get Annie to find out for me if Isabel had lost her virginity, and who it was with, and if she wanted to sit around a campfire or something and tell me about it. Tonight, if possible.

"Have you even heard one thing I've said to you, Ryan Dean?"

Annie was so hot when she got that scolding voice.

"Huh?" I said, suddenly aware that I'd been sitting there for at least five minutes at breakfast with my friends, thinking about Isabel having sex, and then thinking about Isabel talking to me about having sex. And a campfire, which, like having sex, is also specifically against the rules at Pine Mountain.

"Well, clearly you're misleading yourself if you think you're not going to at least be kind to him. Leaving him alone this morning was a very thoughtful thing for you to do," Annie said.

"Huh?" I was still thinking about Isabel and sex, as opposed to Sam Abernathy taking a shower, and my compassion toward him.

"It stands to reason that Winger and the little guy would bond," JP added. "After all, they have so much in common. And besides, you've got to feel sorry for a kid with irrational fears, right, Ryan Dean? *You're* not afraid of anything, *are you*?"

For just a second, I thought I saw a flash of that dude in the black cloak—Nate—looking at me from over JP's shoulder.

I hated JP Tureau.

Annie shifted in her seat and cleared her throat, which was her way of letting us know she didn't appreciate it when JP and I picked on each other around her.

Then Isabel looked at me with her liquid black eyes and said, "You should ask him to hang out with us at dinner tonight. That would be so cool of you to introduce him to some older friends, Ryan Dean."

"What?!!" I was shocked. Also, to be honest, I was imagining Isabel naked.

I just can't help these things. Nobody can, right?

Seanie slapped the table and shook his head decisively. "There are certain social barriers that cannot be broken. Inviting a freshman to sit at a senior table could only end up in total anarchy."

Seanie Flaherty was rarely the voice of reason, but when he rose to the occasion, it was like drifting into a life raft when you're treading water in the middle of the Pacific.

"Nobody wants total anarchy," I said.

Everyone knew the game plan for senior year.

It was supposed to be easy, right? I'd taken my SAT in June (I aced it, thank you very much), had been working on my college apps (as a gesture to my parents, I sent one to Harvard and one to MIT, even though I already knew I wanted to go to school in California, dude), and had completed all the core requirements for graduating from Pine Mountain. To top it off, pretty much all I had to do this year was play rugby and take fluff and breadth classes. Easy report card full of vowels. It was all lined up perfectly.

But Sam Abernathy equaled total anarchy, treading water for the next nine months.

To make matters worse, Sam Abernathy would end up being in two of my classes: Creative Writing, followed by the worst-imaginable scenario, Culinary Arts, which was also the only class I had with Annie Altman. But I didn't find out about this wonderful arrangement until later.

I could not get away from the guy. At least I was safe for first period, Body Conditioning (which was only for twelfth-grade boys) and for Health (also, a new *thing* at Pine Mountain—a class for only senior boys that was a ninety-minute endurance test in discomfort because it was (1) taught by a woman, Mrs. Blyleven, and (2) all about "issues" like sex and consent and being a good young man); and then I could always count on the sanctuary of rugby practice and Coach McAuliffe to make me forget everything Abernathy and Blyleven.

Or so I thought.

So, yeah, it was a shock for me to see Sam Abernathy timidly enter my Creative Writing class, and it was entirely natural for me to assume the little crouton was simply lost in a forest of gigantic lettuce leaves. Or something.

But no. And of course, I had no way of knowing anything about the Abernathy, because *I refused to converse with him.*

Sam Abernathy was an open book as far as I was concerned. I didn't need to ask about any details in the kid's two-sentence biography. I decided then and there to make a chart (that's not creepy of me, is it?) in which I would predict everything about the Abernathy, and then I could check it off during the course of whatever period of endurance I'd have to endure with my unendurable roommate, just to see how very right I could be:

ITEM	PREDICTION	RIGHT?	WRONG?
NAME	Sam Abernathy	X	
AGE	12	X	
PLACE OF ORIGIN	I'm guessing Boise. Nobody comes from Boise, and it may not even exist. But if people _did_ come from Boise, they'd be Abernathy.		
HOBBIES	Collecting porn, saving his ear wax, microwaving things.		
SPORT	Duh. Soccer. Also, probably "tag."		
LIFE GOALS	Give Ryan Dean West an aneurysm. Puberty would be nice.		
PETS	He looks like a Pomeranian owner to me.		

"Oh. Hi, Ryan Dean."

"Hello."

"Is it okay if I sit next to you?"

"No. Because you're not in this class."

The Abernathy unzipped his notebook. He had one of those really big, zipper-shut notebook organizers that nobody would ever willingly be seen with in public. He took out his class schedule.

"Is this Creative Writing, with Dr. Wellins?"

Mr.—Dr.—Wellins, a monumentally renowned pervert, had been my American Lit teacher in eleventh grade. Apparently, over the summer, he had earned a PhD in misidentifying sexual subtext in classic literature. I liked Mr.—uh, Dr.—Wellins, despite the fact that he was really creepy.

I sighed and waved my hand at the empty seat beside me.

Annie would be pleased at how nice I just was, I thought.

Sam Abernathy sat down, all smiles.

"I'm so glad I actually know somebody in one of my classes," he said. "This is going to be fun!"

Fun.

Dr. Wellins came in, wrote his name and the date on the board at the front of the class, then launched into a dramatic speech with lots of hand gestures about how we were only to refer to him as *Dr. Wellins*, and that we were all going to find this the most uncomfortable (he was already right about that) and difficult class of our career—so we might rethink committing to the course right now.

I was used to this type of opener. A lot of the teachers at PM were so full of their own credentials, they tried to scare down the number of papers they'd have to grade right at the start of each term by proclaiming their impermeable magnificence. I looked around at the sets of terrified eyeballs staring at the master of all things creative and wordlike.

There were sixteen kids in the class, and ten of them were girls. Score on that one. Also, I was pretty sure I was the only senior. Everyone else looked really young (Sam Abernathy looked like a fetus with a necktie). But the other kids probably thought I was a tenth grader or something, anyway.

Then Dr. Wellins fired off a machine-gun barrage of requirements for his course, which included specifics on font size and page layout of our work, our responsibilities regarding deadlines, our openness to criticism, and his general prohibition against a list of verbs (he gave the ones he never wanted to see, which included any form of "to be"), all adverbs, and anything ever written in first-person point of view.

"And, if you are not aware of what an adverb is, or one-P-P-O-V, then I would suggest you consider transferring into beginning finger-painting class immediately," Dr. Wellins said.

I was thinking if he only banned a few more language devices, we could all hand in blank pages and ace this shitty class.

Here's another thing: I hate alphabetical order.

Opportunities are supposed to be randomly distributed, right? There are only three possible terminal initials worse than *W* when it comes to the unfair allocation of choice or turn taking, and *nobody* has a last name that starts with *X*. I mention this because as Dr. Wellins called off the names on his roster he asked each student to name the person in the class with whom they would like to be wed for the term as a crit partner.

"'Crit partner' is what WRITERS"—whenever Dr. Wellins said "writers," it always sounded like it was in all capitals, like he was attempting to describe celestial angels to the tongueless half-beast spawns of hell—"call their critique partner. It is a significant relationship, one based on trust, openness, integrity, and support. The commitment is akin to the faithfulness and dedication of a husband or wife. Do I make myself clear?"

I mentally counted the number of "to be" verbs in his proclamation. Don't look back. There were three.

Nobody said anything.

To be honest, I think most of the kids in the class stopped listening to Dr. Wellins when he told us all about his doctoral dissertation, which was an analysis of the underlying themes of homosexuality and narcissism in Robert Louis Stevenson's *Treasure Island*.

Besides that, *husband or wife?*

Was Dr. Wellins already concocting some bizarre fantasies about the kids in his Creative Writing course? Also, who ever says "akin"? Look, I knew how much I'd changed over the summer, and I was certain that Isabel had lost her virginity, but Dr. Wellins, since earning his PhD, had transformed into an even bigger self-absorbed douche than he was in eleventh-grade American Literature, and the scale of that was almost impossible to imagine.

But, to return to the egregious miscarriage of justice known as *alphabetical order*, the first kid on Dr. Wellins' roster happened to be the Abernathy.

"Samuel Abernathy?" Dr. Wellins said.

The Abernathy raised his little pink baby hand. "Here, sir."

"Do you know anyone here in this desiccated wasteland of imbecility with whom you would like to bond as a crit partner?"

Dr. Wellins swept his arm across the breadth of the room like he was scattering chicken feed in slow motion.

Please don't bond with me, Sam Abernathy. Please don't bond with me, Sam Abernathy. Please don't bond—

Then the Abernathy pointed at me and said, "Yes, sir. I would like to partner with Ryan Dean."

Unfortunately for me, Dr. Wellins's factory of creativity—like our (*my!*) dorm room—was on the ground floor, which eliminated the possibility of a desperate leap from the window.

And Dr. Wellins's pervert-tumbleweed eyebrows rose like the spines of twin cats about to fight when he realized the target Sam Abernathy pointed at was the same Ryan Dean who was also in his American Lit class the preceding year.

"Ryan Dean West?" Dr. Wellins was practically salivating.

I apologize for using a "be" verb *and* an adverb.

I also apologize for not being able to deny my existence.

"Hello, Dr. Wellins." I gave him a half-elevated pope wave. "Congratulations on the sheepskin."

"I didn't recognize you! You must have grown a foot!"

"Hyperbole," I pointed out, avoiding first person, be, and adverbial modifiers.

I totally *owned* that old pervert.

"Well, I expect nothing but the best from you, young man! Nothing but the best!"

You see, here's the thing: I had creepy old Dr. Wellins figured out from day one. I knew exactly what he wanted to see from us half-wits. He was an incredibly shallow audience who was so easy to satisfy.

Instant A.

If only I could get away from the Abernathy. But I realized it was beyond hope when Dr. Wellins, beaming, wrote down the first official crit partnership on his whiteboard:

Abernathy/West

I glared at the Abernathy, who smiled at me and bounced up and down in his little Creative Writing desk like he was five years old and waiting to open all his Christmas presents.

CHAPTER TEN

OKAY. EVEN THOUGH I KNEW IN
chapter nine that I'd end up reencountering my crit partner, the Abernathy, in Culinary Arts, I didn't *really* know it until just before the
class began, which is going to happen in a few paragraphs.

So hang in there.

The Culinary Arts room was as big as a grocery store. Instead of
desks, there were prep tables with built-in sinks. There was an entire
wall of gleaming steel ovens and cooktops, and even a walk-in refrigerator and freezer. There were microwave ovens, too, which made me
flash back unpleasantly to the sleep-deprived night before.

This was all new to me, though, especially the teacher, Mrs.
O'Hare, whom I had never seen around Pine Mountain before.
Mrs. O'Hare was the exact opposite of what I'd imagine a cooking
teacher to look like. She was young, with billowing blond hair, and
long slender legs that you couldn't help but notice in her tapered
chef's pants. She also wore one of those perfectly white, double-
breasted chef's tunics with just one button seductively undone.
No boy in his right mind would have to break out the candy ther-
mometer to know that Mrs. O'Hare was the hottest thing in the
kitchen.

I wondered if she was a widow.

Something cool and soft touched my hand, and I snapped out of my stare-down contest with that *one button*.

"I've been waiting for this all day. Well, since breakfast, at least."

Annie.

We held hands beneath our prep table and leaned close enough that our shoulders and legs touched—just innocent enough that Mrs. O'Hare (my new favorite, hopefully widowed teacher) wouldn't think anything rule-breaky was going on.

"Oh man, Annie! I am so happy to see you. Do you realize I had to endure an all-boys Health class, where we were forced to take a pledge and promise that we'd learn stuff like healthy attitudes and behaviors toward our penises, and then I just had the worst experience ever in Creative Writing class," I said.

"What now, Ryan Dean?" (hot scolding tone).

"Well, first off, it's taught by Mr. Wellins, who is now *Dr. Wellins*, which means his obsession with sex is going to be even more creepy and condescending, and then Sam Abernathy turned up in the class—and Dr. Wellins had us *pair up* as permanent writing buddies—and he even made us write something together called a *tandem dialogue*. It was a nightmare. We had to take turns, where the setup was assigned by Dr. Wellins, then we alternated writing dialogue between two supposedly fictional characters. Here. You should read this."

And I slipped Annie Altman the shared paper that Sam Abernathy and I had written our first partner project on.

Nice verbs, guys! Great job!

Sam Abernathy
Ryan Dean West
Creative Writing Assignment: Tandem Dialogue (A)
Dr. Wellins

Assignment: Write a dialogue scene with your partner, taking turns to alternate between speakers. Be sure to utilize proper dialogue tags and punctuation. Limitations: (1) YOU MAY NOT USE ANY FORM OF THE VERB "TO SAY." (2) YOU ARE NOT ALLOWED TO USE "REAL PEOPLE" IN YOUR STORY. The situation is as follows: Two speakers are present, engaged in dialogue. One of the speakers finds out that his/her friend is having unprotected sex.

Ready? Set? Write!

I could not believe what Stan Abercrombie just confessed to me. "You've been having UNPROTECTED SEX?" I asked.

Stan Abercrombie considered the question for a moment and then retorted, "I thought you weren't allowed to write in first person."

I conceded, "Stan, I will overlook your use of a form of 'to be' if you will just go with the one-P-P-O-V. The

BIGGER ISSUE REMAINS THE FACT THAT YOU'VE BEEN ENGAGING IN
UNPROTECTED SEX."

"~~RYAN DEAN~~

"~~RODNEY DAN,~~"

"RICHARD DICK," STAN ABERCROMBIE EXPLAINED, "I DON'T REALLY
KNOW WHAT UNPROTECTED SEX IS."

"WAIT," I EJACULATED, "ARE YOU ~~FUCKING~~ KIDDING ME?"

STAN ABERCROMBIE ~~NERVOUSLY~~ ADMITTED, "NO. I REALLY DON'T
KNOW WHAT THAT MEANS."

"THAT ISN'T WHAT I WAS TALKING ABOUT," I BELLOWED. "WHY
THE HELL WOULD YOU NAME ME RICHARD DICK? NOBODY
WOULD EVER BE NAMED RICHARD DICK! WHO WOULD NAME A KID
RICHARD DICK?"

Annie laughed. Well, she tried not to laugh, but I could see all that
liquid laughter pooling up in her eyes, which I always found to be
incredibly hot. Combine that with Mrs. O'Hare's top button, and I
was certain that Ryan Dean West was raising the internal temperature
in Culinary Arts enough to turn milk into yogurt, and yogurt into
cheese, and cheese into fucking fondue.

"I'd keep reading this," she said. "It's really funny."

"He's going to give me a stroke," I said.

Annie sighed and shook her head. "Just listen to yourself, Ryan Dean. You're being *mean*. I've never seen you be mean to anyone. Not ever. Why have you decided this is how things are going to be this year? I don't like it at all."

If you've never played a sport like rugby, then you might not know what it feels like to get the wind knocked out of you *and* punched in the balls at exactly the same time. But trust me. It was how I felt when Annie said I was being mean. And immediately after that, it also felt like somebody was adding a stiff knee to the kidneys on top of it all, because that's right when Sam Abernathy came into my constricting field of vision.

"Ryan Dean! I didn't know you liked to cook too!"

No. I can't. Just no.

And Sam Abernathy plopped his big-zipper-binder-organizer onto the prep table *right next to Annie* and proceeded to sit down as though it were entirely acceptable.

"Is this—?" Annie started.

"Sam Abernathy, meet Annie Altman, my girlfriend."

And the Abernathy stuck out his sticky little cotton-candy puppy paw and shook Annie's hand. They were actually *touching* each other's skin and stuff.

I studied Annie.

That's when I saw it.

She blushed.

Okay. So, you know how when you completely know someone inside and out (I mean that in a totally non-sex [but it would be with protection, unlike that fictitious moron Stan Abercrombie] way) and then when that person you know actually looks at and touches the bare pink skin of another boy who I will openly admit (in a completely non-gay way) is clearly five out of five baby hedgehogs on the Ryan Dean West Scale of Things That Everyone Is Convinced Are Adorable but Ryan Dean West Thinks Are Totally Disgusting, and then that person who does the skin contact actually blushes and then hedgehog boy blushes too and you're sitting there watching a fucking hormonal blinking blush fest that looks like a flashing railroad-crossing sign and you're thinking to yourself, *Dear God, she thinks he's cute* and *Great Caesar's ghost, he's already got a crush on her* and *Are these ovens gas, and, if so, are their pilot lights out* and *Would it mess up my hair if I stuck my fucking head in one* and *Is this the first time in my life I've ever thought about my hair being messy?*

Yeah. That.

Then hedgehog boy looked at me, his eyes grapefruit-size saucers of admiration and protopubescent lust, and said, "Wow, Ryan Dean, I had no idea you had a girlfriend."

"What the fuck is that supposed to mean?" I said.

Well, to be honest, I didn't say exactly that. In fact, I didn't say anything at all, because (1) I was choking on something, possibly wishful-thinking gas, and (2) Mrs. O'Hare launched into her sermon on the gospel of Culinary Arts.

"Let's get this straight right away," Mrs. O'Hare, whose voice was shockingly manlike, said. "If you think this is going to be an easy class, you are in for an unpleasant surprise."

Annie leaned into my ear and whispered, "She sounds like a man."

"If I close my eyes, I picture a young Ernest Borgnine," I confirmed.

The Abernathy, whose feet couldn't reach the floor because we sat on tall backless stools, kicked and squirmed and bounced, which meant he was either really happy to be sitting with me and Annie or he needed to pee really bad again.

"To begin with," Mrs. O'Hare chainsawed on, "this is *not* a cooking class. Anyone who calls it a *cooking class* is not fit to polish the Vikings."

Side note: Is it just me, or does "polish the Vikings" *sound really terrifying, in a deeply perverted way? I came to eventually find out that Mrs. O'Hare called her stoves "Vikings."*

And I have no problem admitting that I thought the class was going to be easy. I had already categorized it in my mind as a *cooking class*, and, speaking of which, I had never cooked anything in my life, unless by "cooking," you mean "unwrapping and putting in your mouth."

"Furthermore," Mrs. O'Hare said, "in Culinary Arts, we work in *pods* of two students . . ."

Great. Say good-bye to your little pink hedgehog, Annie.

". . . which have already been determined by me . . ."

Wait a minute.

". . . based on alphabetical order."

No. No. No. No. This isn't real, right?

"Pod one: Abernathy and Altman."

Sam Abernathy kicked and bounced with joy.

This can't be happening to me.

CHAPTER ELEVEN

FINALLY. RUGBY.

And I needed to hit somebody, preferably someone who was twelve years old and smelled suspiciously like candy corn, baby powder, and vanilla frosting all at the same time.

But I knew that wasn't going to happen. The first week back on the pitch was always about noncontact drills and Coach M looking us over to decide who went where in the fifteen. Rugby is a very specific sport in terms of where you play based on your build and abilities. I had always been at the wing because I was small and fast, but when Coach McAuliffe saw me suited up for practice that day, his eyes widened, and he squeezed my shoulder and said, "Look at you, Ryan Dean! I daresay I could move you up to flanker."

No. Please, God, do not make me a forward.

There is this thing in rugby called a scrum, which is basically something that looks like a crab with sixteen legs fighting another crab with sixteen legs. The crab is made out of the eight forwards on the team. I guess the flankers would be like the crab's pinchers. Still. Gross. In rugby, it wasn't only about the physical attributes of a player, it also had a lot to do with the psychology. For example, to be a forward, you have to be like a really loyal, big fluffy dog who doesn't mind how much his owner abuses him, with two exceptions.

The number two guy—the hooker (his name was Jeff Cotton, and everyone on the team called him Cotton Balls)—has to not care if he dies, and the number eight guy—the eight-man, a kid who came all the way from Denmark to enroll at PM, John Nygaard, who was nicknamed Spotted John and had a schoolwide reputation for breaking every rule at Pine Mountain, has to not care if he accidentally kills anyone else, including his own teammates.

I was not cut out to be in that pack.

Then there's the guy who gets the ball from the crab, the number nine guy—the scrum half, which is where Seanie played—who is kind of like the crazy and lonely cousin who always shows up at family reunions and tells jokes that nobody gets, and when he leaves everyone keeps saying what a nice guy he is, but you still don't quite understand why you like him.

The back line starts with the fly half—number ten. That was where Joey played. After he died, Coach M moved some guys around, but the whole season was shot for us after that and nothing seemed to click. Then you have a couple of center backs, the wings, and, finally, number fifteen—the fullback, JP Tureau, who we sometimes called Sartre—who basically had to be immune to pain and have a monstrous ego, since fullbacks are so often responsible for saving—or losing—the game. A perfect spot for JP.

There were always new guys coming out for rugby at the start of every year. The general practice was to not bother trying to learn any of their names because most of the new guys would quit after finding out that rugby is more difficult than anything. (One thing's for sure: Coach M *never* had to give the scare-kids-away speeches that I had to sit through in Creative Writing and Culinary Arts classes). It usually only took a day or two for most of the rookies to quit; and besides, most of the guys who stuck it out and made the team got named by their teammates, anyway, which is why they called me Winger.

But after seeing Coach M that day, I was scared my nickname was going to be changed.

When practice was over and we'd all showered and dressed and were heading back to our dorms or to dinner (which was the first time I'd even thought about Sam Abernathy in hours, and I thought, *Why can't every day be like this, all day long?*), Coach M stopped me on my way out of the locker room. He asked if I'd mind coming into the coach's office and having a "little chat."

Okay. Two things here, maybe three: First off, Coach McAuliffe is English, and he has the nicest, most civilized way of saying things. Also, I loved Coach M as much as anyone I ever knew. But I always felt raw terror when any adult asked to have a one-on-one talk with me, and Coach M was no exception to that dreadful fear.

"Sit down," Coach M said.

There were exactly two chairs in the locker room office: one of them was in front of Coach M's computer, which I don't think he'd ever used, and the other was positioned beside a stainless-steel cart with first-aid gear and butterfly bandages on it. Lots of bloody stuff got taken care of in Coach M's office.

"Thanks."

I sat in the chair by the medic's cart. I'd sat there enough times before. If things were ever beyond cart-level repairs, guys would have to go to the health office, a round-the-clock clinic for the students at Pine Mountain that was headed by Doctor Norris, a physician the guys on the team nicknamed Doctor No-gloves for obvious reasons.

A rugby ball sat in the bottom bin of the medic's cart. I picked it up and spun it around in my hands, just kind of waiting to see what Coach M wanted to talk about, hoping it had nothing to do with last year, nothing to do with Joey Cosentino.

There's something about the way a brand new rugby ball feels in your hands. I'm not even going to try to explain it because I don't need to if you've ever played the game, and it wouldn't mean a thing if you haven't.

"There are a lot of good boys on the team this year," Coach McAuliffe said.

"It's rugby, right? There always are."

Coach smiled and shook his head slightly. "I mean the talent, Ryan Dean. It seems we'll have a first fifteen that will be nearly all seniors, and experienced ones at that."

"We have some holes here and there," I said, "but it's only the first day."

As usual during the first week back on the pitch, we'd ended practice with some matches of touch sevens, which is a kind of tag-rugby played with seven kids on a side, and everyone more or less plays like a back. It wasn't too surprising that some of the guys made frustrating mistakes or got winded too easily. Rugby practice just wouldn't be rugby practice without at least one guy puking on the sidelines because he was being worked too hard. That day it was our eight-man, Spotted John Nygaard, who threw up. And he was mad about it too. Spotted John was a tough guy, but he kept the forwards in line. And, like a lot of forwards, Spotted John resented how much Coach M made us run during practices because he said if you were a good team, you shouldn't have to run too much during a game. Everyone knew that was bullshit, though. In a full rugby match, it's not unusual for a player to run more than eight miles.

Coach M sat down and wheeled his chair over so his knees were practically touching mine. I spun the ball around and around.

"And tell me, how are things for you this year, Ryan Dean?"

Well. I could have said a lot to him.

I could have told Coach M that things were terrible, that I didn't know whether or not I could make it through my senior year at Pine Mountain, or how scared I was—all at the same time—about *not* being at Pine Mountain next year and having to go on to college. I could have told him that I felt like I was slipping away from the only friends I'd made since coming here, or—worse yet—that I'd been feeling distanced from Annie, like there was something getting between us. I knew exactly what that thing was because I kept drawing it and seeing it over and over again, but I didn't really want to talk about it with anyone. You know, the dark guy called Nate—the thing that kept telling me to be ready, because just when you think everything's all fine, that would be when he'd pop around and another terrible something else would happen. I could have told Coach M that sometimes I got scared at night, but I didn't tell that to anyone either. And I could have told him that I was pissed off at being assigned a slummy dorm room with a twelve-year-old kid named Sam Abernathy, whom I absolutely refused to allow myself to become friends with, no matter what, or that Mrs. O'Hare was a gleaming five out of five polished Vikings on the Ryan Dean West Scale of Things That Make Me Sweat in Culinary Arts Class. And I could have asked him if he maybe had any idea why I wasn't going to tell him any of this stuff.

But instead of all that, I gave him the vaguely bullshitty synopsis that went as follows.

"Everything's okay with me, Coach."

Yeah. I know.

But it wasn't like I was lying to Coach M, was it? I didn't look him in the eye, though, either. I kept my eyes on the rugby ball I spun around in my grasp.

"You're sure about that, Ryan Dean?"

"Reasonably confident, sir."

"Good, then, because I have a few ideas I thought I'd present to you—things I've been thinking about after seeing you work with the team today," Coach McAuliffe said.

"Oh?"

"I trust the differences between you and Jean-Paul Tureau have been put aside?"

"A long time ago," I kind-of lied.

Man, I was not doing good here, considering how much I respected Coach M.

I needed to get out of there. I shifted in my medic-station seat.

"I'm going to move Mike Bagnuolo to the number eleven wing."

That was no big deal, I thought. Mike—we called him Bags—played backup winger last year. I liked him. He was a good guy, a junior, who was still more than a year older than me. I just figured this meant Coach M would put me over on the right wing—number fourteen.

No big deal, right? Except, as I thought about it, the right wing doesn't get the ball as much as the left wing, at least not according to my calculations, because since most guys are right-handed, the passes out from backs under pressure tend to go to the number eleven guy—the left wing—which was MY SPOT.

I swallowed. "Oh. Okay."

"My plan is to pull up Timmy Bagnuolo to play on right wing."

Now that was a shock. Timmy, Mike's sophomore brother, had played varsity a couple times in relief last year. The guys called him T-Bag—what else? But it all only meant one thing to me: THERE WAS NO PLACE FOR ME.

I felt flushed and sweaty, kind of like I was trapped in after-class detention, all by myself with Mrs. O'Hare, and she was lecturing me on the proper way to use dry rubs on meat—and WHY AM I THINKING ABOUT THIS RIGHT NOW, WHEN COACH M IS BASICALLY CUTTING MY ASS FROM THE TEAM?

"Naturally, this all means, what are we going to do with you, Ryan Dean?"

I tried to play it off like I was okay with anything Coach M wanted to do, but then my voice cracked like a handful of uncooked spaghetti when I said, "Okay," and I felt like such a monumental crybaby loser.

"Of course, I'd want to have some input from the captain," Coach M said, but, to be honest, my head was so gunked up between thinking about being off the wing and thinking about being in detention with Mrs. O'Hare talking about rubbing meat that I couldn't even begin to think rationally, as though that was something I'd be good at anyway.

Coach M clearly noticed I was zoning out. He said, "You know. The captain?"

I suddenly realized I didn't know *anything* about cooking—and how was I *ever* going to get through Culinary Arts, especially with Sam Abernathy, who could probably poop out perfect soufflés in the time it took me to read the instructions on a frozen pizza, paired up with Annie?

"Ryan Dean?"

"Huh?"

"Do you even know what I'm talking about?"

"I'm thinking it isn't about cooking?"

"I'm asking you to be team captain this year."

What?

"Why?"

"Because the players all love you, Ryan Dean. You have a good head for the game, and you set a good example for everyone on the pitch."

"Are you talking about *me*?"

Coach M laughed.

"How can you ask me to be captain if I'm not even in the first fifteen?" I said, trying to sound manly but coming off terribly undercooked.

"That's the other part of the proposal," Coach M said. "Look at you now. The team would be best served moving you off the wing, so you can have more influence in the game. I saw you kicking the ball today. You're tough, you're a match to anyone on the team, you can take anything anyone hits you with, and your passes are strong to both sides. Having you on the wing is a waste of the man you are."

God no, I thought, *please don't move me to the pack, please don't move me to the pack, please don't move me to the pack.*

"But I want to stay on the wing, coach."

"I want to move you inside the line, to number ten."

"No," I said flatly. "I can't do that."

He didn't know what he was asking me. Joey played number ten last year. I could never play that spot.

"I think you can," Coach M said.

"That's Joey's spot. I couldn't be fly half, Coach. Please."

"It's a number, a job, Ryan Dean. It isn't the person. I'm not asking you to be Joey, or to somehow erase what he means to you."

"I—"

Here's another thing about rugby that you might not know: Because the numbers determine the position assigned to a player, the jerseys come off and go back to the team at the end of every game, so getting one of the first fifteen (numbers sixteen to twenty-three are substitute players' jerseys) was an important thing. Being moved around also meant you'd end up wearing a jersey that someone else had worn the last time it had been used in a game. Last year, after Kevin, one of our locks, was taken out of the season, Coach M didn't let anyone else wear the number four jersey for the rest of the season. And after Joey died, our replacement fly halves always wore the number twenty.

But this was a new year, right? And things get put behind us, right?

I stared out through the reinforced windows that looked from the coaches' office onto the empty shower room, half expecting to see some dark dude wrapped in a cloak staring at me from behind a row of lockers.

Coach M stood up and went to a bank of wire mesh shelves.

I knew what he was doing. I seriously thought about leaving. Why was he doing this to me?

"Here," Coach M said. Then, very gently, he placed the number ten jersey on my lap.

I picked it up and looked at it, turning it around. There was a grass stain over the right shoulder. It hadn't been washed since the last time Joey wore it, which was on the day before Halloween last year.

I could almost see Joey there in my hands. I could smell him in that jersey.

I swallowed hard.

Coach said, "You remember that last match Joey played? Against that team from California?"

I looked back out at the empty locker room. It was so quiet in there, all I could hear was the splattering dribble where one of the showers hadn't been turned off all the way. I was getting a little too choked up to be sitting here alone with Coach M, and all I could force myself to say was, "They were shitty, Coach."

"Ryan Dean." Coach M had a stern tone in his voice. We were *never* allowed to cuss in front of Coach M.

"I apologize, Coach." I handed the jersey back to him and said, "I can't do this."

"Nonsense," Coach M told me. "It's the best thing for you, and it's the best thing for the team."

"Spotted John can do it," I said.

"Are you saying you'd like to play number eight?"

I shook my head and bit my lip. Nothing could possibly be more ridiculous than asking me to play a position where you had to scare people and yell at them. Suddenly, dealing with a claustrophobe cooking-show addict didn't seem so tough. I thought about leaving, just going back to my dorm room so I could pout and be alone and think about quitting everything again.

"I'll tell you what, Ryan Dean. If it makes a difference, and I believe it might, we won't call you fly half. We'll call you stand-off. I prefer the name for the number ten, anyway, because it really says what it is you do on the pitch—you stand off from the pack and you design the strategy for the squad to win."

Stand-off. I'd heard the name before. Old-school guys from the north used it instead of "fly half." I couldn't even think of "fly half" and not think of my friend Joey Cosentino, whose jersey I had just held in my hands.

I stood up, a little wobbly.

"I don't know, Coach."

And I left it at that.

CHAPTER TWELVE

I KNEW FOR CERTAIN I DID NOT WANT to do it.

But I was incapable of saying no to Coach M.

So Ryan Dean West, fifteen-year-old Pine Mountain senior and human napkin, was trapped. And I walked away from the locker room in the dying light of evening while one of those heavy Pacific Northwest mists that is neither fog nor rain coated everything in gray. I could hear the sounds of all the kids gathering in the dining hall, and as I looked up at the random silhouettes performing against drawn blinds in the dorms, every voice that ever raised a question, objection, doubt, or observation seemed to shout at once inside my head.

RYAN DEAN WEST 1: It's fucking cold out here.

RYAN DEAN WEST 2: You might consider buttoning your shirt, loser.

RYAN DEAN WEST 3: I bet Stan Abercrombie, he of legendary unprotected-sex carelessness and soccer-ball pajamas, has the goddamned window open again.

RYAN DEAN WEST 2: The kid doesn't even know what unprotected sex is, Ryan Dean One, maybe you should have a talk with him.

RYAN DEAN WEST 4: We aren't ever going to talk to the kid, remember?

RYAN DEAN WEST 1: Yeah. What he said.

RYAN DEAN WEST 5: All I know is, Coach M is crazy if he thinks I can play fly half.

SPOTTED JOHN NYGAARD: Of course you can't play fly half. What's Coach thinking?

RYAN DEAN WEST 6: Coach said to call him the stand-off.

RYAN DEAN WEST 7: That's a perfect name for where we are right now. A real standoff, right? Besides, it's not like you *can't* play fly . . . er . . . stand-off, it's just that you won't let yourself even try.

RYAN DEAN WEST 8: Because you're afraid you might be good at it. You're afraid you might be as good as Joey—or maybe better.

RYAN DEAN WEST 1: Shut the fuck up. Don't ever talk to me about Joey.

NATE: You *should* be afraid, kid.

RYAN DEAN WEST 1: You're not allowed in my head.

NATE: Apparently, the doorman didn't get the memo, kid.

MRS O'HARE: Don't forget, Ryan Dean, tomorrow is the quiz on *units of measure* and how to properly *dry rub a meat!*

RYAN DEAN WEST 1: I . . . I just can't.

SAM ABERNATHY: Oh, hi, Ryan Dean! Annie and I were waiting for you!

"Huh?"

All the voices in my head vanished, except for the one who was really there, who also happened to be twelve years old and was standing maddeningly close to my girlfriend beside a menacing-looking juniper shrub at the walk-up to the dining hall. And they were *sharing Annie's umbrella*!

Rain immediately turned to steam as it struck the forge of my white-hot head.

"You're later than all the other rugby guys. Did something happen?" Annie asked. She looked me over, no doubt scanning for any blood or stitches or bandages, which, considering that I was partially undressed, was kind of hot.

It was an agonizing scene: Here I was, completely confused about everything I had believed I was *okay* about. My hair was still wet from the shower, my shirt was untucked and unbuttoned, hanging open on my damp goose-bumped skin. I was carrying my school socks that I didn't feel like putting back on, and my unraveled tie hung like a dead wet otter around my neck. In contrast, Annie Altman and her apparent dinner–slash–umbrella date, Joe Randomkid, looked like advertisements for Pine Mountain's exquisite lifestyle—all done up perfectly with their impeccably ironed outfits and flawless hairstyles that seemed to magically repel the autumn dampness. If Sam Abernathy weren't so much shorter than Annie, you could swear they were the youthful and healthy offspring of some genetically superior country club billionaires, on their way to the fall cotillion.

I was sweaty, wet, cold, angry, and confused.

"Oh. Yeah. Coach M wanted to talk to me," I said.

"Is everything okay?" Annie asked.

I locked eyes with her for a quiet moment—probably long enough to make it clear to the Abernathy that I really wished it could be okay if I just hauled off and punched him—and I wanted to say so much to Annie, and I wanted to hold her so badly, but I also didn't want her to think that there was something wrong with the little kid she'd fallen in love with, that maybe I was losing it and I wasn't all that good at getting past things.

"Yeah. Everything's great," I said. "You guys can save me a seat. Let me go get some dry clothes on and I'll catch up to you in a couple minutes."

"We'll save you a seat, Ryan Dean!" the Abernathy gurgled.

And as I walked away I thought, *I really wish you would shut the fuck up, Abernathy.*

CHAPTER THIRTEEN

OKAY, I'LL ADMIT IT: I DID NOT GO BACK
and sit down to dinner with Annie and the Abernathy.

I don't know why it made me so angry to see them together, looking
for me. Wait. Yes I do know why it made me mad. It was because of
Abernathy. That's all. Possibly the umbrella, too. And when I walked
away from them, all I could think about was how they were probably
buddying up over giddy dinner conversation about how many teaspoons are in a tablespoon, and then I realized I DID NOT KNOW
HOW MANY TEASPOONS ARE IN A TABLESPOON AND I
WAS FACING THE PROSPECT OF FAILING A QUIZ AT PINE
MOUNTAIN FOR THE FIRST TIME IN MY FUCKING LIFE.

Because here's the thing: Up until this point in my academic journey, nobody had ever tested me on any subject that I didn't already
know something—a lot—about. But all I knew about cooking was
that Sam Abernathy apparently had mad skills when it came to getting
every last fucking kernel to pop inside a bag of microwave popcorn.

And then it was like the next thing I knew, I had gone completely
past the boys' dorm building and was halfway around the lake, dripping wet and standing on the path that led to the front steps of the
old abandoned O-Hall.

I shivered as I came to the realization that I had just been standing there staring at the empty building, replaying mental filmstrips of ghosts from the past. And there was something that seemed to want to pull me even closer. I was absolutely certain that if I just walked up to that mudroom door, it would be unlocked and I could step right inside the biggest fucking haunted nightmare imaginable.

I rubbed my eyes and shook rainwater from my hair. Then I ran back to the boys' dorm.

CHAPTER FOURTEEN

I LAY IN BED, STUDYING THE HANDOUT on units of measure Mrs. O'Hare gave out in Culinary Arts until I couldn't stand it anymore. So I turned off the reading lamp clipped to the windowsill beside my Princess Snugglewarm cot and tried to go to sleep.

Click.

On came the light.

Whoop! Skreek!

Up slid the blind, then the window.

Rattle rattle rattle. Fluff!

"What are you doing, Abernathy?"

"Oh! Are you awake, Ryan Dean?"

I groaned. But in my defense, it wasn't a mean groan.

"I'm just hanging up your clothes. You don't want to leave wet clothes all balled up on the floor," the Abernathy explained.

"Yes. Yes, I do, Sam. Really," I said.

"Why didn't you come down to dinner?"

"Are we really *talking* right now? And, if so, shut the window. I didn't feel like having dinner."

"That's not good for you, Ryan Dean. Annie was worried. I should go tell her you're all right."

Okay. There was just so much wrong with what the Abernathy just said to me that I didn't even know where to begin. So I got out of my little bed and stood in front of the window as gusts of a frigid Pacific Northwest low-pressure system buffeted my previously warm body. I reached up to shut it, trying to not look outside (what was wrong with me?), and someone yelled, "Nice undies, Ryan Dean. What are you, like, twelve?"

Pretty close, I thought.

I recognized the voice. It was our eight-man, Spotted John Nygaard. There was no mistaking the chop-edged Danish accent that always made him sound like he was really pissed off, and also an emotionless serial killer who wouldn't bat an eye about using an electric carving knife on you while mocking you for your choice in undergarments. And Spotted John was one of the very few guys on the team who didn't know that I was only fifteen, which made me feel kind of manly, in a fifteen-year-old sort of way.

"Shut up, Spotted John!" I feebly fired back. "They're comfortable."

Then I slammed the window and shut the blind.

"Dude," I said, "it's raining. *Raining*. We are *not* going to go through this every night."

I squeezed back into bed.

The Abernathy started hyperventilating or something. I couldn't be sure, since I had never been in the presence of a twelve-year-old in respiratory arrest. All I know is it sounded like this: *Hwupp! Hwupp! HWUPP!*

I tried to ignore it.

Okay. So, you know how when you're lying in bed and you're pissed off about so many things, you don't know which one of those things, exactly, tops the list, and then your twelve-year-old claustrophobic roommate who just picked up your fucking clothes from the floor and hung them all up, putting, I might add, a perfect crease down the legs of your official school trousers, and who also has a very obvious crush on your girlfriend, turns all pale (I'm only assuming because I was so definitely *not* looking at the Abernathy) and begins making this most desperate-sounding codfish-in-the-desert wheezing noise and you're thinking *this can't be fucking happening* and you hope it will just go away and work itself out or something, you know, *resolve itself*, but then it doesn't go away and you're, like, *what am I supposed to do when a twelve-year-old kid starts hyperventilating?* and your mind flashes on something you're supposed to do involving a bag and the face of the afflicted child, so you get out of bed and dig through the trash can and—*Eureka!*—you find last night's empty bag from his microwave-fucking-midnight-popcorn festival, and you sniff it because, let's face it, popcorn bags smell really good even if your roommate *does* happen to sound like an old Plymouth with a blown starter, and then you hold the bag out to him and say nicely, "Here, kid, try this," but he's just staring straight ahead with a look of frozen

I-can't-breathe terror on his little pink (but rapidly blanching to off-white) face, so then you actually have to press the bag over his tiny nose and mouth and hold it on his actual head while you're standing there in nothing but your underwear and thinking, *If you die, my whole night's going to be shot, so I may as well not tell anyone about your corpse until tomorrow sometime?*

Yeah. That.

The Abernathy came back to life.

Ryan Dean West, reanimator.

"Mrff mrff wmmmpr fruhh mrrrffibb," the Abernathy said, and the bag expanded and withered, expanded and withered.

"What?"

The Abernathy pushed my hands away from his face.

"I told you I'm claustrophobic," he said.

"I never doubted it."

Let me say here that there was definitely an acidic look on the little dumpling's face too—and I had just saved his life!—but this was a side of the Abernathy I had not seen (granted, I had been trying not to look at him from any side for the past couple of days).

"Well, are you trying to kill me or something?"

The Abernathy's eyes glazed over and he began to wobble a bit. He put the popcorn bag back around his little airholes. As I walked over to the door and turned off the light, Sam Abernathy started wheezing again.

"I'm going to bed. Try to die quickly and quietly if you can."

Okay. I'll admit it that I felt a little bad when the Abernathy started crying, but come on! We could not keep the window open up here in the Cascades. What was he thinking?

He was probably thinking about oxygen at that moment, and how nice it would feel inside his little lungs, and how he couldn't get any, I thought.

Wheeze! Hwupp! Hwupp!

I sighed and sat down on the edge of my bed.

"Are you going to be okay?" I said.

There wasn't much of an answer—just some rumpling of paper and something that sounded like a muffled "mrrffrr." And then I thought, *Did he just call me "motherfucker"?*

"Sam?"

Nothing.

This was total bullshit. I fucking hated everything about Pine Mountain at that moment.

"Sam?"

I gave up. My ass was just kicked by a twelve-year-old.

I stood, pulled the blind up a few inches and slid open the window.

"Is that okay?" I said. "Just a few inches, Sam. I don't need creepers like Spotted John or Seanie Flaherty doing weird stuff through our window all night."

Sam Abernathy calmed down and started breathing again.

"Thank you, Ryan Dean."

"Whatever."

I climbed back into bed.

"Can I open the door?"

"No. The window or the door. One or the other. That's as far as I'll go."

"Okay. Thanks, Ryan Dean. I'll take the window."

I didn't say anything. It was finally quiet and dark, even if it was a little damp and drizzly. I rolled over and put my arm over my head.

"Ryan Dean?"

Really? *Really?*

"What?"

"Will you do me a favor?"

I had already saved his life. What could he possibly want from me now?

"What?"

"Will you go outside so I can pee and change into my pajamas?"

"No. Shut up."

"Please?"

"Dude. Abernathy. Don't you play a sport? Everyone here plays a sport. Don't tell me you have your own private locker room and urinal. What the fuck is wrong with you?"

Okay. You know. I didn't really say "fuck." But I really *wanted* to. I also really wanted someone in our room—and I'll be honest, I didn't care who it was—to be abducted by aliens or something.

"They gave me a one-year exemption on account of how I only weigh seventy-two pounds. I'm the smallest person at Pine Mountain. Girls included."

Bullshit.

Exemption? Pine Mountain never did anything like that for me. And I thought, *I wonder how far I could throw seventy-two pounds?*

Try to ignore him. Try to ignore him. Try to ignore him.

"Ryan Dean?"

"Look. I saved your life. I actually held a bag over your face for you. I gave you the window. I gave you forty degrees inside our bedroom. That's the extent of my saintliness. You can sleep in your school tie and hold your pee till your bladder explodes, but that's it. I am not leaving *my room*."

"Oh."

I had a sudden realization that the world was turning, that I'd undoubtedly be talking to the Abernathy until sunrise if something didn't give.

The something that gave was a fifteen-year-old loser named Ryan Dean West.

And while I stood out in the hallway in my underwear and wrapped up in a Princess Snugglewarm blanket, waiting for Sam Abernathy to manage his affairs in private, just about every guy I did not want to see (because they all lived at more desirable elevations and had to pass me on the way to the elevators), walked past me. And mocked.

SEANIE FLAHERTY: Dude. Ryan Dean. You know my birthday's coming up, right? Well, the only thing I want for a present is for you
to finally be honest with everyone and come out of the closet.
And preferably dressed just like you are right now. Is that too
much to ask of you?

And then—

SPOTTED JOHN NYGAARD: Dude. Ryan Dean. Um, why are you standing in the hallway in your underwear?

RYAN DEAN WEST: My roommate needs some alone time.

SPOTTED JOHN NYGAARD: You should just teach him the hang-a-sock-
on-the-doorknob signal. That's what I do. Everyone knows that.

RYAN DEAN WEST: That's totally gross, Spotted John. I did not need
to know that.

And of course—

MR. BREAM: Well, well! Ryan Dean! Is it too hot in your room for you?
I could adjust the heat down for you!

That was more than enough humiliation for one night.
Unfortunately, dorm room doors are always locked, a fact that I over-
looked before going out into the hallway in my goddamned underwear. So I had to knock.

And while I was knocking on my own door in my underwear
and clutching a blanket with unicorns around my waist, asking Sam
Abernathy nicely if he would please let me back in, JP Tureau came

through the hall. He stood there, staring at me, shaking his head.

JP TUREAU: Dude. That Annie Altman is the *luckiest girl* at Pine Mountain Academy.

Finally, it was over. Little Sam Abernathy, all pajamaed up and smelling like seventy-two pounds of Colgate, let me back inside our refrigerator.

"Thank you, Ryan Dean," he blubbered.

I threw myself onto my bed, mumbling something about how this was *never* going to happen again and the Abernathy had better come to terms with how things worked in the real world.

Then, out of the dark, drifting across the arctic expanse of a 130-square-fucking-foot room like the damp finger of a ghost, came the voice of a claustrophobic, toothpaste-smelling, soccer-ball-pajama-wearing, cooking-savant angel.

"I like Annie."

Blood pressure = off the chart.

"Please. Never talk to me about my girlfriend again."

"Oh. Sorry."

Why did he have to do it? I was suddenly so angry, the rising waves of heat coming from my forehead were likely going to collide with the cold front coming through the window and produce thunder and hail.

There was only one reasonable conclusion: Sam Abernathy was trying to kill me. I made up my mind: One of us was going to have to go.

Calm down, Ryan Dean. Calm down.

"What sport do you play, Ryan Dean?"

"Rugby. Shut up."

Maybe three seconds of shutting up ensued.

"Is it fun?"

"No. Shut up."

One-one-thousand, two-one-thousand . . .

"Did you remember to brush your teeth, Ryan Dean?"

"Shut. Up. Now."

Five seconds passed.

"Would it bother you if I watched TV, Ryan Dean?"

I'm pretty sure I cried myself to sleep after that.

CHAPTER FIFTEEN

AS TERRIBLE AS THE RUN-UP TO bedtime was, what happened to me that night was worse than anything I'd ever been through. And I had no idea where it came from.

No idea at all.

I know this: I was lying on my back when my eyes opened. And even though all the covers had been kicked off my bed, I wasn't cold or anything. I knew the television was still on—someone was saying something about blanching fava beans—and across the room the Abernathy had clearly fallen asleep.

But something was terribly wrong with me, with getting air into my lungs, with the tilt of the earth, with pretty much everything. I couldn't move. I felt dizzy, like I was disconnecting from my body, and everything looked fuzzy and swirling. I was simultaneously sicker than I'd ever been in my life, and so terrified of everything that I felt absolutely certain I was going to die—I was having some kind of heart attack, and if I said anything, or made any sound at all, I was sure it would kill me.

Then I started shaking, and I couldn't do anything to control it. And although it was undoubtedly cold in the room, the shaking wasn't from the temperature, it was from fear. I had never shaken in fright before in my life, and this made me even more convinced that

I was about to die, and I'd be lying there dead in the room, and Sam Abernathy wasn't even going to know it until he woke up. Outside, the wind screamed through the trees.

And the fear got worse and worse and worse.

Oh, God, I need to get out of here.

I can't say I remember trying to get up. The next thing I knew, I was sitting down on the carpet in the hallway in nothing but my underwear and Mr. Bream was standing over me, saying something that I couldn't understand at all.

"Ryan Dean? Ryan Dean? Hey. Can you hear me?"

Mr. Bream shook my shoulder. When he did that, it made me even more terrified, and I thought I was going to throw up, so I slid along the wall and lay on my side.

"Ryan Dean!"

I waved him away from me.

"I'll be okay. Just let me lie here for a minute."

I did not think I was going to be okay. I just needed Mr. Bream to shut up and leave me alone. Then he was knocking on my door, jiggling the knob, telling Sam to let him inside. Finally, Mr. Bream just let himself in with his pass key, then he came back out and covered me with my blanket and top sheet.

It was the worst thing I'd ever been through.

CHAPTER SIXTEEN

I LEFT THE NEXT MORNING BEFORE the Abernathy woke up. There was no way I would even for a moment consider chatting with the kid about what had happened to me.

I went to the Student Health Center. They had an open policy there that allowed students to call home if something was wrong, and something was definitely wrong. I needed to talk to my father. But to get to the phone required filling out a patient admission form and answering questions from Doctor No-gloves's receptionist, Nurse Hickey, whom I'd had countless fantasies about during my less-mature eleventh-grade year.

Now, highlighting that there was something seriously the matter with Ryan Dean West, I hardly looked at her, and when I finally did I saw that she was quite pregnant, which made me feel like I'd been cheated on or something.

"Ryan Dean West?" Nurse Hickey said. "I remember you from last year!"

That's because most people wouldn't forget the only patient they'd ever had who came in with an injury to his ballsack.

"Oh. Hi."

I know I must have looked terrible. I hadn't taken a shower or washed up that morning, my hair was a mess, and I had raccoon eyes.

"Is something the matter, sweetie?"

"Uh. Something happened to me last night while I was sleeping. I think something's wrong with me."

Nurse Hickey looked at the information on my health record printout. "Oh? Let's see . . . you're fifteen?"

"Yes."

Then Nurse Hickey got these really big, compassionate eyes and stared directly at me and patted my hand knowingly.

"Oh, honey. That's just a normal thing that happens to boys your age."

Then I felt really sick. What was she thinking I'd checked myself in for?

"Do you want to talk to Doctor Norris about it? He can explain why these things happen when you sleep. You shouldn't feel scared or embarrassed about it, sweetie. It happens to all boys."

No.

Gross.

No.

I was completely mortified. Once again, Nurse Hickey had it all wrong about Ryan Dean West.

Okay. Well. I ended up not calling my dad that morning. But I did talk to Doctor No-gloves, who insisted that I take off my fucking shirt so he could listen to my chest and measure my blood pressure, which he said was a little high for a fifteen-year-old boy, but it stood to reason if I had been experiencing insomnia, which was *not* what I had experienced, because I've been unable to sleep plenty of times and it never scared the living crap out of me, but this was all a normal thing that he dealt with at Pine Mountain at least four or five times per week during the start of the school year, especially among "younger boys" (and what the fuck did he mean by that?) who tended to have these "episodes" more commonly than girls (and what did he mean by *that*, too?), so I shouldn't worry, because once I got back into my routine and began working out regularly with the rugby team, Doctor No-gloves was absolutely confident I'd feel like my old self again, but if I felt uncomfortable, he said, I could talk to him about anything, or maybe set an appointment with Mrs. Dvorak, and, by the way, Ryan Dean, do you have any concerns about any other issues going on with your changing body?

Why do I even bother?

I put my shirt back on and borrowed a loaner tie from Doctor No-gloves and managed to make it to my Body Conditioning class before the trainers even realized I was late.

PART TWO:

the code

CHAPTER SEVENTEEN

DESPITE GETTING BACK INTO WHAT
Doctor No-gloves called "my routine," after two weeks I did not feel
like my old self again.

I had been working out—the team was in full-contact mode, and
the first fifteen (that's first string in rugby) had been established, with
me at number ten, stand-off, even though I felt like I wasn't going to
be able to handle the pressure of all the guys and Coach M counting
on me to be some kind of leader. Luckily for me, I kind of lost myself
when I was on the pitch and in the game—like I almost could blank
out and forget everything else in the world when I had that ball in my
hand, or when I was getting hit or putting the hit on another guy. But
I was losing weight too, because I'd skip out on meals just about every
day. Annie noticed it. How could she not? So I drew her a comic that
kind of skirted around the issue of what I'd been going through since
the start of the school year, and I tried to make it not so dark, but it
only ended up making Annie sad and concerned about my health. I
told her everything was going to be fine.

But there was nothing I could do if things were going to just stay
the same. Time marches on and all that, right?

I'll admit that the more mature part of Ryan Dean West knew
that I'd be better off talking to someone about what I'd been going

through, but that other, bigger part of Ryan Dean West didn't want to seem weak or needy or broken to Annie, because outside of Annie Altman I felt like I didn't have a single true friend in the world, which made me miss Joey even more and made things worse at the same time too.

So I sat down one afternoon, when, for whatever reasons, the Abernathy was not haunting our dorm room, and I made a little side-by-side comparison chart, adding up the positives and negatives of the first three weeks into my senior year.

It didn't balance out so good.

NEGATIVES	POSITIVES
- Got a D on our Culinary Arts quiz	- Mrs. O'Hare gave me lunch detention
- Coach M. made me team Captain and Stand-off	- Coach M. made me team Captain and Stand-off
- I'm so scared at night I can't sleep	- We have a practice game in a week
- I can't stop drawing and seeing that NATE guy everywhere	- At least I'm drawing again
- I live with the Abernathy	- He hangs up my clothes, which is kinda gross
- My friends don't hang out with me anymore	
- I'm afraid to talk to Annie about what's going on	

And the worst thing of all—the thing I could not even bring myself to commit in writing to the Ryan Dean West Side-by-Side Positive versus Negative Comparison Chart is the one item that tipped the scale and practically caused my little half sheet of composition paper to spin endlessly counterclockwise. It was this: Sam Abernathy volunteered to be manager of the rugby team at Pine Mountain Academy.

Oh yeah.

So maybe all the calculations, the weighing of good and bad, had some kind of influence on fate—if there is such a thing—because on the Thursday of my third week at Pine Mountain (the day before most students got to leave for the weekend and go home to their families and bedrooms with windows they could actually shut), I had come to a decision about making a change for the better. I set an appointment to see Headmaster Lavoie, whose name nobody could pronounce, in order to submit a petition for a reassignment of my housing.

I went to see Headmaster Lavoie at lunch. Another missed meal for our withering stand-off.

By the way, I had to check one box in the error column about the Abernathy. His pedigree did not, as I had theorized, originate in Boise. The Abernathy clan lived in Plano, Texas, which was a slight right turn and about 1,600 miles from Boise.

Close. Well, same planet as Boise, at least.

It may seem mean of me to want to get out of my living situation, but it was not my responsibility to look out for, bond with, share mid-night popcorn chats with, or otherwise fraternize with the Abernathy. It was unfair of anyone to put that expectation on me. This was my senior year, after all, and there were so many other things that I should have been enjoying besides all that icy fresh air from sleeping with our goddamned window open (and no screen, either, by the way), as well as my frequent exiles out into the hallway so that the Abernathy could change, shower, or poop—if he even had a functioning digestive tract.

And I struggled—but only a little bit—with formulating my "It's not your fault; it's mine" speech that I'd inevitably have to deliver to the heartbroken Abernathy, because there was no way to do this and not hurt his feelings. But in the end, Sam Abernathy's feelings were not my concern. I had to look out for number one, or number ten, if that matters. If anything, I had to feel a twinge of empathy for the next cellmate in Unit 113. Maybe I'd leave him a list of pointers on how to successfully navigate the inhospitably storm-tossed and claustrophobic seas of Sam Abernathy.

"Please take a seat. The headmaster will be with you as soon as he's available."

Apparently, even Mrs. Knudson, the administrative secretary at Pine Mountain, didn't know how to say his name.

I'll admit I was nervous. Nobody likes dealing with grown-ups with unpronounceable names who also happen to be in positions of high authority.

Mrs. Knudson handed me a clipboard that had a ballpoint pen leg-ironed to it by a length of chain, so I could complete a Request for Change of Housing form for Headmaster Lavoie. Unfortunately, as I sat there sweating over my penmanship, I was confronted by something I hadn't fully considered: box number seven.

> **7. State specific reason(s) for requesting housing reassignment:**

What could I say?

I ~~HATE~~ DON'T LIKE Sam Abernathy.

My roommate is ~~INSANE~~ TWELVE.

My roommate leaves the window open and kicks me out so
HE CAN ~~POOP~~ PUT ON HIS PAJAMAS.

~~My roommate has a crush on my girlfriend. Just. No.~~

I AM A SENIOR AND DESERVE ~~TO GET~~
~~WHAT I WANT~~ MORE THAN THIS.

Why did all this have to be so difficult?

"Um. Can I have another form, please, Mrs. Knudson?"

I crumpled up attempt number one at box number seven and sat
down again with a fresh start, a tabula rasa, or a box number seven
rasa, as it were. I had absolutely no idea what I should argue to win
my case.

And as I sat there staring at empty box number seven, which is
what teenagers do so frequently on exam days (like when I had to
know how many fucking tablespoons make one fluid ounce), hoping
that words would magically Etch A Sketch themselves into coherency,
Headmaster Lavoie's door opened and a small exodus of humanity
spilled out into Mrs. Knudson's reception area.

To be honest, the exodus wasn't so much along the scale of the
"children of Israel" type of numbers; there were exactly three people
with Headmaster Lavoie: a man, a woman, and a teenage boy. It was a
typical we-are-bringing-our-child-to-abandon-him-on-your-doorstep
scene at Pine Mountain Academy. What else could it be? They were

all the picture of American privilege: tailored clothes, unscuffed shoes, the man in a tie and the woman in an actual skirt. The boy, their son, was maybe a freshman, I thought. He looked nervous and eager to get the hell out of Headmaster Unpronounceable-name's office, which was a good sign that he was psychologically stable.

It turned out I was wrong about the dumping-the-kid off assumption, but I'll stand by the rest of it. But for just a moment when the quiet little family came out of Headmaster Lavoie's office, I made eye contact with the boy and something happened.

No, it wasn't a magical moment.

Somehow, I felt certain that I knew the kid from somewhere.

Okay. You know how when you're wandering around in public and you make eye contact with someone and you know that you know them, but that's all you know (which is a lot of knowing going on there), and your eyes get this hey-I-recognize-you look, and maybe you even smile and the muscles in your tongue actually begin to run through their "Hey, how's it going??!!" warm-up routine and just before you say it, the other person gives you a who-the-fuck-are-you-and-you-should-stop-looking-at-me-right-now-weirdo look so your speech assembly line gets all bottlenecked and you feel yourself turning red and wanting to die because maybe you really *don't* know the dude you were just giving full-on love eyes to?

Yeah. Pretty much that.

But then who the fuck was he? I *knew* I knew him, which again, well, when you know you know something, you just know it, right?

Maybe you can help me out. Here's what he looked like: As I said, I think he must have been fourteen or fifteen years old. He was just a bit shorter than me, but he was fit, with square shoulders that showed me he probably played a sport—maybe rugby, since I had assumed he was enrolling in Pine Mountain, as opposed to doing what he was actually doing, which was canceling his enrollment. He had thick, wavy brown hair that you could tell he spent time on getting it to look perfectly messy, and a darker-than-Oregonian complexion with those kind of picket-fence braces on his upper teeth that looked like dot-to-dots played with a soldering iron. His non-student, non-tie shirt was open two buttons, and he wore one of those lassolike necklaces that attached by magnets at each end, and I swear on all things holy that I knew the kid.

Maybe I'd played against him at some time, I thought. That must have been it.

Anyway, since I was busted, like, practically checking this dude out as I sat there like a dork with my clipboard, I pointed at the kid and said, "I think I know you, don't I?"

He shook his head. "Nah, bro. I don't think so."

He *broed* me. I hate getting *broed*.

At which point I felt like a complete ass. With a clipboard, which only served to magnify my assishness. Bro.

Headmaster Lavoie gave me a suspicious look that also conveyed his do-I-actually-have-another-person-with-a-clipboard-waiting-to-talk-to-me-during-lunch disappointment, and then shook hands with the man and the son.

And he said this to them: "Mr. Cosentino, Mrs. Cosentino. Dominic. I'm sorry things aren't going to work out here for you, son, but I understand completely. It was so nice to see you all again."

And that's where I'd seen the kid before—in photographs my friend Joey had kept in his room in O-Hall. These were Joey's parents, and the kid was his younger brother, Dominic—I remembered how Joey called him Nico—who under any other circumstances would have started school at Pine Mountain this year; and why he was not doing that was a no-brainer as far as I was concerned.

CHAPTER EIGHTEEN

I FELT TORN, BUT I WAS THANKFUL
that some reasonable shred of my command center restrained me from
blurting out something as horrendously dorky as *Hey! I do* know *you!
You're Joey Cosentino's family, and Joey was my best friend in the world and
he saved my ass so many times from doing stupid things like blurting out a
ridiculous and self-serving info-dump about myself in front of decent and
loving human beings, which is why I'm not actually saying this right now,
but only imagining how stupid I would feel if I did!*

Or something.

But I did want to say something to the Cosentinos. To be honest, I
wanted to tell them a lot of things. I desperately wished an opening would
present itself, and when it didn't, when Mr. Cosentino held the administrative center's door open to let his wife and son—*Joey's brother!*—out of
the office, I just sat there with my clipboard and unfilled-out complaint
form that I suddenly could not possibly care any less about, much less
recall, who Sam Abernathy even was, with my mouth hanging open and
eyes glazed over, looking like a Pekingese who'd been left too long inside
a car on a sweltering summer afternoon.

Click.

The door shut behind them. They were gone.

Headmaster Lavoie looked at me.

Mrs. Knudson looked at me.

"Were you waiting to see me, son?" Headmaster Lavoie asked.

"Uh."

I glanced at the blank form pinched to my clipboard.

"I'm writing a piece for the school newspaper," I squeaked. "I was wondering how to pronounce your name, sir."

Headmaster Lavoie laughed.

Mrs. Knudson laughed.

It was all so fucking funny, wasn't it?

I handed the clipboard back to Mrs. Knudson, mumbling something about changing my mind and throwing in an abbreviated apology to both of them for wasting their time. And, fully embarrassed for all kinds of reasons, I ducked out of Headmaster Unpronounceable-secret-name's office and followed the departing Cosentino family to the school's parking lot.

Of course, I had no idea what I might say to them, only that I felt an urgent need to let them know who I was before they left, because I was certain I'd never have a chance to speak with Joey's parents and brother again.

I couldn't let that happen.

So I dashed out into the parking lot just as Mr. Cosentino was getting into the driver's seat of what I guessed could only be a rental car—because it was a red minivan, and there was no way I could picture anybody in Joey's family driving a red minivan. I waved my arm and said something dumb like "Excuse me! Mr. Cosentino? Excuse me! Wait up!"

Which caught Joey's dad's attention, stopping him at his open van door. And when he looked back, I can only assume this is what he saw: He saw me, Ryan Dean West, waving my hand over my head like a dork and looking at him with pleading eyes. Then he probably saw me cutting between one of the first rows of diagonally parked cars. The car I jogged past happened to be Seanie Flaherty's black off-road vehicle (I know, right? Now that Seanie was a senior, not only could he drive a car, but he was allowed to keep his own car here at Pine Mountain, and actually go places—like home on the weekends, since his family lived in Beaverton, to visit his vast pornography collection), and I couldn't help but notice all the inappropriate bumper stickers Seanie had all over the back window, like the one that read RUGBY, BECAUSE YOU'RE ALREADY DRUNK! And I thought, *Man, if Headmaster Whatever-that-dude's-human-name-is ever notices this, he's going to make Seanie take it off.*

And then Mr. Cosentino probably saw the waving, cutting-between-the-cars dorky dude hook the toe of his right foot square into one of those goddamned concrete-turd thingies that like Headmaster Lavoie's last name no human being knows what to call them, and that also separate rows of parking spots, and then lurch forward like the waving, cutting-between-the-cars dorky dude was running away from a German trench in World War I and just caught a Mauser round squarely between his shoulder blades.

I went down.

And while I was noticing the smell of asphalt and considering the acidic sting of a certainly road-rashed knee, I could only imagine the Cosentino family having an in-van conversation that went something like this:

I got up.

When I dusted myself off, I noticed my pants were ripped, and through that newly opened window I could see a bloody right knee.

Great.

Mr. Cosentino just stood beside his car and watched, no doubt wondering what the hell was going on with the kid, the lion pit, and the parking lot.

I waved. "I'm okay."

What an idiot.

Mr. Cosentino turned to get into the van.

"No. Wait. Can I talk to you for a minute, Mr. Cosentino?"

I threaded my way between the next row of cars and crossed to where the Cosentinos sat in their red minivan. When I got up to the driver's-side door, Mr. Cosentino grimaced slightly and pointed at my bloody knee.

"Oh. Uh, wow. Are you all right?"

"I'm fine," I said. Then I stuck out my hand and realized I still had bits of gravel embedded in my palm. I wiped my hand off on my butt and stuck it out again.

"Mr. Cosentino, I wanted to introduce myself. I'm Ryan Dean West, and I . . . well . . ."

Then I realized I didn't actually know how to finish what I was trying to say. In fact, I didn't have any clue as to *what* I should say to him at all.

But Mr. Cosentino, obviously the father of the son, saved me—as Joey had so many times. He shook my hand and smiled.

"Oh! Ryan Dean! Joey used to talk about you all the time! It's so nice to finally meet you," Mr. Cosentino said.

And as I shook Mr. Cosentino's hand, standing there in the slight drizzle that fell over Pine Mountain's parking lot, bleeding from my stinging right knee, I thought, *Hmm . . . I wonder what Joey said about me,* because it couldn't possibly be good, since Joey was constantly saving my butt from terrible fates only a half-wit loser could get himself into, like fooling around with another girl when I was madly in love with Annie Altman, or gambling and being talked into drinking alcohol with Joey and some of the other guys on the team, or having my face busted open a couple of times by getting into stupid fights—well, not *stupid fights,* because God knows I'd always win in a stupid fight, just look right here at my torn school pants and bloody right knee and there's all the proof you'd need, but . . . I really just wanted to know what Joey told them about me!

But I couldn't say anything at all because I was so choked up over the fact that I was actually shaking hands with my best friend Joey Cosentino's father.

Then Mr. Cosentino leaned toward the car and said, "Sheri, Nico, this is the boy Joey told us about—Ryan Dean. Remember?"

I still needed to know what, exactly, Joey had said.

Doors opened on the other side of the van, and I realized that I was now actually afraid of talking to the Cosentino family, but I had kind of painted myself into a corner. And I also managed to get a bloody knee and torn pants in the process.

I got choked up like a thirteen-year-old girl at a boy-band concert when Nico got out of the van and stood between me and Mrs. Cosentino.

He eyed me up and down. He was as unsmiling as he'd been inside the headmaster's office.

"You ate shit over there, bro."

Okay, so my knee was pretty bloody and Nico just broed me for the second time in less than fifteen minutes.

"I . . . Uh . . . Mrs. Cosentino, it's very nice to meet you. And, Nico, Joey used to keep a picture of you in his room. That's why I recognized you. And I just . . . I . . ."

Mrs. Cosentino nodded and smiled at me. "I understand, Ryan Dean. Really. We know how much you all meant to Joey. Really we do, honey."

Joey's mom melted my heart.

Nico began sidling his way back into the van. He said, "Well, nice meeting you. We got to go, though."

And my voice cracked when I said, "I know you probably have to leave, but if you ever come back—maybe to watch us play rugby or something—it would be . . . I mean, I'd really like to maybe hang out and talk to you, Nico. Or, you know, we can't have phones and stuff, but if you wrote a letter to me here at PM, I'd write you back. Or draw something. I draw."

And then Joey's brother, Nico, turned back from the edge of the van's sliding door and said, "Thanks, bro, but I don't really need to talk about things."

Then he climbed inside and pulled shut the door.

Mr. Cosentino gave me an embarrassed glance, and Joey's mom looked a little hurt and saddened.

And before they left, she said to me, "I'm really sorry about that, Ryan Dean."

Yeah. Me too.

CHAPTER NINETEEN

"WHAT HAPPENED TO YOUR PANTS?"

Sam Abernathy—our team manager and the guy I had just nearly filed divorce papers on—caught me on my way into the locker room as he carried out two heavy baskets of water bottles for Coach M. The kid tottered along, grunting from the weight of the bottle carriers, which probably doubled gravity's pull on him.

And somehow the Abernathy had managed to appear there at the big metal double doors to the locker room at the start of practice every day since becoming manager, dressed in baggy shorts and a Pine Mountain Rugby Football Club hoodie big enough to function as his sleeping bag. I never asked him about it—because, you know, I don't actually *converse* with the larva—but I had to wonder if he made Coach M or the rest of the staff leave the locker room at the end of lunch so he could change into his adorable little manager's costume.

The guys on the team instantly adopted the Abernathy as a sort of mascot, too. They couldn't help themselves; after all, the kid gave off this fluffy-baby-chick-in-an-Easter-basket vibe that kind of made you want to hold him inside your cupped hands. Until he ran out of oxygen, in my case.

But I had to be nice at practice. Well, at least I had to not be mean, since I was captain and had to set an example of all the ethical and responsible stuff that frequently went against my gut instincts.

Spotted John walked in front of me and rubbed the Abernathy's head. That was something else everyone on the team did too. Every day on the way into the locker room and on our way out at the end of practice, all the guys rubbed Sam's hair and called him Snack-Pack. JP Tureau seemed to take pleasure in pointing out at any opportunity how Snack-Pack Abernathy also happened to be *my* roommate.

"How's it hanging, Snack-Pack?" Spotted John said.

"Hi, Spotted John. What happened to your pants, Ryan Dean?" the Abernathy annoyingly persisted in his investigation into my trousers.

I fantasized about putting Snack-Pack Abernathy in a chokehold and washboarding my knuckles on his head with enough friction to start a fire. But Captain Ryan Dean outmuscled Immature Ryan Dean. And, speaking of this inner struggle, I was absolutely convinced that Immature Ryan Dean was far more likely to go skinny-dipping with Annie Altman than Captain Ryan Dean, who responsibly and wholeheartedly embraced Mrs. Blyleven's all-boys Health class Ten Commandments to My Penis.

"There's a wolverine back there by the soccer field," I said. "It tried to tear my leg off."

I winced and looked away as I touched the Abernathy's dirty little-boy hair. You know, rituals and customs, you have to do them in rugby, even if they're completely disgusting.

"Really?"

"No. Not really. And stop talking to me."

And while I was getting changed into my rugby stuff, our little manager-fetus told on me. Not because I was mean to him; the Abernathy told Coach M that Captain Ryan Dean was bleeding from his kneecap, which meant I had to go back inside the coaching office and allow manager-grub Sam Abernathy to clean and tape up my cut, since there are very strict laws against playing rugby while hemorrhaging from open wounds and stuff, and taping up semidetached body parts was one of the things rugby managers sometimes had to do, along with collecting up all the dirty uniforms and towels from the locker room floor at the end of a game.

Why anyone would volunteer to do such a thing mystified me, and I refused to consider—as Annie had theorized—that Sam Abernathy only volunteered to manage the rugby team because it was his singular mission to become friends with me.

I'd told her he was more likely trying to give me a burst blood vessel in my brain.

And the Abernathy's hands were too small for medical gloves. When he put them on, it looked as though skin was dripping like melted wax from the ends of his tiny baby fingers. He even got one of the fingertips stuck beneath the pressure wrap when he wound it around my knee.

"So, how did you do this, again?" Sam Abernathy asked.

"I told you. A wolverine."

Sam Abernathy laughed.

"I think you're one of the funniest guys I know, Ryan Dean."

I shrugged and cleared my throat. I was still perturbed about the way Joey's brother Nico had completely dismissed me—worse, he *broed* me—so I was in no mood to entertain the Abernathy's attempt at flattery.

The front-row guys—the props and the hooker—because they were honestly pretty fat, referred to Thursday practices as "hashtag throw-up Thursdays" because they were generally the toughest workouts of the week. That day, the day of my run-in with Joey's family and my scuffed-up knee, was no exception. Our practice seemed to expand through time, with endless suicide sprints and ladder drills until Coach finally relented and divided us up into four teams for sevens.

Playing the game was what we all lived for, anyway, and Coach M knew exactly how to time things so that just as we were all ready to collapse he could use the final reward of some honest and hard-hitting play to get our heads back into what we were there for. Unfortunately for me, my head wasn't where it was supposed to be that day, after missing lunch and hanging out in Headmaster Name-that-shall-not-be-spoken's office and then the terrible experience in the parking lot, as well as having to endure first-aid treatment from Snack-Pack Abernathy.

And my team was poised to win it all, too. I had the brute Spotted John Nygaard playing center for me, and Seanie Flaherty feeding the ball back from the front guys. But during our last game, just after getting the ball out of our three-man scrum, I got distracted by something.

Well, to be honest, it wasn't just *something*. I looked up for a moment and I could swear I saw that dude I'd been drawing—the one in black named Nate—standing in goal at the far end of the pitch, just watching me from behind the posts.

And it was while I was caught in that momentary distraction that JP Tureau, who was playing on the opposite team, sailed shoulder-first into my chest and crushed me into the turf of the pitch. I felt something pop, and I tried rolling over to protect the ball, but JP had his hands twisted in my jersey and he pinned me there, rucking over me so his teammates could poach the ball.

Being on the bottom of a ruck in rugby is one of the worst places a human being could ever find himself. Luckily for me, rucks in sevens didn't involve as many assailants as a ruck in a full game, but still, they gave your opponents easy chances to rough you up with grabs, hair pulls, occasional punches, and frequent kicks. I got a little bit of all that while JP pinned me down. He even put his face next to my ear and called me a bitch before raking the ball out of my arms with his cleats, and then feeding it to Bags, who went on to score and win the game.

I thought about things. I decided that my eyebrows and the inner arch of my right foot were the only parts of my body that were not sending pain signals to my brain.

RYAN DEAN WEST'S
RUCK PAIN PIE CHART

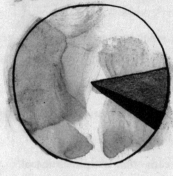

86% – PARTS OF RYAN DEAN WEST'S BODY THAT ARE INJURED OR IN EXTREME PAIN.

12% – PARTS OF RYAN DEAN WEST'S BODY THAT ARE NOT IN PAIN.

2% – PARTS OF RYAN DEAN WEST'S BODY THAT HE NEVER THINKS ABOUT. THESE MIGHT INCLUDE THE WEIRD PIECE OF SKIN THAT ATTACHES HIS TONGUE TO THE BOTTOM OF HIS MOUTH.

Which was just about when Coach M blasted the whistle to end practice.

I was in no mood to get up. I lay on my side, tasting the little bits of grass and dirt that had somehow crossed the border and migrated into my mouth, thinking how if there ever were a flavor of ice cream called Oregon or Failure-Pain Swirl, it would pretty much taste exactly like dirt and grass.

Coach M stood above me as the rest of the guys filed off the pitch.

"Are you all right, Ryan Dean?"

"I just don't feel like getting up yet, Coach."

"All right, then," Coach M said. "You know, he who hesitates . . ."

"Gets rucked," I said.

CHAPTER TWENTY

I WAS PRETTY SURE JP TUREAU
had cracked a rib, but I wasn't going to say anything about it, especially with only one week to go until our first preseason friendly.

A friendly is a rugby match that doesn't count for anything. And, like most rugby matches that actually *do* count, they're usually friendly affairs, because rugby tends to be like that.

"It seems like we hardly see each other lately," Annie said.

She sat beside me in the dining hall as we ate dinner that night. And let me tell you, those preformed fiberglass benches we sat on seemed to shoot spikes of pain upward through my rib cage. It hurt so bad, I could hardly take a breath.

"We saw each . . . other in Culinary Arts," I said, stuttering and gasping through the pain. "Remember? You and the Abernathy . . . won the . . . Coquilles St.-Jacques com—competition. Mine looked . . . like giant scabs."

"You sound strange. Is something wrong, Ryan Dean?"

"I kind of have . . . the hiccups," I lied.

JP leered at me from across the table, no doubt trying to gauge whether or not his tackle had had any lingering effect on me. But I was a rock. Well, a stuttering rock. But there was no way I'd ever admit to being hurt in front of JP Tureau, or anyone for that matter. I turned my face at just the perfect angle so nobody could see the tears pooling in the corners of my eyes.

"You should scare him," Isabel suggested. "That always works when I have the hiccups."

I still hadn't found out if Isabel had lost her virginity over the summer. It was killing me almost as much as my ribs. Actually, more.

And then JP said, "Hey, Ryan Dean, a few of us guys are planning on sneaking over to the old O-Hall at midnight tomorrow and busting in to the place. You game?"

I dropped my fork. It was plastic, so it wasn't very dramatic at all.

"Fun—Funny, JP."

"Nobody told me about that," Seanie said.

To be honest, nobody ever told Seanie anything, unless they wanted the entire planet chatting about it.

"Oh. I guess that didn't work on the *hiccups*, huh, Ryan Dean?" JP said. "Well, can't blame a guy for trying, right Snack-Pack Senior? How about if I said we all found out you broke Penis Commandment Nine?"

Two things: First, JP and some of the forwards were effectively getting the rugby team to adopt Snack-Pack Senior as my new nickname, since I couldn't properly be called Winger anymore. I did not like the name Snack-Pack Senior. It was really creepy, because it almost gave the impression that the Abernathy was my spawn. Besides, the Bagnuolo brothers who played the wings both already had nicknames, so some of the guys on the team couldn't break themselves from still calling me Winger, which I definitely preferred to Snack-Pack Senior. Second, four of my rugby teammates, including JP Tureau and Seanie Flaherty, were in the same all-boys twelfth-grade Health class with Mrs. Blyleven, so we all had to write down and sign and memorize our own copies of the Pine Mountain Academy Ten Commandments to My Penis.

To be honest, the first few penis edicts made sense and were reasonable—kind of—but, by the end of the list, whoever had come up with those decrees (and I am absolutely confident the responsible person was not God) had to have been pulling stuff out of his (or her, because I think Mrs. Blyleven was the original author) ass to stretch the list out to Number Ten. Number Nine, undeniably terrifying, involved motorized household appliances.

But I didn't have hiccups, much less a motorized household appliance, so that didn't work either.

Then Seanie, all deadpan creepiness, said, "Dude. Ryan Dean, did you bring a vacuum cleaner with you to PM?"

And Isabel asked, "You guys have *penis rules* on the rugby team?"

"Grr—Great conversation," I said, and then winced.

"It's a list of rules the boys in Senior Health had to sign," Annie explained. "I'll tell you about them later."

And then she giggled and looked at me, which was simultaneously embarrassing and totally hot, because I would have done anything in the world to be there when Annie told Isabel about our Penis Commandments.

But, unfortunately, that wasn't going to happen.

I told Annie about meeting Nico Cosentino in Headmaster Whatever-you-want-to-call-him's office that day when I wasn't having lunch with her. I didn't tell her why I'd gone to the office in the first place. Annie still foolishly held out this expectation that I would forge a deep and meaningful friendship with Snack-Pack Abernathy.

But, like eavesdropping on Annie Altman's recounting of the Ten Commandments to My Penis to her roommate, Isabel Reyes, that was another something that was too far-fetched to ever consider happening.

We stole a good-night hug behind the screen of shrubbery at the De-Genderized Zone after dinner. I'll admit it hurt enough to make me gasp, and Annie grabbed me by my shoulders and asked, "Ryan Dean, are you *crying*?"

My eyes were watering because of the pain in my ribs, but I still took the opportunity to score major emotional points with Annie Altman.

"No," I said, and wiped my eyes.

But everyone knows *No* is going to be the answer a boy gives to that question, no matter what the truth is, so Annie just stood there, staring at me. Then she put her hand on my cheek.

"I'm sorry about what happened with Joey's brother," she said.

"But he *isn't* Joey, you know. He has to deal with things in his own way. You get that, right?"

"Oh. I know, Annie. Still, it would have been cool if we could have just talked a bit, you know?"

Annie nodded. "I love you, Ryan Dean."

"I love you, Annie."

Then our perfect and quiet moment was ruined by Mr. Bream's punch-in-the-ribs baritone: "Ryan Dean! Are you managing to sleep better these days?"

In the same way I neglected to tell Annie about my torn-up knee-cap and JP cracking my ribs, I also failed to mention to her that I'd been having near-nightly episodes where I'd been terrified of everything. And nothing was getting better.

"Oh. Huh? Uh . . . yes, Mr. Bream," I said. "Much better."

But I could see the pain and concern on Annie's face.

She said good night, and added, "The weekend before your regular season starts, you're coming home with me to Bainbridge Island, okay?"

"You still have that dog?" I asked.

Annie had a pug named Pedro who liked to hump my legs whenever he saw me.

"Don't worry," she said, "we had his balls cut off."

Suddenly, everything in my body, my soul included, was wracked with pain.

Poor, poor Pedro.

CHAPTER TWENTY-ONE

I DRAGGED MYSELF THROUGH UNIT 113's doorway, wondering if it would even be possible to lie in my bed and not feel pain.

The Abernathy, all soccer-jammied-up, was already there watching television, wrapped in his blankets next to the open fucking window. And what a surprise—it was the Cooking Channel.

Mrs. O'Hare would probably dock me points for not calling it the Culinary Arts Channel.

"Hi, Ryan Dean. Want some popcorn?"

"No."

Watch. Watch. Watch.

I sat on the edge of my bed and snaked off my belt, acutely aware that I was unable to bend forward enough to untie my shoes. I kicked them off and stiffly unbuttoned my shirt.

The Abernathy was still watching me, as opposed to paying attention to the riveting feature about marmalade preservation.

"Is something wrong?"

Duh. My ribs hurt so bad, I couldn't even take my pants off. I was not about to ask Sam Abernathy to lend a hand. I lay down on my bed, a mess of unbuttoned, unfastened school clothes.

"No."

"Are you drunk?"

Why, I wondered, was it the case that every syllable from the Abernathy's lips was like a little rusty knife stabbing into my side?

"Stop . . . talk—talking to me."

"Is that why you're sleeping in your clothes? Because you're drunk? I heard some of the forwards talking about getting drunk and smoking marijuana with Spotted John. So if you did, you can trust me. I won't tell anyone."

What kid says "marijuana"? And anyway, Spotted John was from Denmark. That explained everything, right?

Still, I refused to engage. Also, my pain receptors, like the larva in soccer pajamas, refused to quiet down.

"How's your knee?"

NO.

Look, I knew it was going to be a long season and a rough year. The Abernathy wasn't making things any easier for me either. The simple truth is that number ten—the stand-off—gets hit more often than any player on a rugby team, so I couldn't reasonably count on being *out* of pain until May or June. I was also well aware that there was nothing that could be done for injured ribs besides taking painkillers of some kind. I was desperate, too—desperate enough to actually say something to Sam Abernathy.

Painkillers.

That was it. Legendary rule breaker and future Prince of Denmark

Spotted John Nygaard could hook me up. I should have thought of it before getting halfway out of my clothes and lying down. I rolled over and slid my knees down to the floor. I thought about slipping my shoes back onto my feet, but the thought was enough to sway me over to the hell-no camp.

"Ryan Dean! You *are* drunk, aren't you?"

"No. Shut—shut up."

I heard the soft little sound of Abernathy feet hitting the floor behind me.

"Are you okay? Do you need help? Are you going to make vomit?"

Who says "make vomit"?

"No. I . . . my ribs . . . I think I crack—cracked them."

I groaned and stood up. Sam Abernathy's baby cow eyes were as big as billiard balls.

"Oh my gosh, Ryan Dean! Oh my gosh!"

Holding up my pants, I slid my socked feet toward the door.

"If . . . If you say . . . anything to Coach . . . about this, our claus—claustrophobia truce ends. Got it?"

And the Abernathy repeated, "Oh my gosh, Ryan Dean!"

"Let me back in . . . when I . . . knock."

"Where are you going, Ryan Dean? Do you need help? Can I come with you?"

"No."

I didn't even have the strength to grab my room key from my little desk.

I left.

Spotted John Nygaard's room was on the sixth floor, a level in the caste of Pine Mountain that I was destined only to look up to from my untouchable earthbound banishment in the wasteland called Abernathy.

Some random kid with a ketchup stain on his shirt was waiting for the elevator. He looked me up and down and said, "You missing a few articles of clothing, dude?"

Funny.

And I said, "Did you miss your fucking mouth with that french fry, asshole?"

Well, to be honest, I *thought* about saying that, but I didn't.

I buttoned my beltless pants, which wouldn't stay up because I'd dropped a few pounds, and then I did that elevator thing where you just stare directly ahead at the crack in the door and wonder when the fuck the random ketchup-stain kid is going to get the hell out of *my elevator*. And when the random kid got out at floor three, I flipped him off. After the doors were closed, though.

That's how I roll when I have busted ribs, an open (but unstained) shirt, and only one sock on.

Daring.

And my greatest fear was that Seanie Flaherty would be standing in the hallway when I got out of the elevator. He and JP Tureau also lived on the celestial floor six, which I had been to a couple of times but always imagined as some kind of endless pleasure dome of fun, which was a stupid thing to fantasize about, being that there were only boys on the sixth floor and this was Pine Mountain, where pleasure domes—like campfires, kissing, and cell phones—were against the rules.

Luckily for me, the hallway was empty except for the potted palms on either side of the elevator. And then I found myself momentarily seething with jealousy over the sixth floor's foliage, when all floor one had was a claustrophobic, insane twelve-year-old who wore soccer pajamas and knew how to make hollandaise sauce from scratch. Unfortunately for me, there was a sock slung over Spotted John's doorknob, which I understood to be the internationally accepted boys' dorm symbol for "keep out."

Keep out, unless it's an emergency, right?

And as I stood there, debating whether or not to actually ignore The Sock, I thought, *Hey . . . convenient. I could use an extra sock right about now.*

And then I wondered if it was clean and if I could actually stand the pain of putting it on.

Gross.

I decided to bury Spotted John's sock in a shallow, unmarked grave in one of the potted palms.

And again, as luck—or the absolute absence of luck—would have it, just as I was finishing up my sock funeral, the elevator doors slid open and out walked Seanie Flaherty and JP Tureau.

"Ryan Dean! Why are you digging in our palm tree? And why are you practically naked?" Seanie Flaherty said.

"And are you even *allowed* up here?" JP added.

I had to think on my feet, one of which was bare.

"I . . . uh . . . need some palm . . . root . . . for Cu—Culinary Arts class."

Brilliant.

JP stared at me. He could tell he hurt me at practice; I knew it. Then he leaned over the potted palm's pot and looked at me, then at my bare foot, then at me again.

"And why are you burying your sock in our palm tree?" he asked.

Seanie saw it too. He shook his head. "Dude. That's so fucking gross. Why don't you just throw your *special sock* in the trash, like a normal guy would do?"

Seanie made air quotes with his fingers when he said "special sock."

"It's not . . . my . . . sock."

Which was probably the worst thing I could say.

"Dang," Seanie said. "Snack-Pack's got some big feet."

"I hate . . . hate you . . . Seanie."

Then Seanie Flaherty gave me his creepier-than-usual creepy Seanie Flaherty expression and backed toward his doorway.

"Well, it was nice seeing you, and, uh, your sock, Ryan Dean. Or Snack-Pack's sock. Whatever. It's all *okay* with me."

Seanie made air quotes when he said "okay."

And he continued, "I'd invite you in to kick it with some TV or shit, but you probably need to finish doing what you were doing with your sock. Or whoever's sock. Or getting dressed. Or whatever. Dude."

CHAPTER TWENTY-TWO

I WAS ALONE IN THE HALLWAY AGAIN.

I knocked on Spotted John's door.

"Fuck off," came a voice from the other side. "Can't you fucking see the sock?"

"There is no sock, Spotted John," said the guy who murdered and buried Spotted John's sock. "It's me, Ryan Dean."

I heard some movement inside the dorm room, and the door creaked open. I looked up, expecting to see the towering monster of our Danish eight-man, but there was only open airspace where Spotted John's head should have been. Spotted John's roommate, our hooker, Cotton Balls, who stood roughly even with my collarbones, peered out at me.

"Hey, Cotton," I said, "I need to ask Spotted John a favor."

Jeff Cotton—Cotton Balls—looked down at the doorknob, then he looked at my one-sock-on-and-one-sock-off feet.

"Is that our door sock?"

"No. It's mine. My foot sock."

"Why do you only have one sock, Ryan Dean?"

"Long story. Is Spotted John awake?"

"Why is your shirt unbuttoned?"

Hookers get hit in the head an awful lot. To be honest, hookers' heads are the battering ram of a rugby team.

Cotton turned away from his door crack. "Hey, Spotted John, Snack-Pack Senior's here. Should I let him in?"

Oh yeah, hookerballs. Snack-Pack Senior. Great.

From behind the cracked door, Spotted John asked, "Is he alone?"

Cotton stuck his head out the door and looked behind me, trying to see if maybe I was smuggling an Abernathy upstairs to spy on our forwards for Coach M. Then he yawned and let me inside.

I don't know what was more irritating to me at the time: the pain in my rib cage or the intense feeling of outrageous indignation at seeing the interior of Spotted John's and Cotton Balls's apartment—because that's what it was, an apartment. They had a *living room* that was bigger than the entire hellhole I shared with the Abernathy, and each of them had his own separate, doored-off bedroom, both of which were clearly bigger than good old Unit 113. And Spotted John's apartment was like a shrine, a museum for all things prohibited at Pine Mountain Academy. He had two cell phones sitting next to a six-pack of beer on a coffee table, which was in front of the plaid sleeper sofa where Spotted John Nygaard sat in his boxers and a T-shirt that said I WOULD PREFER NOT TO, doing something on a prohibited iPad that was obviously connected to the Internet. It was like standing inside a massive glass-fronted diorama display of "Everything Good Boys Are Not Allowed to Do at Pine Mountain."

Also, the place smelled a little like pot, and I noticed that a plastic bag had been duct-taped over the unit's smoke detector. They also had one of those inflatable life-size girl dolls standing in the corner beside one of their desks, and that really made me feel gross and creepy, because the vinyl girl was naked except for a scrum cap, which is one of those douche-looking foam pads that forwards wear on their heads.

It was almost too much to take in, but at the same time I couldn't look away from all the rule breaking going on in front of me. It felt like the time I'd visited Seanie Flaherty's house in Beaverton and he showed me my first porn film, which I also felt extremely guilty about not looking away from.

I never knew anyone who so flagrantly violated our no-tech contract at Pine Mountain, but, still, with his entire family on the other side of the world, I couldn't really blame Spotted John for smuggling in outlawed communication devices.

Spotted John popped off a beer cap and took a long drink.

"What brings Snack-Pack Senior up to the high-rent district?" Spotted John asked in his clipped and creepy Arnold Schwarzenegger drone.

"I have a broken rib. I don't want Coach to know. I thought you might have some painkillers or something."

Spotted John nodded. "Broken ribs are fuckers."

Cotton Balls said good night to the inflatable girl (her name, apparently, was Mabel) and lumbered into one of the actual bedrooms.

"See you tomorrow, Cotton," I said.

Cotton Balls stopped at his bedroom door and said, "Don't touch Mabel. If I come out and find her popped and slimy in the morning, you're dead, Snack-Pack Senior."

"I never thought anything could be grosser than playing the front row. Until now," I said.

"Yeah. Whatever. Good night."

Cotton shut the door. I noticed the light click off in the bottom gap.

I couldn't take my eyes off the iPad and the cell phones that were just sitting there. It was almost too much for me to resist touching them.

Spotted John looked at me. "Do you want a beer?"

I shrugged. It hurt. But there's an unwritten code when dealing with Mafia dons and forwards, especially if you're the stand-off *and* the team captain.

"Uh, sure. Thanks."

Spotted John handed me a bottle of beer and an opener that looked like a shark.

I grunted when I tried to pry the cap off the beer. Everything I did hurt like hell.

"What rib?" Spotted John asked.

I pulled my shirt back and showed Spotted John the

chrysanthemum-shaped purple blotch JP Tureau had stamped on my bottom right rib cage at practice.

Spotted John nodded. I flinched when he pressed his fingertips against my side. "Yeah. I don't think they're broken. Just a fucker of a bruise. Sit down."

I sat on the couch beside Spotted John Nygaard. It was awkward, because the couch was actually a love seat, which meant our personal space melted us into conjoined twins, and Spotted John was in his underwear, but I kind of wanted to spy over his shoulder to see what he was doing online.

"How's the beer?" Spotted John asked.

"Huh? Oh."

I hadn't tasted it yet. I hated beer. So when I took my first swig, it confirmed what I had already anticipated: The beer tasted exactly like fizzy armpit sweat. Well, to be honest, I haven't actually *tasted* armpit sweat that I know of, but if I did, I'm sure it would taste like beer. Or something.

"Uh . . . it's great." I coughed. It felt like I had stabbed myself in the spleen with a broken pencil.

"It's from Denmark," Spotted John said.

The beer came in a green bottle, and it had an elephant on it. It was terrible, but I drank it, and I wondered how long I'd have to woo Spotted John Nygaard in his museum of illegal shit until he caved in and gave me a knockout pill or two.

I have to admit that I felt guilty about being there in the first place, about drinking beer and begging for narcotics from a Danish guy in his underwear. Annie and my parents would be so disappointed in me, but their potential letdown and my guilt didn't occupy one one-hundredth of the attention I was paying to the pain in my rib cage.

I took another drink. It made me hiccup—a real hiccup—and one of my ribs corkscrewed into my trachea.

"What are you looking at?" I pointed at Spotted John's iPad.

"Shopping," Spotted John said.

I was relieved it wasn't what I thought Spotted John would be looking at.

And in the internationally accepted language of don't-look-over-my-shoulder-when-I'm-online, his answer was as good as permission for me to lean uncomfortably close to Spotted John so I could have a better look. I might just as well have been a four-year-old asking him to make a blanket fort with me. Except that would be gross, considering Spotted John was in his underwear.

"Shopping for what?"

"Ninja stuff."

"Ninja stuff?"

"Yeah. Swords and blowguns and shit like that," Spotted John answered.

"Oh."

Swords? Blowguns?

Spotted John was a psycho. I always knew it anyway. I imagined the beast inside a blanket fort, all dressed in black, dipping blowgun darts into curare[1] poison.

"Are they *real*?" I asked.

"Who the fuck would buy a fake blowgun?"

To be honest, I didn't have an answer to that, so I drank some more stinky beer. It seemed to taste better after the third or fourth swallow. Also, it made my ribs not hurt so much and made me really enjoy hanging out with Spotted John Nygaard while he shopped for ninja equipment, even if he was a psycho in his underwear sitting next to me on a love seat.

At some point, I made the mistake of accepting Spotted John Nygaard's offer of another beer. It was all getting distorted and hazy, but my ribs sure felt better, and I liked Spotted John Nygaard just about as much as I'd ever liked anybody in my entire life. In fact, I was already at that Ryan-Dean-West-is-incapable-of-controlling-himself-after-a-beer-and-a-half point where I wouldn't hesitate at all if he suggested we go out and get buddy tattoos together, except Pine Mountain and Bannock, Oregon, weren't exactly meccas for body art, and that would be gross, anyway.

That's perfectly normal, right?

At some point—I can't recall if it was before or after Spotted John gave me a painkiller—I also ended up with his iPad in my hands and

---

[1] Look it up! It's what people dip blowgun darts into, but I'm pretty sure you can't buy it off an iPad.

found myself having a fantastic experience poking around in every teenager social networking app to see if I could find out anything at all about a kid named Dominic—Nico—Cosentino.

"See? I told you he'd be easy to find," Spotted John said.

We found his picture, his address, everything. And the Cosentinos had moved—to Oregon.

"You're the best guy ever, Spotted John," I said as I floated out over the waters of Idiot Bay. "And you're a ninja on top of everything."

"Will you guys *shut up* out there?" Cotton Balls's voice seeped through his closed bedroom door.

We laughed.

My ribs felt wonderful. In fact, my entire body felt like I was that superhero who could stretch in any direction, like Silly Putty or something.

Yeah, the S.S. *Idiot Ship* had steamed out of port, and Ryan Dean West stood at the rail, waving good-bye to everything I ever knew. For a moment, I could almost imagine the Abernathy waving back to me from the dock. But then he was standing next to Annie, who was also waving to me, and she had her arm around the Abernathy's shoulders while they both giggled and blushed and talked about making gnocchi in Mrs. O'Hare's class.

And at some point, Spotted John Nygaard handed me one of his cell phones and told me I should call Nico Cosentino, which I did, but I can't really remember much of the conversation beyond

Nico's getting pissed off at me for calling him at midnight, and then how I asked him what time it was where he lived in Oregon.

Yeah, I was pretty stupid.

And that was about the point at which I realized I did not remember why I'd come to Spotted John's place to begin with, or how to get back to Princess Snugglewarm and Abernathy Land. But thankfully—because he was such a great guy, as well as a ninja—Spotted John Nygaard offered his pullout love seat bed for me, so thank all things Denmark I was going to sleep in a place with closed windows and no twelve-year-old kids.

Unfortunately for me, at some point, Spotted John Nygaard and Cotton Balls thought it would be really hilarious if they put Mabel, their inflatable doll, in bed with Snack-Pack Senior, their team captain, while I slept. They also thought it would be hilarious if they took lots of pictures of us, which they uploaded to every goddamned website imaginable from Spotted John's iPad.

Hilarious.

I dreamed about being on a boat, sailing farther and farther away from Annie Altman.

At some point—it was just about sunrise—I woke up.

And I didn't wake up due to the rotation of the earth and the subsequent waves of light that streamed down on Pine Mountain from a yellow dwarf star (the sun *is* a yellow dwarf, right?). I woke up because Spotted John and Cotton Balls were laughing so hard, it sounded like someone was going to need a Heimlich buddy and a defibrillator in about three seconds.

And then I had one of the most intense what-the-fuck moments, because I had no idea where I was (although the bed was much bigger and more comfortable than the puppy pad I slept on in Unit 113), and I was snuggled up to something cold and human-shaped, which I immediately believed was the corpse of some girl I couldn't remember meeting.

Awkward.

Also, I had no canned apology prepared for her in case this all turned out to be real.

The other discomforting element was that the only thing I had on was a pair of briefs. And for some reason, I couldn't help but run through the Five-Point Checklist for Consent Mrs. Blyleven had us senior boys memorize in Health class.

Checkpoint one: You and your partner must both enthusiastically *agree to engage in mutual contact or petting.*

Who says "petting"? Nobody says "petting" unless they were born in the Midwest at a time when a rotary-dial phone was a rich-man's toy.

"Ha ha ha ha ha!" came the lunatic cackles from the people in the room with me (I still couldn't remember coming up to the sixth floor).

Click click click! went the fake sound-effect shutter on Spotted John Nygaard's iPad camera.

"I got it on video!" came the voice of Cotton Balls, our hooker.

Knock knock knock! went a set of beefy knuckles on a presumably shut door somewhere.

"John? Jeffrey? Are you boys awake? It's Mr. Bream. Can you let me in, please? We're looking for a student who didn't come home last night."

Oh shit.

"Oh shit!" Cotton Balls said. "I better hide Mabel."

Empty bottles clinked in the wild cleanup frenzy going on around me. Cotton Balls wrapped up Mabel in the sofa bed's blanket, which was the only thing covering me—us—and Spotted John stashed his cell phones and iPad beneath the pillow that was under my very groggy head.

Then a door opened, and there were people.

Lots of people.

CHAPTER TWENTY-THREE

OKAY. SO, YOU KNOW HOW IN THOSE first ten seconds after you wake up from a particularly deep sleep, and you're next to some air-filled plastic stranger in someone else's room and you have absolutely nothing on except your underwear and there are two—no, two and a half—guys in full school uniforms with ties and shit, laughing at you because you're on display for the entire fucking planet like some kind of living motivational poster about things you should never be photographed doing, and the door is wide open and all you want to do is go back to sleep, especially now that the balloon woman has abandoned ship, but the one-half boy in the school tie, who happens to be twelve years old and is named Sam Fucking Abernathy, is shrieking in what could either be joy or horror, "We found him! There he is!" and the adult figure hovering over you is actually touching your naked fucking shoulder (gross!) and saying, "Ryan Dean? Ryan Dean? What are you doing here, son?" and you're thinking, *This all has to be a dream, right?* but it obviously isn't, and you have no way of formulating an answer to Mr. Bream's question about what you are doing here, son, that doesn't begin with the word "I'm" and end with the words "fucking sleeping, what does it look like I'm doing, asshole?" but you would never say something like that to anyone, much less Mr.

Bream, so all you can do is moan and put your hands over your face?

Yeah. That.

"I *was* asleep," I said.

"Why?" the Abernathy, who was definitely not allowed to say anything to me but went ahead and said something anyway, said.

"Because I was tired, and Spotted John keeps his fucking windows shut."

Okay. I didn't actually say "fucking," but I wanted to.

Say it, I mean.

Gross.

I found myself wondering if Inflatable Mabel had been a dream, and, if so, maybe there weren't actually photographs that had actually been taken of me. And her. Together.

But no.

Shit.

What I actually told the Abernathy was this: "Shut up, Sam."

"There are rules about this, Ryan Dean. You can't just sleep *anywhere*," Mr. Bream scolded.

"That's what Mrs. Blyleven keeps telling us boys in Health class," I said.

"Sam was scared out of his mind. You should *never* do things like this to your roommate. I'm going to have to give you a violation ticket."

"It's okay, Mr. Bream," Spotted John, whose eyes were still

dripping with laughter, said. "We were up late studying, and Ryan Dean sort of dozed off. We didn't mind letting him crash here."

And for some unexplainable Scandinavian reason, everyone—*EVERYONE*—over the age of eighteen at Pine Mountain Academy believed every word that came out of Spotted John Nygaard's mouth, which was just another factor in his whole pot-smoking-slash-cell-phone-and-iPad-smuggling magic.

And as I lay there practically naked on a gross, bare, foam folding mattress, wishing I could blink my eyes and then have some clothes instantly wrap themselves around me so I might pocket one of Spotted John's cell phones or his iPad—because there was no way I'd get away with smuggling one out in my briefs—*gross!*—Mr. Bream nodded thoughtfully and then said, "Well, then. You're going to need to find some suitable attire, young man. First-hour class starts in fifteen minutes."

I sat up. It kind of hurt, but it woke me up.

"What?"

"Where are your clothes, Ryan Dean?" the Abernathy asked.

"Don't talk to me," I said. Then I looked from Spotted John to Cotton Balls. "Yeah. Where are my clothes?"

"Fifteen minutes, Ryan Dean," Mr. Bream reminded me. Then he turned around with a disgusted pirouette and slipped outside, into the hallway.

As soon as Mr. Bream left, Spotted John thrust a finger at the

Abernathy and said, "Get out, Snack-Pack, or I'll stuff you inside my underwear drawer."

Spotted John had no idea the degree of terror the prospect of being crammed inside a dresser drawer inflicted on the claustrophobic little maggot, who instantly turned as pale as a . . . well, maggot. The Abernathy momentarily froze. I detected pinpoint beads of sweat on his minnow-size forehead.

"He doesn't mean it, Abernathy," I said. "Just go to class. I'll see you in Foods."

Then two things struck me: First, was I being *nice* to the Abernathy? No. I couldn't do something like actually feel sorry for him. And second, the little grub got this look on his face like he was going to tattle on me to Mrs. O'Hare for calling Culinary Arts "Foods."

"You mean you'll see me in Creative Writing, Ryan Dean," the Abernathy pointed out.

"Whatever. Stop talking to me."

"Did you do your homework? You know—the descriptive poem about your body?"

Crap. I forgot all about Dr. Wellins's perv-poetry assignment. Maybe I should just walk to Dr. Wellins's class in my underwear and call it an unspoken poem. He did, after all, tell us to embrace the idea of writing our body-exploration poems while completely naked, him being the unwaveringly creepy old pervert that he was.

"Time to go, Snackers," Cotton Balls said.

And on his way out, the Abernathy reminded me, "You only have about ten minutes, Ryan Dean. Don't get in trouble."

After Sam Abernathy left, Cotton Balls dead-bolted the door behind him.

"That was close," Spotted John said. "You almost got us in a shit-load of trouble."

"Where are my clothes?"

"They're in the spruce tree." Spotted John hitchhiked a thumb toward the window through Cotton Balls's bedroom doorway.

"Why are they in a tree?"

"We threw them out the window because you admitted that you buried our sock," Cotton Balls said. "It was only fair."

"After you crashed, Cotton Balls woke up and we thought we should throw your only sock in the tree, but then we thought justice would require more than that. You're lucky we left you in your little boy undies. Balls was going to toss those, too," Spotted John added.

On the one hand, I was proud of myself for confessing that I was the one who had buried Spotted John's door sock. It made me feel saintly and absolved. On the other hand, I suppose I couldn't really blame them for getting even, so I was grateful Cotton Balls didn't take my underwear, too. But still, it made me sad to think that my clothes were about fifty feet above the ground, dangling from the limbs of a spruce tree in a cold Oregon drizzle.

"They're not *little boy undies*," I said.

Spotted John countered, "Whatever."

"I don't have any pants," I said.

Cotton Balls shrugged. "Well, duh. Pretty much everyone who has Internet access is currently aware of that, dude."

"Did you really—"

Spotted John's laughter was enough to cut my question short.

"You guys are dicks."

I really *did* say that. That's not swearing, right? I mean, the word "dick" could mean a lot of things, right? Probably not when a teenage boy says it. Well, probably never. I wondered if I should maybe go to the chapel and pray or something.

"Sorry I called you guys a swear word for penises," I confessed again. I was getting pretty good at coming clean. Except to anyone over, like, seventeen.

"Ha ha ha." They laughed like morons.

"You are such a dork, Ryan Dean," Spotted John said.

I hugged my knees to my chest. "The thing is, I really *don't* have any school pants now. I ripped my only other pair when I did this." I pointed out the bandage on my knee.

In the end, Spotted John and Cotton Balls turned out to be solid teammates, even if they did get unreasonably excited by the photos of me and Mabel they'd uploaded to the Internet. But, in the end, I was also a little late to Conditioning class because I had to play Goldilocks-tries-on-pants-that-are-too-fat-and-too-short-and-pants-that-are-too-fat-and-too-tall before deciding that it was probably best if I just borrowed a pair of Spotted John's and rolled them up, which was marginally against the rules.

And I still went to school that day dressed in a Pine Mountain uniform that was so ill-fitted, I looked like a Vienna sausage in a sleeping bag.

I also had to borrow some of Cotton Balls's shoes because my dorm room key was locked inside Unit 113, which was just below the spruce tree that had been decorated with my only clothes.

At least neckties only come in one size.

CHAPTER TWENTY-FOUR

I FELT BETTER THAT DAY. AT LEAST, until I got to Dr. Wellins's Creative Writing class.

For one thing, it was a no-practice Friday, since most of the guys on the rugby team were leaving Pine Mountain and going home for the weekend after lunch. That gave my ribs, which were loosely swaddled in the tentlike outfit hybridized from Cotton Balls's and Spotted John's schoolboy uniforms, three days to tighten up.

Also, I had finally slept without nightmares, and without waking up in the middle of the night terrified about something I couldn't really grasp—that terrible dark figure that seemed to follow me everywhere, waiting to do something else to me. If I was afraid of anything that morning, it was about what would happen to me when I had to go back to my own room, and my own bed, and be alone all weekend with someone I never wanted to talk to—and alone with myself.

Considering he was a psycho ninja, and despite the fact that he posted Internet photographs of me sleeping in my underwear in a compromising situation with the inflatable girl doll named Mabel, Spotted John was an okay guy. He not only loaned me clothes to wear, he also slipped a couple pain pills into the pocket of his too-tall-and-too-fat pants that I had to cinch up with a belt that didn't have enough holes for a Ryan-Dean-West-size occupant. I pretty much had to hang on to Spotted John's belt all day to keep my—his—school pants from ending up around my ankles.

In Health class, Mrs. Blyleven gave the boys a lecture on testicular cancer. Then she made us watch an actual cartoon that showed us how to perform a testicular self-exam, which resulted in Seanie Flaherty being asked to stand out in the hallway for suggesting what our homework assignment was going to be.

He'd said, "Are we going to have to fondle our balls for homework, Mrs. B?"

It was so awkward and uncomfortable being with all those boys in that deathly quiet room, watching a cartoon about our balls. It was also uncomfortable because the pain pill I'd taken in Spotted John Nygaard's drug den had worn off, and I just couldn't sit comfortably in that goddamned plastic desk chair.

Mrs. Blyleven noticed me wriggling and shifting around in my seat.

"I apologize if the subject of the film makes you feel uncomfortable, Ryan Dean, but this really is an important topic for young men over the age of fifteen," Mrs. Blyleven said. Then she patted my shoulder and added, "No need to be embarrassed about it, Ryan Dean."

The other guys in class laughed at me, and Mrs. Blyleven scolded them. "This is a Health class, boys! There is nothing to laugh about here!"

Which made the other boys laugh more.

Crap.

Mrs. Blyleven seemed to take pleasure in watching us boys squirm in embarrassed discomfort when she told us things about ourselves we didn't really want to hear from a middle-aged woman. So I pretended to take notes during the cartoon, but I was really writing a goddamned poem (on borrowed notebook paper, since all my stuff had been locked inside Unit 113) about *my body* for Dr. Wellins's class.

I decided to work in a bit about a self-exam of my balls.

And although Seanie was exiled to the hallway during the ball-check cartoon, he was right about our homework. Mrs. Blyleven really did assign us to perform what she called a TSE over the weekend, and then she said that on Monday we'd have to hand in a paragraph about what we experienced.

What guy could possibly write an entire paragraph about what he experiences while checking his balls?

Gross.

Maybe I could just hand my poem in to her, I thought.

I figured that if I ran, I might catch Annie on her way between classes, since I'd missed seeing her at breakfast. When I found her coming out of her British Lit class, I was sweating and out of breath, and my oversize shirt was coming untucked from my too-loose belt and too-big pants.

"Oh, Ryan Dean! You look terrible! And you missed breakfast again."

I always thought it was hot when Annie scolded me. I was also hot from running through the halls.

I held her hand and stood as close to her as I could without breaking any Pine Mountain required-distance-between-friends guidelines. "Sorry, Annie. I overslept and ended up being a little late to Conditioning class."

"You have to stop missing meals, Ryan Dean. Look at you. Are you losing weight? It looks like your clothes are draperies."

To be honest, *my* clothes actually *were* draperies. On a spruce tree. And I *was* losing weight, not that I had much I could afford to give up.

"I had to borrow these clothes from Spotted John and Cotton Balls because I got . . . um, locked out of my room this morning when the Abernathy left."

Annie laughed. It always made me feel wonderful when my girlfriend laughed, like there was nothing at all that could possibly hurt me, anywhere. "Why do these things always happen to you, Ryan Dean?"

"Admit it, Annie. It's what you love about me. And my body. Which reminds me—you might find this interesting—Mrs. B taught us boys how to do a TSE, a testicle self-examination."

Annie blushed, the same color as when she gazed upon the fetal, hedgehog-like, Sam Abernathy. "And how did Mrs. Blyleven teach a bunch of guys how to do *that*?"

"Well, it was a cartoon, to be honest. And the main character was a fox. Named Timmy, the TSE Fox. And Timmy the TSE Fox had hands. The hands, and opposable thumbs, are necessary things, in case you were wondering how to do one. Oh, and balls, too. Very necessary. I wrote a poem about it, kind of, for Dr. Wellins's class. The old perv made us write poems reflecting on our bodies while we were naked. Here. I better get to class or I'll be late and the Abernathy will probably send out a search team for me again."

I passed a folded sheet of paper to Annie.

"What's this?"

"It's a copy of my naked poem for Dr. Wellins. So you can think about me when you're gone this weekend."

I winked at Annie.

"You're such a pervert!" she said.

"That's the other thing you love about me, Annie." I squeezed her hand. "See you in *Foods class*."

The Abernathy wriggled and squirmed in his seat when I walked into Dr. Wellins's class.

"Ryan Dean! You have gigantic clothes on!"

I held on to my pants. "Don't talk to me."

"I brought your backpack, just in case you had any important homework in there—like your poem about your body. And speaking of your body, how are *your ribs*?"

When he said "your ribs," the Abernathy whispered as though we were sharing some darkly conspiratorial secret.

"Never talk to me about my body again."

And why was this kid so nice to me, anyway? Couldn't he see I neither wanted nor deserved his bubbliness? Maybe he was in an especially good mood because he'd been able to write his naked poem, or shower and poop without having to ask me to leave my own fucking dorm room.

I should probably never think about Sam Abernathy composing naked poetry, or showering and pooping, again.

It's all too much.

"I hope my young scholars are emotionally prepared to share their poetry," Dr. Wellins announced when he walked onto the stage of his classroom, waving his tweed-sleeved arm in a dramatic flourish. "Shall we start with Crit Group One—Abernathy and West?"

Shit.

I took the poem I'd written in Health class out of the gallon-size back pocket on Spotted John's school pants and told the Abernathy, "Alphabetical order, Snack-Pack. You're going first."

Okay. It's like this: I'm not going to try to completely recall the psychological torment of listening to what was actually in Sam Abernathy's poem about his naked body, which is also something I never want to think about again, but it was called "Nude Reclining with Popcorn on a Princess Snugglewarm Blanket," and parts of it included the phrases "What fleshy form lies here reposed, nude, at the mirror by the foot of his bed?" and "These narrow buttocks curve, peachlike in the absent morn"—because, two things: One, the only mirror in our room is at the foot of *my* bed—not *his* bed, *my* bed, and the Abernathy was clearly "reposed" on *my* bed, which also happened to have the *only* Princess Fucking Snugglewarm blanket, which the Abernathy was naked on, which is extremely gross; and, second, *"peachlike buttocks"*? Not only did I never want to think about the Abernathy's fruity buttocks again, I also decided I would never eat another peach as long as I lived. And when the little peach-assed puppy was finished reciting his poem to the class (and he recited from memory, with no paper in front of him, which was even grosser than if he'd read it), Dr. Wellins closed his eyes and lowered his chin, as though he were receiving a message from God. Then he removed his handkerchief and dabbed at the corners of his eyes.

"May I see your paper, Mr. Abernathy?" the pretentious old douche asked. (He always referred to us as "Mr." or "Miss," ever since he became "Dr.")

"Sure!" The Abernathy gave himself a quick little TSE, like he either needed to go pee really bad, or he, well, was giving himself a quick little TSE, which was another thing I never wanted to think about happening on Sam Abernathy's little Ts again.

Dr. Wellins held Sam Abernathy's poem at the perfect bifocal angle so he could read it, and he either read it really slowly or he dozed off for a quick nap, because it was a full three minutes before he said anything to the class.

"What we have here," he began, "is a singular effort—an outstanding example—of what is called a pantoum. Fine work, young man!"

Pantoum. I wanted to shoot myself.

"Thank you, sir!" The Abernathy jiggled his narrow peachy ass in his seat and scratched at his little wiener again.

"And, Mr. West?" Dr. Wellins said. "Please share your poem with us."

I cleared my throat and stood up, hoping some massive volcano in the Cascades would erupt before I could even read the title.

"Well?" Dr. Wellins prodded. "What are you waiting for, Mr. West?"

"I thought I heard a volcano."

Dr. Wellins cocked his head, the way a collie might do when someone blows a dog whistle.

"No. That's the title of my poem, sir. 'I Thought I Heard a Volcano,' by Ryan Dean West."

It went, unfortunately, like this:

I THOUGHT I HEARD A VOLCANO: A POEM BY RYAN DEAN WEST

A half-cooled furloughed devil wriggled up through a fissure
from a volcano that erupted near to Boston's Charles River.
Quite obviously naked as Pope Innocent's nose,
since in the pits of hell not a-one of us wears clothes.

He's gotten very thin due to his metabolic rate,

and sleeplessness caused by a haunting bugbear called

Nate.

If you want to see his body, look at Spotted John's

website,

where he's posted sex photos of him and a girl named

Mabel last night.

He has practically no body hair and his breath smells

like burritos,

President Grover Cleveland had a moustache and a lot

of pocket vetoes.

He doesn't know just why his roommate is immune to

his meanness.

It took all goddamned[2] day to craft a mention of his

penis,

which reminds him that he should try to contact the

board of education,

because in Health class his homework is to do a

testicular self-examination.

"A sonnet!" Dr. Wellins squealed. "And the rhymes are so organic, so unforced!"

What an idiot.

Burritos and pocket vetoes?

---

[2] Look, it's not swearing if it's in a poem. It's art.

"And I'd like to point out that I found a word that rhymes with 'penis,' I worked in a reference to Mark Twain[3], my favorite author, *plus* I avoided the use of one-P-P-O-V," I said.

"Remarkable, young Mr. West! Simply *remarkable*."

"Thank you, Dr. Wellins."

I sat down.

The peach-assed Abernathy squirmed and kicked and smiled and tugged at his balls. "That was awesome, Ryan Dean! But what's a testicular self-examination?"

"Don't talk to me."

---

[3] "A half-cooled furloughed devil."

CHAPTER TWENTY-FIVE

JUST MY LUCK.

Mrs. O'Hare had us make peach crisp in Culinary Arts class. I nearly vomited twice thinking about that which I never wanted to think about—Sam Abernathy's narrow, peachy buttocks—which, as far as I knew, had never actually been seen by any living person. Not that I was on a mission to be the first.

Gross.

"How many pocket vetoes did President Cleveland have?" Annie asked.

"Oh. I take it you read my poem."

"It was really good!" the Abernathy gushed.

I stabbed a bad-dog finger at him and said, "No."

He just didn't have a clue.

And then I said, "About two hundred and thirty, I think."

"That *is* a lot." Annie laughed. "And did you manage to do your health homework yet?"

"What? Sitting at my desk in Dr. Wellins's class? I don't think so, Annie. Anyway, I'd ask you to be my study buddy for it, but I'm not going to see you till Monday."

Then Annie smiled, looked at the Abernathy, and blushed.

What was she thinking?

Totally gross.

"If you want to hang out at my house with me this weekend, my parents wouldn't mind. I think they like you more than they like me, Ryan Dean," Seanie said. At lunch, I walked out to his car with him and Annie.

Seanie Flaherty was Annie Altman's airport chauffeur this year, which didn't really worry me, because Seanie was so weird, and I knew Annie didn't think he was cute or anything. And really, Seanie did not like girls. If he didn't want to admit it, I didn't care. It wasn't going to change our friendship.

But hanging out at Seanie's house was really boring because he never did anything except creep around on the Internet and play shooter video games. What was worse was that his parents always tried to start conversations with me about going to college or growing up, and after they'd run out of things to say they'd start talking about church, which is something I'd always have to go to with them if I ever spent the weekend at Seanie Flaherty's house.

So, no.

"What are you planning on doing this weekend?" I asked.

"Besides my TSE and reflective ball-grabbing paragraph? Nothing. Just hanging out. Me and my balls," Seanie said. "But Spotted John told me to look at his website, though. He said there was stuff on it that's funnier than shit."

I knew I was never going to hear the end of the teasing about the night I spent with inflatable Mabel.

After I watched Seanie drive off with my girlfriend, I bit off half of one of the pain pills Spotted John had left in my pocket. My ribs were feeling better, but then again I hadn't been hit yet. Still, I was pretty sure I'd be okay by practice on Monday, so I wouldn't have to fake it or lie to Coach M.

Then I did what I almost always did on Friday afternoons after saying good-bye to my friends: I got depressed and mopey, and walked slowly back toward the boys' dorm.

Alone.

And on my way there, as a cold wind blew across the lake and stung my nonfruity facial cheeks, some of my other Ryan Dean Wests invaded the wasteland of my head to have a go at me, as so often is the case when I am alone.

RYAN DEAN WEST 2: Bet you're scared about being alone this weekend, aren't you?

RYAN DEAN WEST 1: I'm not alone. I have the Abernathy.

RYAN DEAN WEST 2: Oh yeah, your good buddy. And don't forget, you have Spotted John, too—the guy who posted pictures on the Internet of you in your underwear cuddling with his inflatable girlfriend.

RYAN DEAN WEST 3: I've seen them! They're hilarious.

RYAN DEAN WEST 1: Screw you, guys.

NATE: I've seen them too. I'm always watching you, kid.

RYAN DEAN WEST 1: You're not allowed in my head.

NATE: You can't get rid of me, kid. It's as simple as that.

RYAN DEAN WEST 2: Why don't you kick his ass? What are you afraid of,

    Ryan Dean? You can't let that dude run your life.

RYAN DEAN WEST 1: I wish you'd all just shut up and leave me alone.

I ran back to Unit 113. I think the pain pill must have been kicking in, because I couldn't feel my ribs at all. To be honest, I couldn't feel much of anything beyond being upset and pissed off, which are things pain pills can't do too much for. I needed to get out, away from everything, and the only thing I could think to do was to go for a long run.

But, of course, I had to knock. My key was still locked inside, where I'd left it the night before.

"Oh! Hi, Ryan Dean!" the Abernathy said when he opened the door, dressed in his obvious weekend leisure outfit: camo sweatpants, plaid flannel bedroom slippers, and a hoodie with a rainbow print of cats wearing space helmets and shooting lasers at each other.

"Hi."

Then I was, like, *Did I just say "hi" to the Abernathy?*

It was a reflex. Sometimes guys just can't stop themselves from saying hi when someone wearing slippers surprises us with a greeting at an open door. I had to shake it out of my head.

Do not talk to him. Do not talk to him.

I kicked off Cotton Balls's shoes and climbed out of the tent of clothes he and Spotted John had loaned me. Then I got into my running gear.

"Are you going for a run?"

"Yes."

What was I doing? That pain pill must have had some kind of truth serum in it or something. That must have been why I confessed to Spotted John and Cotton Balls about burying their goddamned sock in the hall palm.

Think about peaches, think about peaches.

Totally gross.

My stomach hurt.

"Can I come with you?"

What was he saying? I couldn't just allow the Abernathy to run with me. What if somebody *saw us*? What if Spotted John's poison nice pills made me say yes?

I had to get control.

"Maybe next time."

I already had a hand on the doorknob, but then, cursing myself for apparently having no ability to ward off the politeness side effect of Spotted John's goddamned pill, I had to turn around and grab my key off the desk.

Wait. *Lack of interest in sex????*

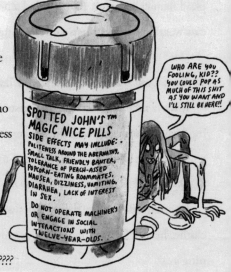

WHO ARE YOU FOOLING, KID?? YOU COULD POP AS MUCH OF THIS SHIT AS YOU WANT AND I'LL STILL BE HERE!!

SPOTTED JOHN'S ™ MAGIC NICE PILLS
SIDE EFFECTS MAY INCLUDE:
POLITENESS AROUND THE ABERNATHY, SMALL TALK, FRIENDLY BANTER, TOLERANCE OF PEACH-ASSED POPCORN-EATING ROOMMATES, NAUSEA, DIZZINESS, VOMITING, DIARRHEA, LACK OF INTEREST IN SEX.
DO NOT OPERATE MACHINERY OR ENGAGE IN SOCIAL INTERACTIONS WITH TWELVE-YEAR-OLDS.

"Okay! Next time, then," the Abernathy burbled. He pointed out the open window.

Shit.

Two girls were walking past our building, giggling because they'd been watching me undress. Whatever. Porno Ryan Dean was probably already at ten thousand hits and counting on Spotted John's fucking website, anyway.

And the Abernathy prattled on, "Oh! By the way, I noticed your clothes were hanging up in the tree out there. What were your clothes doing in a tree, Ryan Dean?"

"Hiding from bears."

I needed to shut the hell up.

The Abernathy was jiggling with joy over the fact that he'd engaged me in conversation. A quick Little-Sam TSE, and he went on, "Ha ha! You're so funny, Ryan Dean! Anyway, Mr. Bream helped me get them down. I'm doing laundry right now, so I put them in with my stuff. I don't mind. It's no bother at all! I like doing laundry. Is there anything else you need to have washed, dried, and folded?"

My clothes taking a bath with the Abernathy's? So gross.

"Uh, no thanks."

What was I *doing*? I had to get out of there before I actually got into a full-blown civil conversation with the boy with an ass of peach.

"I gotta go, Sam."

I was a babbling fountain of idiotic niceties.

CHAPTER TWENTY-SIX

IF I WASN'T SUCH A COWARD, I'D have punched myself in the face. But I managed to get out of Unit 113 before I let go any more unrestrained, pleasant chitchat with Sam Abernathy.

I jogged off, away from the boys' dorm on the trail along the lake.

The rain felt like a stranger sneezed cold spit-mist on me, and I was feeling a little guilty (and spit on), thinking about how guilty Annie would make me feel for being so mean to Sam Abernathy, which would probably make him feel sad if he had any clue about how I felt about everything.

That's a lot of feeling going on there.

Look: It's not like the Abernathy was a *bad guy*. That's what I said to myself, at least.

What everyone—Sam Abernathy included—just couldn't understand was the simple fact that Ryan Dean West was not going to make friends with anyone else this year. What's the point in friendship? When bad things happen to your friends, it hurts worse than if it was your own heart breaking. So it was a matter of practicality. Dominic Cosentino obviously understood that. That's why he treated me like a piece of shit, which was an entirely appropriate reaction to my own over-the-top-Sam-Abernathy-give-myself-an-excited-little-TSE-tug-and-let-me-be-your-best-pal idiocy. In the same way it wasn't my task to help Sam Abernathy through the rough patch that was destined to be his freshman year at Pine Mountain, it also wasn't Nico's responsibility to help me get over what happened to his brother Joey.

I got that, okay?

The world would be so much better off if nobody cared for anybody, ever.

Nico knew that. Lesson learned.

I ran.

When I got away from the main campus, I slipped off my shirt and left it hanging on a trail marker. I liked running in the rain without a shirt, no matter how cold it was—it was like taking a shower outside and letting the universe spit on me, which is something that the universe always seemed to get a kick out of. Headmaster Dude-with-the-unpronounceable-last-name invoked a new rule last semester: that boys could not go running without shirts on if we were anywhere near the campus. He said it was "inappropriate." I'd like to see him run in his fucking Brooks Brothers suit and shiny loafers. What an idiot. He was most likely some kind of ghastly monster, I decided, who only ever showed skin from the cuff links down and from his collar stays up. His real skin was probably grotesquely pocked with pus-oozing boils and would blind any mortal human who gazed upon it.

And I don't know what happened, but somehow, something lured me toward the old abandoned O-Hall, which the school had closed down after Joey died, when they reintroduced all of us "bad" kids back to PM's general population.

O-Hall never did anything to reform me. I was living proof of its failure. I drank beer with Spotted John last night, and then I passed out on his dirty sofa bed, practically naked, with a girl of some tarnished history that obviously involved Cotton Balls's affections and maybe multiple other suitors that I didn't want to know the first thing about. What O-Hall did do to me, though, was make me realize how human we all are, how we all have weaknesses and little empty spots that are almost impossible to fill.

The windows on O-Hall's bottom floor—the one that had been constantly empty because it was the designated girls' floor, and God knows girls never do anything bad—were all tightly boarded over with thick plywood. The upstairs windows had been left uncovered. I suppose the people in charge of shutting down O-Hall figured the only way someone might break in or vandalize the place would be through the ground floor.

That was dumb.

They could have asked an O-Hall survivor like me, or any one of the guys who graduated last year. We boys had no trouble climbing up and down the stacked logs of O-Hall's walls if we wanted to get in or out of our rooms after lockdown.

Dripping wet, and wearing nothing but a pair of nylon running shorts and my trail shoes, I went around back and stared up at my old window, half expecting to see some dim ghost of the person I was before all the bullshit of last year, looking down at the skinny pale kid who couldn't sleep at night.

Everything around O-Hall was wild and overgrown. No need to send out groundskeepers to maintain this old decrepit tomb of a building. I had to snake my way through brush and spruce saplings just to get to the spot where we boys used to climb down, next to the boarded-up, fogged windows of the never-used girls' showers.

My fingers remembered. My toes found their way into the familiar ladder-rung gaps between the logs.

Ryan Dean West: dripping wet, practically naked; cat burglar.

They hadn't thought to secure the upper windows.

It was a little difficult forcing my old window open from the outside. To be honest, my fingers slipped on the wet glass, and I nearly fell to what would certainly have been another pain-pill-requiring injury, but I managed to push the window up far enough for me to wriggle through. And never once did I think to myself, *Hey, Ryan Dean, what the fuck do you suppose you're doing?*

It was as though some primal, unspoken urge had driven me to go back inside O-Hall.

My room was the same as I'd left it that day they came and moved me and Chas Becker—my old roommate—back to the boys' dorm. Neither one of us wanted to go back to O-Hall, and all the other boys had been gone that weekend, so their rooms would have been cleaned out later—if ever. The sheets on Chas's and my bunk beds were still messed up, exactly how we'd left them that morning when we got out of them to help find Joey.

A calendar from a Ford dealership in Los Angeles, where Chas would sometimes go with Megan, his girlfriend who used to make out with me for reasons I could never fully understand, still hung on the wall, open to November of last year. And there were things hidden between my mattress and the wall—an unopened FedEx mailer containing condoms and a pamphlet about how to have sex the first time that my neurotic and grossly concerned mother had sent me, and a Gatorade bottle with about three inches of piss in it that had turned the color of motor oil after seven thousand miles of hard driving.

Who knew a guy's piss turns black in a year?

I was like Louis Fucking Pasteur when it came to pee in a plastic bottle.

It made me feel like I was fourteen again. Not the pee, just being back in O-Hall, where, as bad as it all was, I wished I still lived. But I was in twelfth grade and fifteen now—Snack-Pack Senior—and fifteen-year-olds are way too mature to pee into Gatorade bottles, right?

To be honest, I wanted to pee into the bottle, but I shuddered, thinking about the death cloud of gas that I would release into earth's innocent atmosphere if I uncapped it. So I put my old nighttime urinal back in the space between the mattress and wall.

"Maybe next time, pee bottle," I said. "Maybe next time."

I looked inside our closet. I saw a sock and a pair of Chas Becker's boxers rumpled up on the floor. I thought about giving the sock to Cotton Balls and Spotted John as a gesture of reparations, but decided not to, on account of having no pockets in my shorts to carry it home in.

I tried the light switch. There was no reason for them to have turned off the electricity. The light came on. I opened my old door and went out into the hallway.

I'll admit that I was afraid. I always had the feeling O-Hall was haunted, and not just by the crazy old woman who'd lived downstairs and watched over the empty girls' floor. And if O-Hall was going to pick up any new ghosts, well, it would definitely have one now.

And I wasn't even telling myself to turn around and leave, or calling myself an idiot loser for needing to walk down that hallway again. I could have done it with my eyes closed. To be honest, I think my eyes were closed, because the hallway light was turned off and I was so afraid of the dark there. Because it wasn't just dark, it was *abandoned building dark*, which is something else altogether. And for some reason, empty buildings also generate cold like fucking refrigerators.

Why does that always happen?

I found the switch to the hall lights next to the entryway to the boys' showers and toilets room. I ducked inside for a quick pee.

Flush.

Nice water pressure.

Everything was still the same. Everything. There was even a pale blob of dried Crest toothpaste on the edge of the sink nearest the door—the one I usually had to use because I was the littlest guy in O-Hall—which made me everyone else's bitch.

That last morning I spent here, I brushed my teeth in front of that sink and looked at myself in this same mirror.

I remembered everything that ever happened to me here, just like it had all only been a few minutes ago.

A gust of wind peppered raindrops against the windows.

Of course I went to Joey's room. I had to.

It was fossilized in time. Like my room, it was only partially cleaned out. It was almost as though there was some plan in the future to have a bonfire of O-Hall, to get rid of everything we'd left behind.

The beds were perfectly made. Joey was always so organized and neat. I could never be like that. One of the desks—it would have belonged to Joey's roommate, Kevin—sat with its drawers gapped, with crumpled papers and half-empty spiral notebooks scattered over the surface, but Joey's was neatly squared; so tidy. There was a pen and a pencil, perfectly lined up, lying parallel beside a yellow legal pad and a torn paperback copy of Roget's *Thesaurus*.

Tucked inside the front flap of the thesaurus was a bent photograph of Joey's mother, father, and brother. The photo was one of those coax-our-waiter-into-taking-this-for-us jobs, where the three of them sat together at a table. They all looked lighter and younger than the people I'd seen in the headmaster's office a day earlier.

Joey was a list maker. It was one of the things that made him such a good team captain—his sense of organization. There was a list of things he needed to do, on the top sheet of the legal pad. It choked me up a little to see Joey's writing, and to think about the kid who had sat here at this desk, holding a pencil and drawing perfect little boxes to check off the things he needed to get done.

☐ Calc - Review worksheet. Page 62:
    5, 31 Page 91: 6, 7, 28, 43, 46

☐ AP Econ - Markets. Graph problems
    7, 8, 10, page 48-49

☐ Do laundry for Monday.

☐ TELL RYAN DEAN!!!

What the fuck?

Tell me *what*, Joey?

You can't just fucking do that to me.

And yes, Mrs. Kurtz always gave us too much Calc homework. But what did you need to tell me?

I must have stood over Joey's desk staring at his list for several minutes, just listening to the rain and playing back in my head everything that happened on the last day I saw Joey. Maybe he *did* tell me what he wanted to. Maybe it was nothing important, like he wanted to tell me to stop acting like such an ass or something like that. But he wouldn't have written it down in that case, because Joey used to always tell me to stop being such an ass. It was like instinct for Joey Cosentino.

I ran my fingers over the letters and felt how the point of Joey's pencil had furrowed the page.

It made me very sad.

I decided I was going to tear the sheet off and take it with me, no matter what—even if I had to wait for the rain to stop so I could carry his note back without getting it wet. And then I thought, what if I have to stay in O-Hall all night, waiting? That would mean serious trouble with the Abernathy for not coming home two nights in a row. I'd need to have a serious how-to-cover-your-roommate's-ass discussion with the little worm.

I found a rumpled school shirt, and a Pine Mountain necktie wadded up on the floor of Joey's closet. I picked them up. They had to have belonged to Joey; and I wondered why anyone would have just left them there. And then I wondered why anyone *wouldn't* have just left them there. His shirt would probably just about fit me too, and Joey wouldn't mind. I decided I'd take his shirt and tie back with me too, but not the sack of dirty laundry someone had left in the back of the dark closet. I shook my head at the thought of even looking inside. That would be too weird.

And just as I'd slipped Joey's folded to-do list into the pocket on his shirt, I heard something moving around below me, on the lower floor of O-Hall. Something down there got knocked over, and then I heard a scuffling, scooting sound.

No.

This couldn't really be happening, could it?

It was a trip back through every haunted-house nightmare I'd ever had after being banished here to O-Hall, and why did these things only ever seem to happen to me?

I shook it off. It was the rain or something, right? I rolled Joey's clothes up and stuffed them inside his pillowcase—just like any half-naked cat burglar would do—and then I went back into the hall.

I heard something moving down there again.

I was all kinds of stupid that day. I'm convinced of it. I couldn't stop my feet leading me along the creaking floorboards of the hallway toward the door at the top of the stairwell that would take me down.

I went in.

Click! I turned on the light.

Kuh-chunk! The door swung shut and latched behind me.

Wait. I pushed back against the door. It had been locked from the boys' floor side.

The door was locked and I was stuck in the stairwell down to the girls' floor.

Where something was moving around on the other side of the door.

CHAPTER TWENTY-SEVEN

CHAPTER TWENTY-EIGHT

I PANICKED. I COULDN'T BREATHE.

The stairwell was a vacuum chamber and all the air was gone.

Scritch scritch! went the thing on the other side of the door.

I got dizzy. My knees buckled, and I went down.

I don't know how long I was passed out on the floor at the bottom of the stairs. I woke up because I was shivering so hard, my right knee performed a thumping firing-squad drumroll on the floor.

The upstairs door to the boys' floor was locked, so, as terrible as it was, I knew that the only way I'd get out of O-Hall would be if I sucked it up and walked through the girls' floor and out the front door.

Easy, right? Well, assuming I wasn't locked inside the stairwell from both sides.

But something—or someone—was out there.

I looked through the narrow window onto the hallway of the girls' floor, but it was too dark to see anything with the entire lower level boarded up. So I held my breath and pressed an ear against the door.

Nothing.

Nothing except the voices inside my own head.

RYAN DEAN WEST 2: So, are you planning on spending the night here, or what?

RYAN DEAN WEST 1: Shut up. I don't see you volunteering to go out there.

RYAN DEAN WEST 2: Oh yeah, good one. You're a mess, kid.

RYAN DEAN WEST 1: What do you know about anything?

RYAN DEAN WEST 2: I know enough to tell you that you need to get help, Ryan Dean. I know enough to say that sometimes you just can't fix things on your own. And I know a few more things too.

RYAN DEAN WEST 1: Like what?

RYAN DEAN WEST 2: I know that guy Nate isn't real and he can't hurt you. I know you don't want to face that, do you? I also know that you're going to drift away from Annie if you don't straighten up and admit that you need help.

RYAN DEAN WEST 1: I don't need anything. Just shut the fuck up.

RYAN DEAN WEST 2: I'll make a deal with you: I'll shut up if you'll open the door and get us out of here. I'm hungry and cold. Open the door.

NATE: Yeah, kid. Just open the door.

RYAN DEAN WEST 1: Fuck you. I hate both of you.

RYAN DEAN WEST 2: Same to you, Snack-Pack Senior.

But he was right. I *was* hungry and cold. And he was probably right about the other stuff too. I just didn't know what to do.

So I put my hand on the cold steel push bar across the door.

I held my breath and opened the door.

As the light from the stairwell spilled across the girls' floor, something dark ran toward me from the far end of the hallway.

To be completely honest, I screamed. I probably would have pooped my pants if I'd eaten enough in the past day or so. And I don't know why I did it, but I raised the pillowcase with Joey's stuff in it over my head as though I could use it as a weapon.

It was probably Sun Tzu, or someone who lived a hell of a long time ago and wrote philosophical texts on how to go into battle, who most likely included in chapter fucking one, *Never go to war with a monster, prepared for a pillow fight, Ryan Dean, you dumb fucking loser.*

Yeah. Chapter one.

But the monster turned out to be a Sam-Abernathy-size raccoon. And all at once, the following things happened to me:

1. Relief—I wasn't going to die yet. Probably.

2. Because what do raccoons eat, anyway?

3. But I was so happy that the thing on the other side of the door wasn't Nate, I actually started crying.

4. I also ran so fast, one of my shoes nearly came off.

5. I didn't just run; I ran and jumped, and ran and jumped, and ran and jumped, like a prancing unicorn or something that runs and jumps, because I was terrified that there were hundreds of hungry raccoons down there and they wanted to grab my legs, so I had to run. And jump.

6. I screamed all the way down the hallway.

7. And I screamed in the mudroom.

8. Then I screamed again when I made it out of O-Hall.

9. I was alive! I was alive! I was alive!

10. Shit. How long had I been in there? It was still raining, and it was dark outside.

11. I decided I could probably stop running and jumping.

CHAPTER TWENTY-NINE

"RYAN DEAN! I WAS ABOUT TO GO out looking for you!"

The Abernathy pointed a flashlight at me. He was bundled up in a fisherman's raincoat and full-on rubber boots when I opened the door to our frigid open-air dorm room.

I wagged a finger at him. "Look. Never go looking for me. That is *not* allowed. And never, *never* tell Mr. Bream if I don't come home. That's, like, number one on the Code of Roommates."

The Abernathy wiggled inside his shower-curtain outfit. "Do we have a *code*, Ryan Dean?"

"No. Stop talking to me now."

"What's in the pillowcase? Do you want to do laundry with me?"

"No. I'm taking a shower and I'm going to get something to eat before they shut down the mess hall."

Then the peach-assed grunion said, "Can I come with you?"

I didn't answer him. I closed our fucking window and watched as the Abernathy bleached pale and quivered. Then I dropped Joey's pillowcase on the floor by my bed, stripped out of my cold and wet running stuff, and slipped into the coffin of our shower-stall-slash-toilet-slash-sink.

•••

Knock knock knock.

"Hey, Ryan Dean, is everything all right?"

Okay. You know how when you're cold and wet and have within the last thirty minutes nearly scared yourself to death by confronting man-killer raccoons, when there are not too many things more soothing than half of one of Spotted John Nygaard's magic truth-inducing pain pills combined with an inordinately long hot shower, followed by an equally inordinately long getting-dry-and-making-my-hair-look-sexy-but-not-for-Tootsie-Roll-Midgee-with-limbs-Sam-Abernathy session, and there is one—well, two—other things you're spending some quality time with and then a non-Irish leprechaun invades your moment of zen?

"Leave me alone. I'm doing the first part of my health homework for Mrs. Blyleven."

Fuck those pain pills. I never wanted to take one of those talk-to-Sam-slash-pain-pills again. But they did make me feel good.

"Oooh! What's your health homework about, Ryan Dean?" came a birdsong of little Abernathy chirps through the bathroom door.

So, you know how sometimes you can tell yourself—insist, in fact—that you must not participate in conversational overtures from a gerbil-size twelve-year-old, especially because you happen to be in the middle of your required testicular self-exam, which, by the way, we were all advised to perform *after* taking a hot shower (then to actually be expected to write a paragraph-long reflective response on the gross awkwardness of what Mrs. Blyleven assigned us boys to do), and all of a sudden you can't help but answer automatically, as casually as if you were phoning for take-out pizza, "My health homework was to examine my balls, Snack-Pack," and then, all excited, he asks, "Oh, what do you have to do to examine your balls, Ryan Dean?" and then you have this entire through-the-door chat about the all the details of the TSE you're in the middle of giving yourself because you can't kick the spill-your-guts side effects of Spotted John Nygaard's goddamned pain pills?

Pretty much exactly that.

And then the Abernathy said, "Well if it's *that* important for all boys to do, I'm going to do one too! And right now, so don't come out of there till I tell you it's okay, Ryan Dean!"

No.

I never, never wanted to think about that, or talk about our balls with Sam Abernathy again.

And I was such an idiot, I didn't do anything to stop the Abernathy from following me to dinner. What could I do? Without an easy excuse like Annie around, I was either stuck with the kid, or I'd have to end up punching him. And how could I do that? Punching the Abernathy would be like stepping on a newly hatched baby duckling with rugby cleats. On me, not on the duckling.

"The corn dogs at Pine Mountain are the best thing in the world, don't you think, Ryan Dean?"

Not one time in my life did I ever rate corn dogs anywhere near the apex of the Ryan Dean West Best Things in the World List.

I watched as the Abernathy swabbed his meat stick through a puddle of blue cheese dressing.

So gross.

Also, I wanted to cry because I suddenly realized the depth of my catastrophic social downfall: Here I was, alone on a Friday night, having a corn dog dinner with the Abernathy, who had just examined his balls while I was, like, three feet away from them, examining mine.

"Hey, Ryan Dean, do you know what these cherry tomatoes remind me of all of a sudden?"

No. Just no.

Now cherry tomatoes were officially on the Ryan Dean West Things-I-Will-Never-Ever-Eat-Again List.

"Aww. This is very nice. The Snack-Pack boys are having dinner together!"

I didn't even notice that Spotted John had been hovering behind me and my corn dog and TSE cherry tomatoes buddy.

"Hey, Spotted John!" the Abernathy squeaked. "We're having corn dogs!"

Whatever.

"Hi, kid," Spotted John answered.

"Spotted John," Sam Abernathy began, "I was wondering—why *do* they call you Spotted John?"

I was horrified of where this conversation would go. Because like every other guy on the rugby team, as well as a few twelfth-grade girls at Pine Mountain, I knew the answer to the Abernathy's question about Spotted John's nickname.

"I'll show you how I got that name in the locker room after practice on Monday, okay?" Spotted John said.

"Thanks!" The Abernathy wriggled.

Here's the thing. The guys called Spotted John Spotted John because he had a birthmark that was perfectly round and about the size of a dime. And the birthmark was on Spotted John Nygaard's penis. Which he was going to show our manager, Snack-Pack, in our locker room, on Monday after rugby practice.

Well, the Abernathy did ask for it, I guess.

Gross.

"You're welcome! You can't possibly be an effective manager of a rugby team and not know these kinds of things!" Spotted John chirped back.

The Abernathy kicked his little legs that couldn't reach the floor in the air. "I really like being manager of the rugby team!"

Gross. He had to clean up our dirty towels and socks off the locker room floor every day after practice. That's what managers do.

I shook my head and tried to concentrate on my dinner and nothing else, which was kind of impossible to do. Then Spotted John put his hand on my shoulder and said, "Actually, I was looking for you, Ryan Dean." And Spotted John gave an evil eight-man eye to the Abernathy and rubbed his head. He added, "Why don't you take your corn dogs and run along to bed, Snack-Pack. I need to talk to Ryan Dean about something, and it's kind of confidential, if you know what I mean."

The Abernathy looked wounded, but he could never argue with Spotted John. Actually, I don't think the Abernathy could ever argue with anyone. So, dejected, the Abernathy gathered up his batter-dipped, blue-cheese-dripping meat stick and headed off.

"I'll see you at home, Ryan Dean," he half whimpered.

Home?

No.

And Spotted John sat down next to me. He made a couple spy-like conspiratorial is-the-coast-clear glances around the nearly empty mess hall.

"What's up?" I said.

Spotted John lowered his voice, even though there was really no reason to. All the cool kids were gone for the weekend, and nobody was within earshot of us, anyway. "You know that boy you called from my phone last night? He called back about an hour ago. He thought I was you."

That snapped me out of my post-TSE-and-corn-dog-feast-with-the-Abernathy-social-suicide haze.

Now I whispered too. "What did he say?"

"When he realized I wasn't you? Not too much. But he must have thought we were roommates or something, because he asked me if you were there, and if he could talk to you."

This was huge. I felt like there was some hope that maybe I could get rid of all the bad stuff that was happening to me, invading my head, and following me everywhere. And maybe Nico knew what it was that his brother had wanted to tell me. Or maybe he was just going to cuss me out for stalking him and calling him in the middle of the night and he was going to tell me the Code of Strangers: that I should never try to fucking speak to him again. Because we had that code, right?

"He *did*?"

"I told him I'd give you the message."

I squirmed like the Abernathy in a poetry reading frenzy, but stopped short of grabbing my wiener. Well, almost. Stupid teenage boy instinct.

"You have to let me borrow one of your phones, Spotted John."

"Screw that shit. Nobody takes my phones. I have private stuff on them."

I could only imagine. Gross. And some of that "private stuff" included photos of me and Cotton Balls's inflatable girlfriend, Mabel.

But I needed to talk to Nico.

"John. Please?"

"No. I'll let you call him, though. But you're not taking my phone. You have to do it in my room so I can keep an eye on you. And if you screw around and look at any of my personal shit, I'll fuck you up, Ryan Dean."

"I promise, John. Thank you."

"All right. Whatever. But you owe me big-time."

I honestly didn't think I wanted to owe Spotted John Nygaard big-time. That sounded potentially frightening. But Spotted John had been a pretty decent guy to me, despite the whole bedtime photo-shoot thing. That was just one of those dumb rugby guy things intended to entertain and amuse, as opposed to torment and humiliate, which is a fine line that all rugby players can see. Like a dog whistle to a pug. Which made me think of Annie's poor dog, Pedro, the frisky little pervert who'd just had his balls cut off.

That was very sad.

I swallowed. "Whatever you want, name it."

Spotted John nodded. "Okay. Whatever I want."

Okay, so you know how sometimes when you really want to do something and so you make a promise to someone you don't completely trust because somehow that person has just magically evolved into, like, the greatest human being you have ever known but there's still some deep-down warning signal saying *what the fuck did you just promise to do, Ryan Dean* but you don't care because you really want to believe that whatever Spotted John wants is not going to include multiple things that will ruin your life, so you hurriedly grab the pen and sign the contract on the dotted line?

Yeah. That.

"Anything. I promise," I said.

Spotted John wiped his palm across mine. "It's a deal. Come over when you're done with your corn dogs. Alone. Without your little buddy."

I wanted to fire something back at Spotted John about how the Abernathy was as far away from being my "little buddy" as Pine Mountain was from Copenhagen, but I wasn't going to risk pissing him off and losing the chance to use his phone.

"I'm done. Let's go now," I said.

I tossed the uneaten half of my dinner into the garbage and walked back to the dorm with Spotted John.

CHAPTER THIRTY

"DO YOU WANT A BEER?"

How the hell did Spotted John Nygaard keep a steady supply of beer inside the boys' dorm at Pine Mountain?

Oh yeah, he was a ninja.

I wondered if he'd ever assassinated anyone.

We sat down on the awkwardly close-quartered love seat. Spotted John kicked off his sneakers and turned on a video game called Battle Quest: Take No Prisoners, which was an absolutely inane contest involving murder, ninjas, a World War Five battle in future Stalingrad, and women whose clothes were apparently not as professionally stitched together at the seams as what the male characters wore.

"I better not," I said. "Wouldn't want to get crazy with Mabel again."

"Oh. No worries. Besides, Balls took her home with him for the weekend."

So totally gross.

"Do you ever play this game?" Spotted John asked.

Let me be clear: I *never* play video games, but I know a bit about diplomacy.

"I'm terrible at it. I'll just watch you play."

"I'm the bisexual ninja with the flame gun," Spotted John said.

That confession was definitely five out of five rogue asteroids on the Ryan Dean West Things-I-Never-Saw-Coming Scale. "Uh. You actually smuggled a flame gun into Pine Mountain?"

"In the *game*," Spotted John said.

"Oh. Yeah. I knew that's what you meant. In the game."

I figured we were going to make small talk before Spotted John broke down and did what he agreed to do. Maybe he was lonely without Cotton Balls around on the weekend. I got that. Being alone at Pine Mountain was rough sometimes. Weekends could be insufferably long.

"Since you're a ninja and all, I was wondering, have you ever killed anyone?"

"Not in this country," Spotted John answered. He bit the edge of his lip and flipped buttons on his game controller. "Do you ever smoke weed?"

I shook my head. "Nah. Not in Oregon."

He said, "How are your ribs?"

I shrugged. "I think you were right. Just bruised. They're a lot better now. Thanks for the pain pills, though."

"Anytime, dude."

Spotted John touched my side where JP Tureau had splattered my ribs. I kind of did what any guy would do and leaned away from him. Then he let his hand rest on my thigh.

What?

No no no no no.

I tried to make a joke of it. "Um, Spotted John, you are never going to get to checkpoint one on Mrs. Blyleven's roadmap to consent, dude. So forget about it."

"Ha ha," he laughed.

"Heh." I laughed back at him.

So fucking awkward.

And he left his hand there on my thigh for just a little bit too long for it to have been a Danish mistake, or a rogue five-fingered asteroid for that matter.

It was way too weird. What did I get myself into this time?

Spotted John paused his game. He pressed his hands into his knees and stood up. He cleared his throat and said, "Well, I'm going to have a beer, then. I'll get the phone for you."

"Okay. Thanks."

Spotted John sat beside me and drank his Danish beer. He watched to be certain I didn't get into the personal stuff he was concealing on his phone, and he listened, at least to the Ryan Dean West lines in the conversation I had with Nico Cosentino.

And I'll admit my voice was a little shaky, because *what the holy crap was Spotted John thinking*?

NICO COSENTINO: Hello?

RYAN DEAN WEST: Hi. Nico? This is Ryan Dean West, Joey's . . . uh . . . friend. Is this Nico?

NICO COSENTINO: Yeah. Hi.

RYAN DEAN WEST: Hi.

NICO COSENTINO: Is that all we're going to do? Just keep greeting each
other, back and forth?

*Side note: To be honest, it was a fair question, and one I was asking
myself, which made me realize that I liked Nico Cosentino for thinking
the same way I did, at least about stuff like saying "hi" and stuff.*

RYAN DEAN WEST: I hope not, because this is a borrowed cell phone
and I probably don't have all night.

NICO COSENTINO: Yeah. I didn't think you guys were allowed to have
shit like cell phones at Pine Mountain.

RYAN DEAN WEST: We're not. The dude I got it from's a ninja.

NICO COSENTINO: That must explain it, then. Did he kill anyone for it?

RYAN DEAN WEST: Not in America. But who knows?

NICO COSENTINO: (*He laughs. I made him laugh.*) Look, Ryan Dean, I
just wanted to say that I've been thinking about my brother a lot
since yesterday. And, well, he'd probably be mad at me about the
way I acted. So, I know you were his friend, and you meant a lot
to him, and I'm sorry I was such a dick.

RYAN DEAN WEST: It's no big deal. I guess I was pretty annoying. I
should have left you and your family alone. I'm sorry.

NICO COSENTINO: So now we're just going to apologize back and
forth all night?

RYAN DEAN WEST: No. No.

(There is a really awkward five seconds of silence, during which time

I avoided looking at Spotted John, who was really, really close to me on his couch.)

NICO COSENTINO: So, anyway, I talked to my mom and dad about it, and I asked them if they'd let me come up to Pine Mountain next week to watch your friendly. My team hasn't even started practicing yet, and I thought I'd like to see how you guys play.

RYAN DEAN WEST: You play too? I knew you did as soon as I saw you! What position do you play?

NICO COSENTINO: Winger.

RYAN DEAN WEST: I did that for a couple years.

NICO COSENTINO: I know. Joey talked about you and your team all the time. In fact, he almost never shut up about you. The game's on Thursday, right?

RYAN DEAN WEST: (*Side note: I'm a little choked up thinking about Joey never shutting up about me. It was probably really embarrassing stuff Nico knew about me too.*) After school, at four.

NICO COSENTINO: Maybe we could hang out and talk after the game.

RYAN DEAN WEST: I'd really like that. That would be fucking awesome.

Side note: Okay. You know. I didn't really say "fucking," but I did feel like kicking my feet in the air and doing one of those little Sam-Abernathy-quick-tug-TSEs on myself.

NICO COSENTINO: Okay. My parents really want me to talk to you for some reason. You know. Well, I'm taking a bus up from Portland. If I needed to spend the night, could I crash on your floor?

Side note: Things like visitors sleeping over were entirely against the rules at PM. And then there was the issue of the size of our dorm room. Not to mention the Abernathy and open windows and shit. But Mr. Bream was kind of clueless, as my beer-drinking, pot-smoking, ninja love-seat-mate proved on an ongoing basis.

RYAN DEAN WEST: Dude. Yes. You can. That would be great.

NICO COSENTINO: Okay, then. Sorry I was such a douche to you, and I'll see you Thursday.

RYAN DEAN WEST: Hey, if you need to call or text me, just use this number and the ninja will get the message to me.

NICO COSENTINO: Okay, bro. See you, Ryan Dean.

RYAN DEAN WEST: See you Thursday, Nico.

And, yeah, he *broed* me.

Again.

I thanked Spotted John for the phone and didn't wait for him to say anything else before I got the hell out of there.

CHAPTER THIRTY-ONE

I ENTERED THE ICEBOX OF UNIT 113.

Something was going to have to fix itself inside the Abernathy's little short-circuited brain before the first snowfall or I was going to change the lock on our door.

"Hi, Ryan Dean! I wasn't sure if you'd come back home tonight, but I already decided I wasn't going to say anything to Mr. Bream. You know, because of our *code*."

The Abernathy was bundled up in his soccer jammies, wrapped in his Super Mario Bros. blanket, sitting cross-legged at the head of his bed beside the open goddamned window, watching a program about risotto with truffles.

I absolutely wanted to take off a shoe and bung it at his head.

But I was in a pretty good mood after talking to Nico and managing to escape Spotted John's ninja video-arcade-slash-pot-den-slash-adult-toy-shop without being pressured into doing anything I never would have thought Spotted John might want to do with me. I already convinced myself that Spotted John Nygaard *did not* actually make a pass at me. Right?

No way.

"It's freezing in here, and stop talking to me."

See? Ryan Dean West: a good mood personified.

"I was going to make some popcorn. Would you like to share a bag of popcorn with me?" The Abernathy wriggled like a chubby maggot in his blanket.

Actually, I was hungry. So, whatever.

"Look, if you want to share your popcorn with me, that's fine. I *am* hungry. And I'm also *cold*. So I'm changing into my pajamas and getting into bed," I said.

"You have *pajamas*, Ryan Dean?"

"No. That's exactly what I mean, Abernathy." I didn't even need to unbuckle Spotted John's belt to get out of my deflated giant suit. I kicked off my shoes and dropped my too-big school pants on the floor. "I am taking off these stupid pants and shirt and I'm going to try to climb into my bed before hypothermia sets in."

"Ha ha," the Abernathy laughed. Then he got out of bed and rustled around in his desk to find a packet of popcorn.

I shivered in my icy Princess Snugglewarm sheets, and while the microwave was *pop-pop-popping*, the Abernathy picked up my borrowed clothes from the floor where I'd abandoned them and hung them up.

"I also did your regular-size school laundry, Ryan Dean!" he chirped.

My clothes had come down from the tree. Heartwarming.

I sighed. And then I said what was probably the longest stream of nonirate words I had ever coherently woven together for Sam Abernathy.

"I really wish you could do something about this claustrophobia thing."

The Abernathy stood in front of the microwave, just looking at me. Half of his face pulsed in the microwave's light-shadow-light-shadow as the bag of popcorn spun around and around on the carousel of radiation.

He shook his head. "It's pretty much incurable, Ryan Dean. Please don't hate me."

"But this is getting to be ridiculous. No, it's *been* ridiculous ever since the day you moved in and opened everything in our room and then I actually allowed you to talk me into waiting outside so you could change your clothes or poop or take a shower or do your little TSE or whatever."

"You taught me how to do that, Ryan Dean!"

I really, really, really wanted to punch him.

"But, Sam, it's going to start snowing here soon. You know what that's going to be like?"

"I've never seen snow before!" the Abernathy said.

He opened the microwave and shook the bag.

I rolled over in bed and faced the wall because I didn't want to look at Sam Abernathy's sad little cocker spaniel eyes.

"I'm sorry, Ryan Dean."

"Whatever."

"Do you want me to turn the TV this way so you can see it too, Ryan Dean? I really love making risotto."

"I don't care about risotto. I'm trying to stay alive."

The Abernathy laughed. "You're so funny, Ryan Dean!"

Then Sam shook some popcorn into a plastic bowl and handed what was left in the bag to me.

I sighed again. This whole being-nice thing was wearing me out, but I said it anyway. "Thank you."

"Thank *you* for having popcorn with me!" the delighted little weasel said. Then he climbed back onto his bed and resumed his cross-legged pose.

"Could you just please shut the window, Sam?"

I must have sounded pathetic. But the Abernathy didn't answer me. He got up, went to the window, and—miracle of miracles—slid it shut. And then he walked across the room and opened the front door.

"How's that, Ryan Dean?"

"Don't talk to me."

But the popcorn was pretty good.

And I still fucking hated Sam Abernathy, no matter what.

CHAPTER THIRTY-TWO

I WAS A WRECK FOR THE NEXT two days.

I couldn't sleep at all, and the terror at night kept getting more and more intense. When Sam Abernathy left our door open on Friday night, I was certain that every guy who passed in the hallway was Nate. I couldn't take it. If I started to doze off from exhaustion, I would see Nate and my lungs would stop working.

And I ran into Spotted John at breakfast on Saturday morning when there were no other kids around. He sat down right next to me and his knee bumped mine, so I scooted away from him. It was so awkward and uncomfortable. And then Spotted John Nygaard came right out and told me that he hoped I'd still be his friend, at which I assured him that of course I was his friend—we were teammates after all, and besides that, he was a pretty decent guy who was always there to help out. So Spotted John admitted to me that he really was bisexual—and not just in the video game—and he also hoped that one day I'd maybe be interested in "hooking up" with him for fun.

Just like that—that's what he said.

Fun.

This was something I had no experience in dealing with.

I said no thanks, but Spotted John persisted in asking if I'd spend the night on Saturday—he told me we could drink beer and play around online with his iPad and do whatever we wanted—because Cotton Balls wouldn't be back until Sunday.

What could I do?

"Really, no thanks, Spotted John. Snack-Pack would tell on me if I didn't come home again."

Home?

Ridiculous. I was using the Abernathy as some kind of protection against Spotted John's advances.

"Well, you should come over this afternoon, then."

"I don't think so, Spotted John. Annie and Mrs. Blyleven would not approve of me 'hooking up' with our eight-man."

I tried to make it sound all locker room jokey—just two dudes shooting the shit—but it was so fucking uncomfortable because there was so much more going on that was entirely unsaid.

And I had this kind of Health class epiphany that would have made Mrs. Blyleven so proud of me: Consent applies in every direction, not just between straight guys and the girls they pursue. Those happened to be the only types of consent scenarios Mrs. Blyleven had bothered to cover in class. I realized how ridiculous that was, and that just because you're a straight guy, it doesn't necessarily mean someone else—anyone else—won't ever go a little—or a lot—overboard with pressure and make you feel like you're the bad guy for saying no. Now, if only Spotted John got that message too, I could get on with just being Ryan Dean West and ignore everything about Spotted John Nygaard's . . . um . . . attraction.

"Do you feel like maybe lifting some weights with me today?" Spotted John asked.

"Look, that's three strikes, John. Remember the poster in Mrs. Blyleven's class that says "CONSENT: The first NO is the LAST WORD"? Give me a break, man. I like you and all, but that's about it, Spotted John. I could never be into it."

"Really? I think under the right circumstances, any guy could be into it."

"Is that what you think? Because I don't. It's a no, dude."

And Spotted John said, "Okay, Ryan Dean. I won't pressure you. Because I really *do* like you. Just remember you still owe me a favor."

"I won't forget," I said.

How could I forget?

This was bullshit.

"And the other thing—I mean, I wasn't an asshole about it or anything. My friends, the guys on the team, they all know I'm bi. So if you're going to say anything—"

"Why would I say anything about it? You're my friend, John. It's no big deal. I just never thought about stuff like this. But, to be honest, you *were* an asshole[4] about it. You took pictures of me in my underwear and posted them online. Do you realize you could get

---

[4] Yes, I really *did* say that.

kicked out of Pine Mountain for doing stuff like that? I mean, I know it was a joke and all, and I even think it was pretty funny, to tell you the truth. But it was a real dick[5] move."

Spotted John reddened and looked down. "I . . . I'm sorry, man. I'll remove the pictures. I promise. Really, I'm sorry."

"Thank you."

And we shook hands and left it at that.

So I asked, "Does this count as my anything-you-want favor?"

I made air quotes when I said "anything you want."

"Ha ha," Spotted John laughed.

"Heh."

---

[5] And that, too.

CHAPTER THIRTY-THREE

I could *not* believe I was actually hanging out with the Abernathy on a Saturday afternoon.

A sudden Indian summer had set in that day, so everything felt like we'd gone back in time to July, which would have been fine with me because (1) I'd be at home, and (2) I would have no awareness of the existence of the kid my team named Snack-Pack. The Abernathy could open the window all he wanted to tonight. Hell, I'd even suggest it.

Maybe the warming of the weather caused some mystical increase of my tolerance, or maybe those pain pills Spotted John gave me had serious long-term, niceness-inducing side effects.

Who was I kidding?

To tell the truth, I was just trying to avoid Spotted John, and the Abernathy was the best deterrent I could come up with. Because now, on top of my anxiety, night terrors, fear of the dark shadowy guy who was following me everywhere, and sharing a coffin-size room with a claustrophobic twelve-year-old, I also had to deal with Spotted John's horniness.

So awkward.

Mrs. Blyleven could not possibly have dreamed up a better practical lesson for straight guys about consent. Now I totally understood what

I must have seemed like to so many girls last year when I was fourteen. You'd think Spotted John, at seventeen, would be grown-up enough to make it clear to his penis who was the bigger boss, which was Penis Commandment Three, according to Mrs. Blyleven, by the way.

To be perfectly honest, in my case, I believe my penis and rational brain were twin copilots on the same plane, and I couldn't really tell *who* was flying for Ryan Dean West Airlines. But at least we both flew fairly level. Well, most of the time.

So on Saturday afternoon, with our window open and the outside temperature warm enough for us to wear shorts (and I voluntarily left the room when Sam Abernathy wanted to change—I was such a well-trained loser), we sat at our desks and—unthinkable as it may sound—did homework together.

"What are you working on?" the Abernathy asked.

"Health. Don't talk to me."

I caught the Abernathy as he took a quick glance under my desk.

"Not that part, Snack-Pack," I said. "I am supposed to write a reflective paragraph about performing my TSE."

"Oh! What are you going to say?" he asked. "Do you want to share out with me, like we do in Dr. Wellins's class?"

"Never."

"Maybe I'll write a paragraph, then, too. Would you like to read *mine*?"

"Stop talking to me."

It was so embarrassing, writing that goddamned paragraph for that stupid class.

"Ryan Dean?"

"What?"

"Are you any good at calculus?"

"What part?"

"Derivatives of implicit functions?"

I had fashioned a kind of barrier using a row of novels between our desks, which otherwise may just as well have been connected. I moved the books out of the way and sighed. "Let me see what you're doing."

The Abernathy slid his notebook and text across the now-unfortified border between our desks so I could see.

"This is pretty hard stuff, but I can show you how to do it," I said.

The Abernathy squirmed with joy.

For the next hour and a half, I did math with Sam Abernathy.

Fun.

To be honest, I missed doing calculus and being in Mrs. Kurtz's class.

By the time we were all homeworked-out and I was midway through my what-I-think-about-fondling-my-balls reflective paragraph for Mrs. Blyleven, the Abernathy said, "I have to tell you something, Ryan Dean."

"No you don't."

"I live in Texas."

"I'm happy for you."

"Well, the reason I'm claustrophobic is because when I was four years old, I fell into an uncovered well that was about sixty feet deep and only this big around."

When he said "this big around," the Abernathy made a circle the size of a soccer ball between his curled hands.

"Oh. That would suck."

"It took them three days to get me out. I almost died."

"Oh."

Why was he telling me this? I was actually beginning to feel sorry for him, so I had to keep reminding myself that Risotto Boy was currently alive and that he was also my roommate.

"And the other thing is, the reason I don't ever get undressed or take showers around other boys here is because . . . well . . . I'm not really starting to . . . um, change yet, and I don't have, you know, any hair around my wiener or under my arms. And it's embarrassing."

No.

He actually was talking to me about his *wiener*.

I never wanted to talk to Sam Abernathy about his *wiener*.

But I also recalled, with deep horror, what it was like to be the only twelve-year-old freshman in a pretty much entirely sixteen-year-old-boys' locker room. I had nearly blocked it out of my mind, and I decided then and there that if I ever had a son (which meant I would eventually have the opportunity to actually breed with a noninflatable living female human being), I would never, never,

never allow anyone to suggest the idea of moving him forward in school.

Trust me, it was the most God-awful thing that could ever happen to a boy.

"Nobody cares about that, Sam," I said, which was kind of a lie, and also unwarrantedly kind.

"Sometimes I feel like I shouldn't have come here to Pine Mountain, because I don't belong with all you grown-up boys."

Why the hell was he telling me this?

I couldn't even respond to him, because I felt so bad for the kid. I was such an asshole to him.

I was *not* supposed to feel sorry for Sam Abernathy.

But Sam Abernathy was a living photocopy of all the terrible shit I had experienced for three solid years at Pine Mountain. Now that I was fifteen, and a senior, I had finally started to feel like I was on a level playing field with all the other boys at PM, and here that little bastard Sam Abernathy had to disinter all the shitty loser feelings I thought I'd buried over the summer. To be honest, I was getting a bit choked up, so I turned my face down at the page I'd been writing on and focused my attention on a description of rolling my testicles between my fingers (Mrs. Blyleven had strict rules about using correct vocabulary terms, so we had to include words like "penis," "testicles," and "scrotum," regardless of how stupid those words sound in comparison with the preferred, simpler vernacular).

And then Sam Abernathy said, "If it weren't for you, I'd feel so lonely, Ryan Dean."

That was it. Time for Ryan Dean to go. I had to leave.

I finished my goddamned balls paragraph and stood up, clearing my throat.

"Thanks for the calc help," the Abernathy said.

I did not answer him. I put on my sneakers and changed into a tank top. I stuffed some clean socks, underwear, and a T-shirt into my gym bag.

"Where are you going?"

My voice cracked a little when I answered, which made me feel like a stupid loser, so I stared at the door that would get me out of here.

"I need to go work out or something. Lift some weights," I said, which was a lie, because there was no way I'd ever want to get caught alone in the locker room on a Saturday with Spotted John on the prowl.

And the Abernathy said, "Can I come with you?"

I paused at the door. Goddamn that little kid.

"Sure. I guess."

CHAPTER THIRTY-FOUR

ON SATURDAYS, WHEN NEARLY ALL
the students are away from Pine Mountain, a custodian named Red
stays in the boys' athletics area to do things like hand out clean towels
and tell guys to wipe down the weight machines after we use them,
and to keep an adult eye on the PM boys.

We were required to always sign in and sign out if we used the
locker room and athletics facilities on the weekends, just so they knew
where we were.

Pine Mountain had become very "supervised" following my friend
Joey's death the year before. So after we lifted weights together (God!
I was now officially such a loser—*lifting weights* with the Abernathy!),
Sam Abernathy and I went into the locker room.

I took a towel from Red's perfectly folded stack. The old man eyed
us suspiciously, like our sole purpose for being there was to make a
mess of the place.

The Abernathy said, "Why are you going to take a shower *here*,
Ryan Dean?"

"Because our bathroom—no, our *shower room*—sucks, Snack-
Pack. It's ridiculously gross and small."

Sam Abernathy sat down on the bench in front of the bank of lockers where I'd undressed. "Okay, Ryan Dean. I'll just wait for you here."

"Fine."

And when I came out of the shower to get dressed, I found the tiny little hedgehog undressed and wrapped in a towel of his own (it went around his waist two or three times), with his arms folded tightly across the pencils of his rib cage.

The Abernathy was out of breath with nervousness, practically on the edge of a panic attack. "I decided to take a shower here too, like regular PM boys do. Only, will you stay here? You're not going to look at me taking a shower, are you, Ryan Dean?"

"I told you nobody cares about that stuff, Abernathy."

The pale little barefoot salamander padded off in the direction of the showers.

I added, "And stop talking to me."

"I thought you said you weren't going to work out today, *Snack-Pack Senior*."

Spotted John Nygaard stood at the end of the row of lockers. I guess he'd been watching the Abernathy and me for a while. And now that I was naked and just about completely unwrapped from my towel, I felt especially naked. Like, supernaked. Nakeder than I'd ever been in my life.

Now here was a real standoff. I heard the water come on in the shower, and then I thought, *I never, never want to think about the Abernathy in the shower.*

There was nothing I could do—my towel was already hanging in front of me like a curtain in my hands. If I put it back on, it would look like I was all weirded out by Spotted John standing there, looking at me, which I *was* weirded out by, but I didn't want to look like it to Spotted John, which was a very complex internal/external stalemate involving all kinds of straight-guy hangups.

"I didn't say I didn't want to work out. But I'd already promised Snack-Pack I'd take him to the weight room and show him how to lift," I lied.

I inhaled deeply. My shoulders tensed up like the backbones of two alley cats getting ready to fight. Then I dropped my towel on the bench and got dressed as quickly as I could without even glancing at Spotted John Nygaard. Well, to be honest, I watched his feet. He stood there, leaning against the lockers and looking at me the whole time. What a piece of shit.

"You took *Snack-Pack* to the *weight room*?"

I shrugged. "He kinda needs it, don't you think?"

The water in the shower turned off.

"Look, I'm sorry I was an asshole, Ryan Dean. About everything. And I want you to know I took down those pictures of you from my blog."

Spotted John looked genuinely sorry.

"Thanks, John. That's really decent of you," I said.

"You're welcome, dude. And, um, anytime you want to use my phone or Internet, well . . . you know you can. I promise I won't bug you about . . . you know . . . anymore."

Pat-pat-pat! came the sounds of the Abernathy's bare wet puppy paws on the concrete floor of the locker room.

I grabbed my gym bag and wadded up the towel so I could throw it into Red's hamper. Guys *do not* want Red getting mad at them for leaving a mess.

"Let's go outside so the kid can get dressed in peace," I said.

I felt better about the whole Spotted John thing. He really was an okay guy. He just needed to study his Penis Commandments a little harder.

Weekend dinners were fend-for-yourself affairs at Pine Mountain Academy.

If only I'd known that sucking it up and hanging with the Abernathy provided all kinds of spillover benefits besides having him serve as bisexual-shark repellent to the great white Spotted John, I might not have dropped as much weight as I had since the school year began. Because whereas my typical Saturday evening meal consisted of frozen microwavable burritos or toaster-oven pizza rolls, the Abernathy—just utilizing what the cafeteria staff left on hand for us abandoned kids—was able to craft a spicy ginger-orange sauce, which he drizzled over boneless chicken and fried rice.

The kid may have been endlessly annoying, but he could cook better than anyone I'd ever known.

When we finished eating Sam's remarkable dinner, I was so tired after all I'd been through in the past few days, I felt like I would sleep for twenty-four hours. The Abernathy opened our window and switched on a program about eating exotic foods in Mongolia. I undressed and climbed into bed.

"Do you want to watch TV with me, Ryan Dean?"

"No. I'm too tired." And then I said the unthinkable. "Good night, Sam."

"You can call me Snack-Pack. I like it when the guys call me that."

I yawned. "Whatever."

And then the Abernathy did the unthinkable too: He actually changed into his pajamas with me lying there, awake, in the same room. And he didn't even attempt to hide himself or ask me to leave.

Ryan Dean West, child therapist. Well, child therapist who probably needed to see his own child therapist, to be honest.

The Abernathy, all soccer-jammied out, climbed up into his little corner atop his Mario Bros. bed and said, "Good night, Ryan Dean. This was the best day ever."

No no no no no.

What had I done to myself?

I shut my eyes and fell asleep.

And that night, it happened again.

Worse than ever.

the jumping-off spot

CHAPTER THIRTY-FIVE

CHAPTER THIRTY-SIX

"OH MY GOSH! RYAN DEAN! OH MY gosh! Please be okay!"

I couldn't move my arms and legs, and I had this dim, swirling vision of Sam Abernathy in his soccer pajamas, kneeling on my bed—*my bed!*—grabbing me by the shoulders, his face just inches above mine. He shook me, trying to wake me up or snap me out of whatever was happening to me.

"Ryan Dean!"

The Abernathy got off me and scampered across the floor to switch on the lights. Then he ran back and put his face up to mine.

"I'm going to call someone for help!"

"N-no. No."

The fuzzy black fist that had closed around my field of vision began to loosen up. I tried to take a deep breath, tried to will my heart to slow down. I managed to get my hands to my face. It was wet. I had been crying. I had been crying in front of the Abernathy. Nothing—not even waking up in the middle of a photo shoot in my underwear with inflatable Mabel—could *ever* be more humiliating than crying in front of the Abernathy.

I wadded my sheets in my hands and wiped my face.

The Abernathy kneeled on my bed next to me. I also never wanted to be in the same bed as the Abernathy. I kept my face covered. This was worse than anything.

"Are you okay, Ryan Dean? You screamed. It really scared me. Are you okay?"

"Get off my bed. This didn't happen. Get off me. I'm fine."

Then I blindly pushed the kid away from me, and Sam Abernathy fell hard against my desk chair. It sounded like it hurt him. I was sure it did.

I got out of bed and stepped over the Abernathy, who was rubbing his head. Then I pulled on some pants and a sweatshirt and slipped my bare feet into my sneakers. I ran out of the room.

It was two in the morning.

I ran, and the farther away I got, the more disgusted with myself and scared I became.

CHAPTER THIRTY-SEVEN

ON THE PATH THAT LEADS TO THE old O-Hall, there is a small ledge on a bank beside the lake. It's a place the boys of Pine Mountain call the Jumping-Off Spot.

A bench cut from a split tree trunk sits in the grass here, so carved up with initials and epithets—the cryptic hieroglyphs of hundreds of Pine Mountain boys from the past six decades.

It's hard to imagine, sometimes, the marks that boys can leave in passing.

The more recent additions were all done by O-Hall boys.

Ever since Pine Mountain expanded and built the larger dorm buildings, the normal kids at PM rarely come out this way. A few times when I just needed someone to talk to, Joey and I would sneak out of O-Hall in the middle of the night and sit here and throw rocks into the water.

I want to throw rocks again.

I want to throw the biggest rock I can find, watch it smash into the windshield of my life and cast a jagged net of spiderweb fractures that multiply the pinpoint stars hanging in the fathomless black over the lake.

Why won't my heart slow down?

Why won't it slow down and let me catch my breath, so I can be happy to sit here again, so I can feel good about Annie Altman, so I can talk to my friends, so I can be okay?

I throw one and another and another, listen as they hit the water and sink. I throw so hard, it feels like my arm is separating from my body, and it hurts and feels good at the same time, but it still is not enough and my heart won't stop doing what it wants to do to me.

It's not enough.

I kick off my sneakers and drop my sweatshirt and pants on the bench, just there, beside Joey's name and my stupid initials—RDMW—where we'd carved them last fall. Then I run toward the edge of the bank and jump as far as I can.

The water is stunningly cold. My chest, everything, constricts.

I am collapsing—a star becoming a black hole. My head spins, and I can't find up, but I'm not looking for it either. I stay beneath the black surface and I scream as loud as I can, until all the air empties from me and I begin to sink and collapse even more.

I am not thinking about dying, and I'm not thinking about living, either. For just that slight moment when all I know is the cold and the dark, I can finally sense peace, can imagine myself catching a glimpse of my decelerating heart trying to run away from me as I get closer and closer to it.

Slow down, heart.

My arms pull me up through the water; my feet kick until I break the surface and take in a breath.

How did I get here?

How did I come to this place?

I'm out near the middle of the lake and I'm shivering. My teeth are chattering and I can almost feel the blue seeping into my lips. And I hear something soft and sad—it sounds like a bird calling from the shore near the bench.

"Ryan Dean? Ryan Dean? Please come back."

It's Sam Abernathy.

I can hear him crying.

CHAPTER THIRTY-EIGHT

I SAT ON THE BENCH, DRIPPING AND shuddering, wearing nothing but the briefs I'd been sleeping in an hour ago.

Sam Abernathy sat beside me, folding and refolding, on his ironing-board knees, the hooded sweatshirt I'd discarded.

"You should put this on, Ryan Dean. You're going to get sick."

I couldn't talk. My jaw was locked shut from the cold. I wanted to put the sweatshirt on, but my arms were too tightly clenched across my chest. I think Sam must have sensed I tried to move a hand to get the shirt from him, but my arms would not let go of my chest.

I shook and shook. I felt snot running down my upper lip.

Sam Abernathy rubbed my hoodie to warm it up in his hands, and then he slipped it over my head, pulling it down until I was reason-ably covered. Then he put the hood up to cover my wet hair.

"What's wrong with you, Ryan Dean?"

I shook my head and stared at the lake.

"Are you going to be all right?"

I shook my head again. I couldn't talk to the kid.

What could I tell him, anyway? Oh yeah, Sam, I'm fine. I'm just losing my fucking mind is all. Just fine.

I don't know how long we sat there saying nothing. When my chest warmed up enough that I could move, I slipped my arms through the sleeves and wadded the cuffs in my fists to glove my hands.

"Here." Sam Abernathy tried to get my feet into my pants. He managed to pull them halfway past my knees as I sat there shaking and not saying anything to him.

He shouldn't have been such a nice kid. There was no reason for him to treat me with kindness—not Joey, and not Sam. I was an asshole, and I went out of my way to keep Sam Abernathy from caring about me, but his heart was bigger than mine. I was an asshole.

I kept thinking that, over and over. *I'm such an asshole.* I needed to tell Sam Abernathy how sorry I was for pushing him, and for all the other asshole shit I'd done since school started, but I knew if I opened my mouth to say those words, I would start crying like a little kid, and I was never going to cry in front of Sam Abernathy. Again.

I pulled my pants up and buttoned them.

And Sam said, "I won't say anything about this, Ryan Dean. It's the code, right?"

I wiped my nose on my sleeve. I was gross and wet and shaking, and I was such an asshole.

The kid grabbed my shoes and lined them up in front of my feet so I could slip them on.

Sam Abernathy stood in front of me, his hand extended to pull me up.

"Come on," he said. "We'd better get back."

I couldn't look at his face. I'd hurt him, and I was such an asshole, and here he was—after the best day he'd ever had—offering me a hand. He pulled me up. I was wobbly. My muscles still jittered constrictions against the ice water I'd been swimming in.

I was such an asshole.

"If you need a hand, you can put your arm on my shoulder, Ryan Dean. I'm not uptight about stuff like that."

I couldn't lean on the kid. I couldn't even look at him.

But before we got out of the woods, I stopped and put my hands over my eyes.

"I'm really sorry for what I did, Sam."

"It's okay, Ryan Dean. It's okay."

CHAPTER THIRTY-NINE

I WAS MOPEY AND USELESS THE whole day on Sunday. I didn't want to say anything else to Sam Abernathy, but it wasn't because I hated him. It was because I hated myself.

Also, I was filthy and smelled like algae.

The Abernathy tried to get me to go to breakfast with him, but I refused to get out of bed. So he made me feel even worse when he came back with a toasted bagel and a cup of yogurt for me.

"You should eat something, Ryan Dean," he said.

I wanted to stay away from Sam Abernathy, so I got dressed to leave.

"Did I do something wrong?" Sam asked.

I shook my head. "No."

Okay. So you know how sometimes your feelings can be all messed up for so many reasons, and you just don't want to talk to anybody but it's not because you're mad at other people, it's because you're really disgusted with yourself, and then you get waylaid by an innocent question like *did I do something wrong?* and you instinctively answer "no," but you also instinctively make eye contact with the person you've been trying not to talk to or make eye contact with and you've been doing pretty good at that since, like, three in the morning, and that's when you notice the person you haven't been speaking to or making eye contact with has a black eye because you were mad and embarrassed and you shoved him off your bed because you didn't want him to see that you were crying—even though he did, and even though you *know* he would never give you shit over it, because Sam Abernathy would never give shit to anyone—and then you realize OH MY GOD I GAVE SAM ABERNATHY A BLACK EYE?

Yep. Pretty much that.

It froze me. I had never done anything as terrible as what I did to Sam Abernathy. And why the hell was he putting up with it? Why the hell was Sam Abernathy nice to me?

"I gave you a black eye."

My stomach knotted. I seriously looked around for a vomit landing site.

And the Abernathy joked about it. "Technically, it wasn't you. Gravity plus your chair gave me a black eye, Ryan Dean."

I felt sick.

I should have been kicked out of Pine Mountain for what I'd done to Sam Abernathy. And I didn't answer him when he asked where I was going. I grabbed my book bag and left Unit 113. Then I went out to the parking lot and sat down in the shade to wait for Annie to come back.

I drew something for Sam while I waited there.

CHAPTER FORTY

I FELT A SENSE OF RELIEF, A LIGHTENING, when I saw Seanie Flaherty's Land Rover pull into the parking lot. Annie was with him.

It was almost as though I'd been holding my breath since Friday afternoon and now I could finally take air into my claustrophobic lungs.

And, of course, the first thing Seanie said to me was this: "Dude. Ryan Dean. Nice photo spread of you and your blow-up girlfriend on Nygaard's blog. By the way, you're totally hot, Ryan Dean."

Annie blushed.

That was totally hot.

Then she said, "Yeah, Ryan Dean. What was *that* all about?"

Of course Annie knew this was one of those things that only—and *always*—happened to losers like me.

I shook my head. "Spotted John and Cotton Balls are . . . well . . . I suppose Mrs. Blyleven would insist I call them penises, as opposed to what I'd like to call them. 'Penises' isn't swearing, is it, Annie?"

Talking to Annie about penises was also kind of hot.

My brain—Copilot One—was a total mess.

Annie laughed, and then we threw our arms around each other and hugged. It was one of the best feelings ever, especially because there were rarely any official eyes watching PM kids on weekends.

"I missed you so much, Annie." I was choked up, and she could feel it. It had been one of the worst weekends of my life.

Annie bit my ear and whispered, "I love you. And those pictures *were* pretty hot."

That was majorly hot. I mean, the ear-biting thing. Annie had never done anything like that before, and it was completely arousing. I pushed my hips into hers and we kissed long and deep.

I'm sure she felt the . . . um, something that was going on down there with Copilot Two. Annie smiled and said, "Oh my, Ryán Dean!"

Score one for consent!

And then, naturally, Seanie Flaherty had to ruin the moment by saying, "Dude, watching you guys make out is hot and everything, but if you're thinking I'm going to leave my keys so you can mess up the backseat and lock up for me, you're both high or something."

"Oh. Uh, sorry, Annie," I said.

We were both a little embarrassed. And Seanie Flaherty wouldn't stop looking at me—at Copilot Two—my crotch, to be specific, which is probably an okay word as far as Mrs. Blyleven was concerned.

Seanie said, "This reminds me, I still have to do my Health homework!"

"You are so gross, Seanie," I said.

"I'll bet you five dollars and all those photos of you I printed out from Spotted John's porn site that you already did yours, Ryan Dean."

"Shut up, Seanie."

Sometimes I could forget everything when I was with Annie Altman.

I guess that's how you know when someone's the right person for you, but what do I know? I suppose you could just as easily forget everything when you're in a fistfight with your worst enemy, too, or when you're drowning in a freezing lake at three in the morning.

It was such a warm day that as soon as we were out of sight of the campus I took my tank top off and hung it from a tree branch. Annie and I had gone out for a run up to Buzzard's Roost, although I could barely keep up with her. I'd really lost a lot of my strength. Not eating will do that to you, I guess. I'd have to start forcing myself to do better, or I'd be toast in our rugby match coming up on Thursday.

And maybe that was the key: *forcing myself to do better*.

"Is something wrong?" I asked. I caught Annie staring at me when I took off my shirt.

She blushed again. So she didn't only do that for Sam Abernathy. This was an important discovery.

Annie said, "You know, I agree with Seanie. You *are* pretty hot, Ryan Dean."

That was twice in one day she called me hot.

"I blame it on the Indian summer affecting your judgment, or maybe they gave you drinks on the plane, Annie. Are you drunk?"

She laughed (that was very hot too), then took off on the trail up into the mountains.

We stopped at the creek, and I washed my face and chest with the cool water. It made me think back to jumping in the lake the night before, and how that seemed like it was another Ryan Dean from some other time, that I almost couldn't believe it was really *me* doing that.

Then Annie said, "You want to go swimming?"

Jackpot.

"What?"

"You know. Take off our clothes and go for a swim."

It felt like my throat was attempting to give birth to a basketball. A square one. With really sharp corners. And coated with Velcro.

I hate Velcro.

"You mean actual *skinny-dipping*?"

Annie, her eyes all wet with smiles, nodded her head.

That was the first yes. An enthusiastic one at that.

"Only if you want to," she said.

(Jump-cut to the interior of Ryan Dean West's head, Copilot One)

RYAN DEAN WEST 2: Interesting. Someone must have had the "consent talk" with your girlfriend.

RYAN DEAN WEST 1: Shut up. She's your girlfriend too. But is this actually happening? I can't believe this is actually happening.

RYAN DEAN WEST 2: Stop being such a loser, dude. Tell Annie you want to get naked and go swimming with her. Dude. Score.

RYAN DEAN WEST 1: To be honest, I'm scared.

RYAN DEAN WEST 2: To be brutally honest, it looks like Copilot Two is into the idea, if you know what I mean.

RYAN DEAN WEST 1: (*Looks down, mortified*) God! I am so embarrassed.

RYAN DEAN WEST 2: Dude, you've been thinking about this for years, and now that your girlfriend is actually suggesting you both get naked together, you can't tell me you're actually going to chicken out.

RYAN DEAN WEST 1: I . . . I . . .

(Jump-cut to the exterior of Ryan Dean West's head: a scene by a creek)

"I want to if you want to," I said.

That was an awful lot of conditional wanting going on there.

I kneeled down to undo the laces on my shoes. I tried thinking about baseball and stamp collecting, with a little bit of risotto preparation and gardening thrown in just to make Copilot Two lower the altitude a bit on Ryan Dean West Airlines Flight 0001, but he was having some serious control issues, and Copilot One, like I said, was in no condition to fly my plane.

I sat on the ground and removed my shoes and socks and watched Annie Altman undress beneath the trees right in front of me.

Oh my God. This is real, and Annie is really taking off her top right

in front of me, and this is the scariest and most thrilling thing I have
ever done, and oh my God, I never knew Annie wore a blue bra when
she ran, because I never knew what bras were actually for, anyway, and
OH MY GOD, she's taking it off and I actually see Annie's breasts and
they are so beautiful, I want to kiss them everywhere, and her tummy,
too, and OH MY GOD she is taking off her shorts—and why do girls
wear so many clothes when they run, because boys can get away with
nothing but running shorts, if they have a support liner, that is, other-
wise Copilot Two would experience some extreme turbulence, and Annie
has the hottest little panties on—and OH. MY. GOD. Annie Altman is
completely naked and I can't take my eyes off of her everything and she
has the most perfect pubic hair that looks so soft, and do I really have to
stand up now???

I felt every pulse of my heart pumping blood as thick as mashed potatoes up through my neck.

I stood up.

It was embarrassing, even though I knew that Annie and I had nothing to be embarrassed about. Then I pulled down my shorts and stepped out of them, and we were both completely naked, standing there beside our running trail next to the creek.

I had never been naked in front of a girl in my life. Well, except for my mom. But I never wanted to think about that again.

I kept my hands at my sides as much as I wanted to cover myself up.

Annie took a deep breath. "Wow."

"Wow what?"

"You're a lot, um, bigger than I thought."

"You *thought* about how big I was?"

She smiled.

"Well, you're a lot more beautiful than I ever imagined. Way more."

"You *imagined* this?"

"One or two times. Hundred, I mean. Maybe thousands. If I had some *alone time* in the bathroom."

When I said "alone time," I made air quotes.

Annie laughed and held out her hand. "Are we going in, or what?"

To be honest, I would have preferred the "or what," considering there weren't too many whats out there involving the two of us being alone and naked together, and the "going in" part meant water. Cold water. Again. I took Annie's hand, and, carefully, we walked to the edge of the creek.

We got in up to our ankles. Honestly, that was deep enough for me.

"This water is so cold, it hurts," Annie said.

"I'd guess that going all the way in is going to hurt a lot, then."

"Well, this counts as skinny-dipping together, right, Ryan Dean? Because you're the first boy I've ever skinny-dipped with."

"It counts for me," I said. And I was so relieved I wasn't going to have to endure Copilot Two making a water landing. There had to be icebergs in that goddamned creek. And the cold water . . . just, no. Copilot Two's jet would have become a hang glider. Maybe a box kite. Copilot One did not want to deal with that.

Then Annie said, "I love you."

"I love you so much, Annie. Who else in the world would I ever get naked with and stand in a freezing creek?"

"Probably anybody, Ryan Dean."

I shook my head. "Not Spotted John."

We both laughed.

Annie Altman and I stood in the water, completely naked, holding hands. I realized I trusted her more than anyone I had ever known.

"Annie? Would it be all right if I kissed you?"

Consent Boy, great American superhero.

"Yes," she said.

That was enthusiasm as far as I was concerned.

So we kissed. Our assorted parts touched. In fact, I touched her everywhere, and she touched me everywhere too.

And I forgot everything in the magnificent wonder of this pinpoint moment.

CHAPTER FORTY-ONE

CHAPTER FORTY-TWO

I'LL COME RIGHT OUT AND SAY IT:
Annie Altman and I didn't actually have sex that day.

Well, to be honest, we kind of did, but it wasn't the kind of sex that could bring about what might have been a June[6] surprise for us and our parents, and for everyone else attending the Pine Mountain graduation ceremony for that matter. Don't get me wrong, we definitely *wanted* to have that kind of sex, but since condoms are not something you normally carry along in your running shorts (Annie did have ChapStick, though), we both agreed that *that kind of sex* was out of the question.

Consent Boy strikes again.

But Annie taught me things about places where girls like to be touched, which I never knew about, and we both liked that part very much. And I showed Annie how to give me a TE (without the *S*). Don't judge—it was a lot more fun and felt much nicer than doing the *S* version alone in my shower room. That was something Mrs. Blyleven and the cartoon TSE Fox failed to point out to us boys in Health class. But when Annie put her hands on me, it made Copilot Two order an emergency evacuation of the passengers, so afterward there was a bit of washing off in the icy creek that couldn't be avoided.

---

[6] It was September. So I think I'm doing the math right.

It was fun. It was the nicest thing I had ever felt in my life.

So there. I told you.

We lay on our backs in the grass beside the creek, staring up at the sky through the treetops. Annie rested the back of her neck in my armpit, so her hair tickled my chin. We didn't bother to put on our clothes yet. Neither of us wanted to.

"Thank you for that, Annie. I've never . . ."

Annie put her fingers on my belly. "I never have either, Ryan Dean. It was nice."

I said, "Next time, Copilot One is going to remember to bring some condoms."

"Copilot One?"

I pointed at my forehead. "My upstairs brain."

"You have condoms?"

"Yeah. Remember? My mom gave them to me last year. Awkward."

"My mom gave me a box of them just this weekend," Annie said. "We had a long talk."

So that's where the whole let's-go-swimming-naked-together idea came from. Thanks, Doc Mom (which is what I called Annie's mom)!

"You had a safe-sex talk about me? That's superawkward, Annie."

"Not about *you*. Just a talk. In general. But I knew my mom was really talking to me about you, Ryan Dean."

"Generally speaking," I said.

Thinking about Annie and her mom—who was incredibly

hot—talking about condoms and having sex and *me* was really hot, but I wasn't about to say that to Annie. Copilot One was back in charge, while Copilot Two took a well-deserved nap.

"I like you very much, Ryan Dean West," Annie said.

"Thank you, Annie Altman. I think you're pretty swell."

"I'd be so lonely here without you."

"I . . ." And that was all I could get out of my mouth, because I was so strangled by emotions that nothing else would come.

Why did Annie have to say that? It was almost the exact thing Sam Abernathy had said to me yesterday before I melted down, and now all I could think about was the black eye I gave the Abernathy and about Nate wanting to suffocate me at night, and how afraid of everything I'd become. I also was suddenly self-conscious and ashamed of what Annie and I had done together.

It was happening again, another panic attack out of the blue at the worst possible time—while I was lying down naked in the grass with Annie. I forced myself to concentrate on not being scared.

Think about Annie. Think about Annie.

I was shaking.

"What's wrong?"

Annie could feel the tightening spasms in my chest.

I am not going to cry in front of Annie. I am not going to cry in front of Annie. I am not going to cry in front of Annie.

It all came rushing at me: I was terrified at the thought of trying to go to sleep that night, and especially of having to face Sam Abernathy again. I was such an asshole. And I was an asshole to Annie, too. I was going to ruin her life, and I couldn't let myself do that to her.

"Ryan Dean. Are you crying?"

I squirmed out from under Annie's head and sat up. I took a deep breath.

"I don't know what's up with me. Um. I think we better get dressed."

I rubbed my eyes and kept my face turned away from her while we put our clothes on.

Annie said, "Did I do something wrong?"

"You're the most perfectly right thing in the world for me, Annie. I'm sorry I'm such a disgusting mess."

The run was over. We held hands and walked out of the woods, toward the trail leading back to school. Holding on to Annie's hand was like a lightning rod for me—it kept me safe and grounded so I didn't get lost in the panic.

I could breathe again.

"Well. When my mom and I *weren't* talking about you and about having sex and using condoms, I told her I was worried about you, Ryan Dean."

I felt myself tightening up again. I knew where this was going, and I did not want to talk about it.

Annie continued, "You know, we have a psychologist here at

school. Mrs. Dvorak. Lots of kids go to see her. You can imagine how tough it is for some kids to adjust to being here."

I shook my head. "I'll be okay, Annie."

"She's really nice, you know. I've gone to see her."

"About what?"

I couldn't imagine Annie Altman ever needing help from anyone.

"Last year. It was about you. Mrs. Dvorak helped me trust how I felt about you."

I'd never met her, but I thought I owed a silent prayer of thanks to Mrs. Dvorak.

We stopped at the tree where I'd hung my tank top. Now we were both just as dressed as when we'd left—like nothing had ever happened. Even if what Annie and I did was the biggest thing that had ever happened in my pathetic life, and now I was all confused and embarrassed—guilty—about what we'd done.

"So. What do you think? Do you think you'll go see her?" Annie asked when we were back on the main campus grounds.

"Could we just not talk about this right now, Annie? Today was so nice, and I don't want to do this right now. Please?"

Annie let go of my hand. She folded her arms across her chest. I imagined seeing her without her clothes on. I would never get that picture out of my mind.

But Annie was mad.

"Fine, Ryan Dean. Fine."

And just like that, Annie Altman turned her back without saying another word and walked off toward the girls' dorm.

"Hey! Annie?"

She kept walking.

What could I say? I felt like I'd been kicked in the balls, and I was scared to go back to Unit 113.

CHAPTER FORTY-THREE

"THANKS FOR THE COMIC, RYAN DEAN! It's awesome!"

I was hoping—unreasonably—that the Abernathy wouldn't be there when I got back to our room. I'd left a note for him—the comic I'd drawn while waiting for Annie—as some kind of means for apologizing beyond just saying *I'm sorry*, which didn't feel adequate.

So I'm not sure if it was knowing that Sam Abernathy had read my comic, which was kind of personal (and it was thumbtacked to the wall above his bed), or thinking about what Annie and I had just done an hour ago, and being here in the same room with a twelve-year-old kid, but I felt my face getting hot and damp with embarrassment.

"I need to take a shower," I said.

"Do you want me to leave?"

I'd been wanting Sam Abernathy to leave since the first moment I saw him.

"Don't be dumb, Sam."

But I felt really weird, and really guilty, taking off my clothes in front of him.

What had I done to myself? To Annie?

CHAPTER FORTY-FOUR

CHAPTER FORTY-FIVE

"DUDE. SNACK-PACK. WHAT HAPPENED to your eye?" Seanie asked.

Here are the depths to which I'd descended: Annie was apparently mad at me—or *something* was going on. She didn't come down to eat that evening. I was so distracted, wondering what was wrong with me—and with Annie—and maybe if she'd regretted what we did by the creek that day. I couldn't help but worry if she felt as terribly guilty and *changed* by what had happened. And there was no going back now, but I couldn't tell if that was a good thing or a bad thing.

I didn't feel like it was good, but like I said, there was no going back.

Seanie and I sat in the dining hall after finishing dinner, when the Abernathy came down and joined us at our table, just like that. And nobody said anything about the inappropriateness of a freshman—a twelve-year-old freshman, no less—sitting at a table with two senior boys.

That's how low I'd sunk.

"Oh. Nothing, really," Sam Abernathy answered. "Ryan Dean and I were just wrestling around, and I bumped my eye against his desk chair."

Seanie gave me one of his patented I-know-you-secretly-must-be-gay-Ryan-Dean looks.

Whatever.

"Wrestling?" Seanie chuckled.

And the Abernathy, for reasons that escaped me, felt compelled to give Seanie more details.

"Yeah, well, actually, I fell off Ryan Dean's bed."

This was a gold mine for Seanie Flaherty. He wriggled in his seat like Sam Abernathy contemplating fondue recipes, or bonding with me over a creative writing session. I think Seanie even gave himself an excited little Sam-Abernathy-tug-slash-TSE.

Seanie's ears raised slightly. "And what were you wearing when this intense bed-wrestling session took place?"

And the kid would not shut up.

"I was in my pajamas. Ryan Dean doesn't have pajamas. He was in his underwear."

Seanie Flaherty looked at me, then at Sam Abernathy, then back at me.

"Dude. Seriously. Come out, Ryan Dean. Admit it and move on. You'll feel so much better about yourself."

Seanie Flaherty had serious issues. And I know that it's totally normal (at least, it's normal according to Mrs. Blyleven) for teenage boys to wonder if their guy friends are maybe a little bit into guys, but Seanie never let up, which kind of made me think that deep down Seanie was the one who needed to come out or shut up, or something. So I put that in my little mental notebook of things to ask Annie: if Isabel had sex over the summer, and, if so, who did she do it with; and, after all the alone time she spent in Seanie's car with him, if Annie thought maybe Seanie was into guys but so hung up on shit that he could never relax and be himself.

"If you must know, to be perfectly honest, Annie Altman and I got completely naked together and had sex in the woods this afternoon."

Okay. To be honest, I did not say that. But I really wanted to. It would have felt so good to see the looks on Seanie's and Sam's faces if I let that out.

What I actually said was, "Feel free to fantasize as much as you want, Seanie. Yes, I was in my underwear. Briefs, in fact. Wrestling. With Sam Abernathy, on my bed. At two in the morning."

Seanie took a deep, thoughtful breath. "Fair enough. Still, it's a nice shiner, Snack-Pack. But if I were you, I wouldn't tell the guys you got it wrestling in bed with Ryan Dean in his underwear. They might not be as open-minded as me, you know."

Yeah. Open-minded Sean Russell Flaherty.

I was so sleepy, but I was afraid of going back to my room alone. So even after Seanie got up to leave, I—and this is hard for me to admit—stayed and hung out with the Abernathy while he ate his dinner. And how that kid managed to prepare a dish of pasta with ham, peas, and fresh mint in a microwave oven was something I simply could not wrap my head around.

"Would you like some of this pasta, Ryan Dean?"

I shook my head. "No, thanks."

"I never knew you drew comics. I seriously love that comic you made for me so much, Ryan Dean. How'd you ever learn to draw like that?"

I shrugged. "I'm not really sure. I just wanted to let you know how sorry I am for being such an asshole. Things are really fucked up for me, Sam, and I'm sorry I took it out on you."

And, yes, I really did say that.

Sam Abernathy stopped eating and looked at me with his large bunny-about-to-be-wolf-food eyes. "I've never heard you swear before, Ryan Dean!"

"Sorry. I don't usually cuss."

"Well, you should stop it right now."

"Things have just been so messed up for me."

"Well, I told you I won't say anything to anyone, because it's part of *the code*, right? But if you ask me . . ."

The Abernathy stopped as though he was suddenly aware that maybe he was going too far and that maybe he should shut up.

"Ask you *what*?"

"I'm sorry. It's none of my business, Ryan Dean."

And the kid filled his mouth with more pasta.

Whatever.

I needed sleep. I was scared to try, though. So I actually *hung out* with the Abernathy, all because I was afraid of being alone. It felt so uncomfortable, too, like we were on a date or something. Because Sam Abernathy was just so damned excited about spending time with me.

When he finished eating, the Abernathy said, "What do you want to do now, Ryan Dean? Lift weights or something?"

No. No.

"I'm supertired, Sam. You know, after last night and all."

It wasn't even seven thirty, another indication of how decayed my life had become.

"Cool! Let's just kick back and watch TV, then!" He was, as always, just a little too tolerant of me, a little too overjoyed.

CHAPTER FORTY-SIX

"NO WRESTLING TONIGHT, SAM."

I crawled between my sheets and lay down with my hands folded behind my head.

"Ha ha! You're too funny, Ryan Dean!"

Sam Abernathy turned the TV at an angle. He assumed I wanted to watch it too.

Whatever.

Of course the window was open. But a partial breakthrough had been established. I didn't have to leave the room when the Abernathy changed into his soccer jammies, and when we did the whole brushing-the-teeth prelude-to-bed thing, he even told me he was going to pee (naturally, the boy from the well left the door to our tiny toilet closet open) and asked me to please not look at him.

I was really hoping the program Sam had on—it was about a foodie traveler who ate roasted scorpions and curry from street vendors in Myanmar—would bore me to sleep. Just the white noise of the show I wasn't following, and the flashing colors of the images I wasn't really looking at, distracted me enough that I actually felt pretty good about things.

"Would you ever do *that*, just because someone *asked* you to?"

"Huh?" I was mortified. At first I thought the Abernathy was talking about what Annie and I had done by the creek that day. To be honest, I really wanted to tell someone about it, what it felt like. Maybe that's a gross guy thing, though, but I did kind of want to tell Sam Abernathy, and especially that creepy Seanie Flaherty. But Copilot One knew saying anything to anyone was a sure way to get Copilot Two grounded for life.

"What?" I said.

"Eat a scorpion. Would you ever eat a scorpion?"

"Would *you?*"

"Yes. I'd eat a scorpion."

"I guess I would too."

The Abernathy wriggled on his bed.

Then I said, "Can I ask you something?"

"Sure."

"Tonight at dinner, you said that it was part of the code that you wouldn't say anything about me to anyone, and then you said 'But if you ask me . . .' and you didn't finish. I need to know what you were going to say to me, Sam."

It got really quiet. Except for scorpion-curry dude on TV.

"If I asked you *what*, Sam?"

"I feel sad for you, Ryan Dean. Something bad happened to you, didn't it?"

Quiet again.

"Yeah. Something pretty bad."

"Well, there's nothing wrong with asking someone for help, you know."

"You're twelve years old. You can't help me, but thanks."

"I wasn't talking about *me*, Ryan Dean. I was talking about Mrs. Dvorak, the school psychologist," Sam said.

"Did Annie say something to you about me?"

"Um . . . I don't know," the Abernathy said. "Would that be breaking the boyfriend code if she did?"

"Just talking to your roommate's girlfriend is a violation of the roommate code, Sam."

"Oh. Sorry. Well, I go and talk to Mrs. Dvorak about once a week."

"You? Why?"

Now scorpion-curry foodie dude was drinking beer, at sunrise, and eating something brothy in a bowl. And there was an actual chicken head in the bowl. Gross.

"You know, Ryan Dean. I told you. It's because I feel like I don't belong here with all you older guys, and my claustrophobia, and how embarrassed I am about everything."

Someone like the Abernathy could keep a psychologist gainfully employed for a long time, I thought. And then I found myself wondering if the Abernathy also told her about the no-hair-around-his-wiener thing, and then I really wanted to slap myself because the Abernathy's wiener was something I *never* wanted to think about again, even though—since it was the Abernathy—I was certain he did tell her exactly that.

And he continued, "Anyway, I think Mrs. Dvorak is nice. She's helped me a lot."

I yawned. "Okay. Whatever. Sam? If my thing happens again tonight . . . well, I'm sorry in advance if it does."

"Don't be scared, Ryan Dean. I'll be here. And you know what?"

"What?"

"I would have never gotten out of that well when I was four if people didn't come to help me."

No. Do not say something smart now, Sam. You're only twelve; therefore, you are not allowed to make such observations to me.

"Good night, Sam."

"Good night, Ryan Dean. Thanks again for the comic, and for being my friend."

Also, no. I could not be friends with Sam Abernathy.

Right?

I shut my eyes and went to sleep. I dreamed about being with Annie Altman by the creek in the woods. The dream was a solid five out of five yapping Pomeranians on the Ryan Dean West Scale of Things That Keep Copilot Two Up All Night Long.

But Copilot One slept like a comatose sloth.

And *my thing* did not happen.

CHAPTER FORTY-SEVEN

I GAVE A NOTE FOR SAM TO PASS ON to Coach M, explaining that I'd be late to practice.

I also wrote a note to Annie, which I gave her at breakfast. And breakfast was awfully weird and quiet. I hated it.

I think Annie and I were both embarrassed and weirded out by what we did the day before. Also, I couldn't quite figure out if she was mad at me, if I did something wrong, or what was going on. And the whole thing was even weirder because Spotted John Nygaard sat right beside me (and he *accidentally* touched my knee, the douche), while Seanie Flaherty sat right next to Annie, which, all things considered, created a Jupiter-size planet of weirdness around our little breakfast group. And Copilot Two took the opportunity to make an announcement from the flight deck that he was taking over the controls of Ryan Dean West Airlines for a while and wanted to let me know that the best way for Annie and me to get over the weirdness we felt would be for us to do it again, but this time with condoms, which—as weird as it made me feel— I thought was a pretty awesome idea, considering it came from Copilot Two, who usually only had terrible ideas.

So, that's a lot of weird. And it was only breakfast.

Dear Annie,

How are you? I am fine. Well, kind of. I hope you are not too weirded out by what we did yesterday, because I am just a little weirded out, but not so much that I wouldn't do it again in, like, a second. Well, I'm pretty sure I would. I hope you're not mad at me about yesterday, Annie. That would kill me.

Can I tell you one thing?

(Ryan Dean West waits for an answer, which I am assuming will be a yes.)

Okay, it is this: I love you more than anything or anyone in the world, Annie. Just saying it (well, writing it) makes me feel happy inside.

But you know, there are other things going on in the Ryan Dean West interior that are making me not very happy, and I really don't know what to do about them, so I am going to take your (and Sam Abernathy's—God help me!) advice. I made an appointment to see Mrs. Dvorak today at twelve thirty, which, as you know, is during lunch, so I will not be able to spend the whole hour with you.

It is okay with me if you hang with Sam Abernathy, as long as you keep telling him to stop talking, which is something he needs to be reminded of almost constantly.

Maybe you could write me a note, so I can read it while I'm
waiting outside Mrs. Dvorak's office, which I am already
getting nervous about, just thinking about being there. And
maybe your note will tell me that you aren't mad at me, and
that I didn't do anything bad or clumsy with you yesterday.
I really want to kiss you so bad right now.
I also totally wouldn't mind "going for a run" too. (Ha ha)
Sometimes I really hate this school.
Love,
Ryan Dean West
PS—Remind me to ask you two questions (not about you or
me), about Isabel and Seanie. And you better spill what you
know, girl.

I'll be honest: I did not want to go see Mrs. Dvorak.

But I wanted Annie to be happy with me, so I figured if the
Abernathy had the balls to spill the intimate details of his hairless
wiener to a school psychologist, then maybe I could do it too. Well,
not the hairless-wiener part. But you know what I mean.

I seriously have to never think about that again.

Anyway, like I said, I had to *force myself* to get better. You can do
that, right?

I mean, I hadn't skipped any meals in over a day, and I even
grabbed two sandwiches from the lunch cart where I met Annie, so

I could take them with me and eat one before my *therapy session*, and then one more before rugby practice.

Annie understood when I told her I didn't want her to come with me to Mrs. Dvorak's. She had a softer, more relaxed look in her eyes that told me things were okay and maybe we should just get over ourselves and stop being so freaked out about the fact that we'd had real, one-on-one, mutually pleasing sexual contact. Because as far as Copilot Two and I were concerned, it was something that needed to happen again—and soon. And that was probably the biggest reason why I took Annie's advice about speaking to Mrs. Dvorak. I had to show Annie that I would do anything for her, in case there was ever any doubt.

So I sat in the waiting area outside Mrs. Dvorak's office, worrying about everything she might want to dig into, and wondering if maybe I had a disgusting piece of sandwich lettuce stuck to my front teeth. I gave them a quick index-finger brush, then unfolded the note Annie had handed me before I left.

Her note was written on the back of one of Annie's British Literature assignments—a paragraph about some dude tearing the arm off some monster named Grendel.

Dear Ryan Dean,
Thank you for the note today. Do you realize
you wrote it on the back of your Health class

homework paragraph? So, you actually did
your TSE in the bathroom while Sam was
on the other side of the door doing the same
thing on himself???

Boys are sooooooo weird.

Really. Really. Weird.

Anyway, in response to your first question, I
am fine, thank you. Also, I am not "weirded
out" about what we did yesterday. I think you
are beautiful.

I'm happy.

I'm happy because I love you so much, and
I'm proud of you for being brave and open
with me, and for having the courage to talk
to Mrs. Dvorak. This will be good, Ryan Dean.
You will see. You need to be happy again.
I love seeing you when you're just your
normal, extremely goofy self, because it makes
everything so much brighter. ☺

I was a little bit mad at you last night because
you wouldn't consider talking to someone about
what's going on, but mostly it made me sad
because there was nothing I could do about
it if you insisted on being stubborn, which is

something you're very good at. I wonder what happened to change your mind? Did Sam talk you into it?

I like hanging out with Sam Abernathy, by the way, and I don't think he talks too much. He really likes you, Ryan Dean. You're his hero, do you know that? You know what he said to me? He told me he wishes he could be like Ryan Dean West. You should really try to be nice to him once in a while.

As for the last part — I really want to kiss you right now too, Ryan Dean. And, you know . . . next time we "go for a run," we should find somewhere nice and indoors. ☺

Love,

Annie Altman xxoo

First off, it was not actually my Health homework that I'd written my note on—it was just a *draft*. I thought Annie would appreciate it. At least I didn't write it on a page where someone is tearing someone else's arm off. And, second, the Abernathy could be more careful of what he wishes for. He already was *exactly* like me, which is a completely pathetic confession to make. But, more important, Annie said "next time," and that made me feel all tingly and conspiratorial about finding some indoor place where we could be alone. Copilot Two was definitely enthusiastic about the idea, which was probably not good timing, because just then Mrs. Dvorak came out of her office and smiled at me.

"Are you Ryan Dean?"

Gardening. Risotto. Baseball. Sam Abernathy. Please go away, Copilot Two!

I desperately wished there were some effective means by which I could deny being me, so I could remain seated for, like, ten more minutes.

"Uh. Uh. Yes. Yes, I am."

I am really stupid sometimes.

Most of the time.

"Nice to meet you. I'm Mrs. Dvorak."

She put her hand out to shake, which meant I *had* to stand up. I wasn't raised by wolves, after all.

I pretended to "drop" (picture me using air quotes) my book bag so I could momentarily avoid the handshake, bend down, and try to get Copilot Two parked at the gate.

Did it.

The seat belt sign came off. I stood up and shook Mrs. Dvorak's cool, soft hand.

Okay, so, I had never seen Mrs. Dvorak before, but just hearing the name caused me to conjure a mental image of an old hunchbacked woman in a lab coat, when, in fact, Mrs. Dvorak was a piping hot five out of five bowls of Ethiopian Doro Wat on the Ryan Dean West Totally-Hot-Things-Whose-Names-Make-No-Sense-to-Me Scale.

What was wrong with me?

Mrs. Dvorak said, "You don't need to feel nervous, Ryan Dean. We're just going to talk about whatever you're comfortable talking about. Relax."

Tell that to Copilot Two, I thought.

CHAPTER FORTY-EIGHT

MRS. DVORAK: So. You're in twelfth grade, and fifteen years old?

RYAN DEAN WEST: Yes, ma'am.

MRS. DVORAK: You must be very smart.

RYAN DEAN WEST: (*Blushes. Yes, I do that too sometimes.*) Oh. Thank you.

MRS. DVORAK: Can you tell me a little bit about yourself?

RYAN DEAN WEST: Like what?

MRS. DVORAK: Oh, just like where you're from, what your family is like, your friends, the things you do here at school, and maybe the kinds of things you enjoy doing when you're on your own.

Side note: I am a fifteen-year-old boy. If she thinks I'm going to tell her everything I do during—air quotes—alone time, she's out of her mind.

RYAN DEAN WEST: Let's see. I live in Boston when I'm not here at school. I don't have any brothers or sisters. My dad's an attorney and my mom does volunteer work for charities and museums and stuff. And I don't hate my parents, which is probably the bread and butter of psychology. I love them both very much. I hope that sounds not-insane. Does that sound normal to you?

MRS. DVORAK: (*Laughs*) I always like it when students bring along a sense of humor. How about friends?

Side note: I did not want to talk about friends.

RYAN DEAN WEST: Did you want me to bring along my friends, too?

MRS. DVORAK: (*Laughs*) No. I mean, tell me about your friends.

RYAN DEAN WEST: Oh. Well, I have friends on the rugby team. And I have a girlfriend. We've been together (*Momentarily forgets what he is about to say, because he's thinking about what having "been together" means*) since last year, but we've been best friends since ninth grade.

Side note: I really need to stop turning red in front of Mrs. Dvorak, but thinking about Annie, and what we did yesterday, and what we were talking about doing again, all in front of Mrs. Dvorak, who I was thinking about in a highly inappropriate way, was making me dizzy.

MRS. DVORAK: Oh, that's so terrific! What's your girlfriend like?

RYAN DEAN WEST: (*Swallows*) She's the most beautiful person I know. She's artistic, funny, smart, and I love her.

MRS. DVORAK: Sounds like you've got a situation that most boys only wish they could have.

RYAN DEAN WEST: It could sound that way, I guess.

MRS. DVORAK: How about your roommates?

RYAN DEAN WEST: I only have one roommate, but I don't like him.

MRS. DVORAK: I suppose that can be rough, living with someone who isn't a good match.

RYAN DEAN WEST: No big deal. I can handle it.

MRS. DVORAK: You must be easy to get along with.

RYAN DEAN WEST: I have my bad moments.

MRS. DVORAK: What are those like?

RYAN DEAN WEST: Just bad luck, mostly. Weird things just always seem to happen to me.

MRS. DVORAK: Do you mean weird like funny, or weird like bad?

RYAN DEAN WEST: (*Shrugs, and shakes his head without answering*)

MRS. DVORAK: What kinds of things do you like to do, Ryan Dean?

RYAN DEAN WEST: I like to play rugby. I'm captain of the team. I like to go running with my girlfriend. (*Starts to choke*) Um, I enjoy writing stuff. I like to read. And I really like to draw and write comics.

MRS. DVORAK: Comics? You sound like a very creative boy.

RYAN DEAN WEST: I think I am.

MRS. DVORAK: Maybe next time we talk, you could show me some of your comics.

Side note: Next time? No. No next time. This is unbearable.

RYAN DEAN WEST: Sure.

MRS. DVORAK: I have this theory about creative people. They tend to be very sensitive to things—like changes in vibrations around them. That's one reason why creative people oftentimes get anxious or sad.

RYAN DEAN WEST: You probably know more about that stuff than I do.

MRS. DVORAK: Do you ever feel anxious or sad?

RYAN DEAN WEST: I have a pulse.

MRS. DVORAK: Can I ask you something?

RYAN DEAN WEST: You mean besides all the other somethings you've already asked me, Mrs. Dvorak?

MRS. DVORAK: (*Laughs*) I like your sense of humor, Ryan Dean. I'll bet all your friends love that about you. But what I wanted to know is this: We—you and I—are going to try to do something together. So we need to think about a goal, just like you think about how to score in rugby, or how to finish the comic you're working on. What I want to know is, what do you want me to help you do?

RYAN DEAN WEST: (*Looks at the comfortable couch against the wall*) Could me and Annie use this office for about an hour—no, two. Two hours—tonight? That would help me do something I really, really want to do!

Side note: Okay, I'll be honest. I didn't really say that.

RYAN DEAN WEST: I'm not sure I know what I want.

MRS. DVORAK: Well, when you called in this morning, you said you were having a hard time with things, right?

RYAN DEAN WEST: There are some people who are kind of worried about me. I'm doing this for them.

MRS. DVORAK: Who are the people that have told you they're worried?

RYAN DEAN WEST: Well. My girlfriend. And my roommate.

MRS. DVORAK: But you don't like him.

RYAN DEAN WEST: I know.

MRS. DVORAK: What would they say they're worried about, Ryan Dean?

RYAN DEAN WEST: I get scared at night. I feel like something terrible is going to happen, and I want all that to stop.

MRS. DVORAK: (*Nods her head*) That's a good goal for us to have, and I think we can do that together. Those kinds of things—anxiety, and feeling helpless—they happen to young people when they go away from home and have to get along on their own. We can do this, Ryan Dean.

RYAN DEAN WEST: If you say so. It would be nice.

MRS. DVORAK: You know, I'm going to need to speak with your parents to let them know you've come to see me.

Side note: NOOOOOO!!!!

RYAN DEAN WEST: Oh. That would be fine, I guess.

MRS. DVORAK: Great. And we'll set something up for next week, then.

Side note: How did I EVER get myself into this?

CHAPTER FORTY-NINE

OKAY. SO, YOU KNOW HOW SOMETIMES you arrive late to a party, or, let's say, to rugby practice, and you see two of the guests—or in this case, two of your teammates—involved in a heated confrontation that you can't really hear but you know is heated because of the way they're standing and how the veins on their necks are sticking out and they've got their hands on their hips and one foot angled back like they were maybe already thinking about boxing, even though there is a calm mediator, a *boy whisperer*—in this case Coach M—trying to get between them, and just as you get through the door to the party—or, in this case, out onto the pitch—all three sets of eyes turn and look at you and you instantly know that the fourth—in this case invisible—participant in the heated confrontation happens to be YOU, and you're all, like, *what the fuck did I do now?* because if there was actually going to be a fight between Spotted John Nygaard and JP Tureau, it would be a real bisexual-ninja-versus-testosterone-drunk-hammerhead-shark death match because those two guys happened to be without a doubt the toughest guys on the team?

Exactly. You know where I'm coming from.

But I had no clue what it was all about. Not that I was particularly eager to find out. So I went over to where the backs were working on drills and got into line for some up-and-under kicking practice. I kept the corner of my eye on Spotted John and JP, until Coach M sent them off on a "buddy run," which was something Coach would make guys do if they got into arguments during practice. He gave them a ball and told them to go, and JP and Spotted John had to run laps around the practice field, passing the rugby ball between them until Coach M was satisfied they were over it.

That afternoon, JP's and Spotted John's buddy run lasted until practice was nearly finished.

We ended with a game of touch. That was more than fine with me because my ribs weren't 100 percent yet, and Coach informed us that this would be a noncontact week leading up to Thursday's friendly, because he wanted us to be hungry and healthy.

And speaking of healthy, I felt pretty good about things. Maybe it was the sandwiches, and the "next time" note from Annie, but I also knew that the uncomfortably awkward hour I'd spent in Mrs. Dvorak's office did something for me too. It opened me up in some ways, and it felt good.

Could I actually be *looking forward* to seeing Mrs. Dvorak again next Monday?

Still, there was this heavy, muted vibe going on during practice, like everyone knew what was up between Spotted John and JP, but nobody said a word about it to me.

Until we got inside the locker room.

I had just come out of the shower and was drying off in front of my locker, when JP Tureau walked up to me and said, "You're a bitch-faced pussy, Ryan Dean."

At once, the following struck me:

1. Bitch-faced pussy. I have been called lots of things. This is high school, after all, and more pointedly, this was a high school boys' locker room, where name-calling is as atmospheric as B.O. But I've never been called a "bitch-faced pussy" before. Also, I didn't really know what "bitch-faced pussy" meant, but I had to give credit to JP Tureau for coming up with a name-calling name that sounded really, really bad.

2. Scanning my recently opened files. What the fuck did I do now? I couldn't for the life of me remember having done something that would piss off JP since, like, last spring or so, unless he was still totally after Annie, and by some weird chance he'd followed us on our run into the woods the day before and saw what we had done—which was an extremely creepy thing that I never wanted to think about again.

3. Are you kidding me? I had been in a couple fights with JP Tureau last year. They were short, and I got lucky because JP should have killed me on several occasions, but—*come on!*—JP was still dressed in his sweaty rugby gear. There were actual chunks of grass and mud stuck to his knees. He had cleats on. And I really, really did not want to get into a fight with JP Tureau while I was

naked. Nobody ever wants to get into a fight while he's naked.

4. Witnesses. There weren't any. My locker's row was empty. All the other guys were either in the showers or had dressed and gone back to the dorms. This was JP Tureau's golden opportunity to pay me back for everything he hated about me.

"What did I do to *you*, JP?"

"Spotted John got all up in my face. He said you were whining that I hit you too hard last week. He told me he'd fuck me up if I didn't go easier on our *stand-off*, because the team *needs* you. Bullshit. You're a fucking pussy. Nobody needs a fucking pussy."

Okay. I knew JP didn't like me, but that kind of hurt my feelings.

"Look, I never said anything at all to Spotted John about you, JP. I thought my ribs were broken is all, and I asked John for some pain-killers so I could sleep. That's all that happened. I never said nothing about you being an over-the-top, think-with-your-dick asshole, so fuck off."

Yes, I really said that. It was pretty good, considering my inexperience with swearing out loud.

I also knotted my towel tightly around my waist because I was 99 percent certain I was about to get into an I'm-naked-and-you're-in-rugby-gear fistfight with JP Tureau.

"Hey. Do you want a towel, JP?"

The Abernathy, our manager and towel boy, appeared at the end of the bench behind JP. He held out a nice, folded Pine Mountain towel and displayed an innocent little Shar-Pei puppy look on his face.

JP Tureau turned around. He looked at the Abernathy. Then he looked at me.

I didn't say anything. I had my hands at my sides. I looked at the Abernathy, then at JP.

The Abernathy looked—at JP, then at me.

That was a hell of a lot of looking, considering we were inside a boys' locker room, where excessive looking is a social felony.

It was like living through the pregnant few seconds just before a three-way gunfight in an old black-and-white Western.

Sam Abernathy's presence was like a punch in the gut to JP Tureau.

JP mouthed "fuck you" to me. Then he said, "Thanks, Snack-Pack."

JP took the towel from the Abernathy and sat down in front of his locker. Guys started coming back from the showers. JP had missed his moment.

And JP touched his eye and added, "You should be careful about wrestling around in bed with loser stand-offs, Snackers."

JP unlaced his cleats. The Abernathy just stood at the end of our bench, watching us.

He said, "I know! Nobody should *ever* get into a fight with Ryan Dean!"

Did the Abernathy know what was going on?

No. There's no way. The kid couldn't have known I was about to be murdered. That would mean he'd just stuck his neck out for me, and that would never happen. After all, he was only twelve, and it would have been inconceivable for him to effectively decode the kind of shit that goes on between older boys, because the Abernathy just wasn't that smart. And, besides, he had no reason to care about me.

Right?

CHAPTER FIFTY

THAT NIGHT A COLD STORM BLEW IN
while we lay in our beds and watched a Cooking Channel program
about searing meat with a blowtorch after cooking it *sous vide*.

Don't ask.

But the weather was like a freaking hurricane gusting in through
our open window. And there was some dude on TV with an actual
blowtorch, spitting ninja flame-gun fire at a piece of meat. I didn't
know if it was supposed to make me hungry or scare the shit out
of me.

Who keeps a fucking blowtorch in their kitchen? Murderers,
probably.

The Abernathy, without being asked, got up from Super Mario
Land in his soccer jammies and socks, and shut our window. Then he
padded across the floor and swung the door ajar.

Whatever. At least I wasn't getting hit by occasional windblown
hailstones.

This was going to be my life until June.

"You've been really quiet tonight, Ryan Dean."

"I don't want to talk."

"What did you think of Mrs. Dvorak?" the Abernathy asked.

I thought about it.

"She was really nice. And I think she's kinda hot."

"You *do*?"

I nodded. "Yeah. Totally hot, dude."

"Well, do you mind if I make some popcorn?"

The kid never ran out of microwave popcorn.

"Knock yourself out."

"It's cheese flavored. Do you want some?"

"Sure."

After the popcorn finished popping, Sam poured some out for me.

"Thanks."

"You're welcome, Ryan Dean!" The Abernathy climbed back on top of his bed. "Oh! I forgot to tell you. Spotted John showed me. You know. He showed me why all the guys call him Spotted John. It was . . . well . . . really gross."

"Spotted John is totally gross, Sam. I should have warned you. Sorry, I forgot."

"It's okay. He's a nice guy, but that's a really weird thing to show off to someone."

I said, "I know. What can I say? He's from Denmark."

"Oh. Do lots of guys have birthmarks on their wieners in Denmark?"

"Sam? I don't ever want to talk about wieners with you while we're in bed, okay? Well, anytime, to be honest. But especially not now."

The Abernathy laughed. "You are so funny, Ryan Dean!"

Whatever.

I ate some popcorn.

And the Abernathy went on, "I will never talk to you about wieners again."

"You're doing it now. Stop talking to me."

"Okay. Well. I wanted to ask you one thing, Ryan Dean, and I hope it doesn't make you mad at me."

"Is it about wieners? Because if it's about wieners, I'll be pretty mad, Sam."

"Ha ha! No! It's not about wieners."

And Sam Abernathy laugh-choked for a good fifteen seconds.

Hilarious.

It had almost gotten to the point where, in my mind, I began running through the steps for applying the Heimlich maneuver to a seventy-two-pound twelve-year-old who was choking from laughing so hard about wieners while eating popcorn. But then Sam Abernathy regained his composure and said, "That JP Tureau really hates you, doesn't he?"

"Yeah. He does."

"That's not good. Why would anyone hate you, Ryan Dean?"

"It's a long story. Sometimes, that kind of stuff happens between boys, you know."

"I hope it never happens to me. I was scared for you in the locker room."

"God knows, JP probably would have punched me in the wiener. That would not have been good."

Sam choked again for at least half a minute.

"Ryan Dean, you are not supposed to talk about wieners!"

"Yes. Mrs. Blyleven would get mad at us for calling them wieners."

"I would hate it if I ever got in trouble for talking about wieners and then PM called my parents and told them," the Abernathy said.

"Okay. Stop talking to me now."

"Yeah. But why? Why did JP want to start a fight with you?"

I rolled over in bed so I could look across the room to where Sam was sitting. "We got into a few fights last year. It wasn't good. I made him look bad, I guess, and he won't let go of it."

"What was the fight about?"

"Annie. JP likes Annie too. He was trying to get her away from me."

The Abernathy said, "Oh." It sounded like something you'd say when seeing your hero receive a medal or something. And that made me feel weird.

"Sam?"

"What?"

"That was really cool, what you did in the locker room."

"What? Looking at Spotted John's wiener?"

"Stop talking to me."

I threw my pillow across the room. It splattered into the kid.

And I'll admit it: Sam Abernathy was a lot smarter than I wanted to believe.

CHAPTER FIFTY-ONE

GAME DAY CAME AT LAST.

I almost had myself convinced that after my one little chat about goal setting with Mrs. Dvorak, my night troubles wouldn't come back. Easy fix, right? Well, I was wrong again.

Anyway, I never could sleep soundly the night before a game, so I guess I kind of set myself up for it. Because just when I was starting to think I was maybe in the clear, I woke up at three in the morning on Thursday with that smothering weight on my chest.

It really sucked.

Shaking and dizzy, terrified, I lay there, frozen in place, staring up at the ceiling. The night seemed endless, and as scared as I was that I was actually going to die, I willed myself to stay put and not make a sound. I didn't want the Abernathy to know what was happening to me. So I stayed there, shivering and scared all night, waiting for morning, and waiting for the next terrible thing that was bound to happen.

I knew exactly what those three days in the well must have felt like to Sam Abernathy.

I think I started to calm down just as the light from our window spilled oyster gray into the room. I was a sweaty wreck. The Abernathy climbed out of his bed. I could feel him looking at me from his side of the room.

"Are you okay, Ryan Dean?"

"Yes."

"Excited for the game today?"

"Uh-huh."

"Well, I'm going to take a shower and get dressed."

"Oh."

I started to sit up in bed, so I could leave, and the Abernathy said, "It's okay, Ryan Dean. You look tired. You don't have to leave. Just promise not to look at me."

"Whatever."

I lay back down as Sam Abernathy rearranged his claustrophobic escape routes from our room by opening the window and shutting the front door. To be honest, the cold outside air felt good, like I'd been dug up from a sixty-foot hole in the ground.

The water came on in the shower.

Maybe the kid was getting better. Maybe Headmaster Dude-whose-last-name-nobody-knows was right about me being able to help Sam Abernathy. Maybe I was a sponge for his neuroses, soaking them all up.

The morning was dreadful, and the morning was wonderful.

I am supposed to be Joey today. Coach is going to make me wear Joey's jersey. I don't know if I can do this. I can't let myself look bad in front of Coach M and the team, or in front of Annie or Nico or Sam Abernathy and especially not in front of that asshole JP Tureau.

I am supposed to be Joey today.

"Done."

I didn't realize I hadn't moved at all. And when I looked at him, there was the Abernathy all Pine-Mountained up in his tie, creased slacks, and school sweater, looking like a *you-can-have-one-of-these-too!* lawn ornament for a fertility clinic.

"Are you sure you feel okay, Ryan Dean?"

"Yeah. I'm fine. Stop talking to me."

I dragged myself out of bed and went into the bathroom—no, shower room.

That day, I wore the shirt and tie I'd taken from Joey's old room in O-Hall. It was a weird thing to do, but I somehow hoped that Joey's spirit might be lingering on it, that he might calm me down and help me get through the game without totally blowing it. And I could almost hear him scolding me like he used to do—telling me that I worried about things too much, and that I'd put all this work into getting here, so there was no way I'd let myself down by not trying my hardest.

It made me kind of sad to think about Joey telling me off, which was something he was always really good at.

And all day long, I kept looking around distractedly, trying to see if Nico Cosentino would just magically appear, like he said he would. Spotted John never said he'd called back (and Spotted John wouldn't lie to me about things), so I had to believe Nico would keep his word and show up sometime before kickoff.

It was all I could do to slog through the day. Annie understood. She knew I always got quiet and nervous on game days. What rugger doesn't? It would be better afterward, when all the bashing back and forth was done and we could sit down to dinner with the boys from the other team while we stretched the boundaries of acceptable Pine Mountain content and attempted to out-sing each other.

In the locker room before the game, it was the Abernathy's job to pass out the jerseys while Coach read his roster for the first fifteen and the subs. Not everyone would get to play, but that's how things are in real life, too. Right?

Coach skipped from nine, Seanie, to eleven, Mike Bagnuolo. He was saving my number for last, and I was dreading having to say something as captain to the guys about playing the game. Here's how our numbers worked out for the first fifteen:

NUMBER	POSITION	NAME	NICKNAME
1	Loosehead Prop	Steven Murphy	Little Wood
2	Hooker	Jeff Cotton	Cotton Balls
3	Tighthead Prop	Doug Wilson	Dougie
4	Left Lock	Jack Jefferson	Basketball
5	Right Lock	Kyle Cortez	Bunbun
6	Blindside Flanker	Georgie Herrera	Bucket
7	Openside Flanker	Eli Koenig	Tarzan
8	Eight-Man	John Nygaard	Spotted John
9	Scrum Half	Sean Russell Flaherty	Seanie
10	Stand-Off	Ryan Dean West	Snack-Pack Senior
11	Left Wing	Mike Bagnuolo	Bags
12	Inside Center	Matthias de Clerq	Corn Dog
13	Outside Center	Javier Mendez	Swordfish
14	Right Wing	Timmy Bagnuolo	T-Bag
15	Fullback	JP Tureau	Sartre

And, in case you've never seen rugby, this is how the positions line up on the pitch:

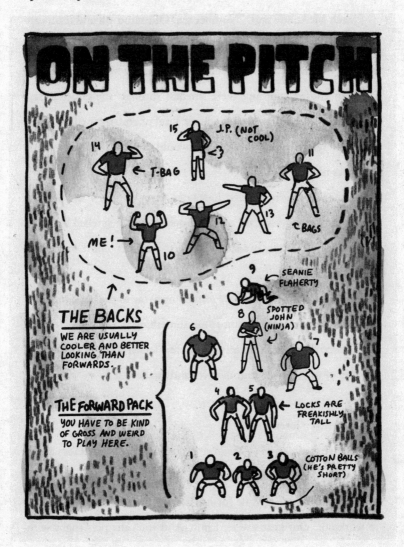

At the end, even after the subs' jerseys had been given out, it was finally my turn, and all those eyes turned toward me.

Coach McAuliffe said, "Number ten. Our stand-off and team captain, Ryan Dean West."

The guys clapped and slapped my shoulders, which stung because I had to endure standing there shirtless through the entire jersey-passing-out routine. Also, it made me kind of embarrassed because I never thought the guys on my team would clap for me.

It was nice.

So the Abernathy handed Joey's old jersey to me. I unfolded it. There was still a grass stain on the shoulder, and it smelled like Joey. I pulled it on over my head. I knew what was next, and I was feeling pretty sick about it.

Coach M said, "Do you have something to say to the boys, captain?"

I really, really did not want to say something to the boys.

I looked down at a spot on the concrete locker room floor between the toes of my cleats. I shut my eyes and swallowed.

My voice cracked.

I am such a loser.

"Last year, after we lost Kevin, and then Joey, we kind of lost a sense of who we were as a team, and it felt like we didn't want to play anymore. I can't blame anyone for it—it's the way things just happened to work out. Our hearts weren't in it. And you can't play rugby without your heart, because the game is so much more than just a contest about where the numbers end up when that last whistle blows."

Side note: What the fuck am I saying? You're not starting to cry, are you Ryan Dean? You better not fucking start crying.

"I've been trying to find my heart since last year. I don't know if I have yet. Maybe we'll find out after seventy minutes of rugby. We've always been a great team, but too many things got in our way last year. Now it's a new year, right?"

Some of the guys said, "Right!"

It made me feel weird. I didn't think anyone was listening to me. I don't even know if I was listening to myself.

I said, "It's supposed to be fun. Joey would want us to have fun. I'm pretty sure he'd give us some serious shit if we didn't have fun out there today, no matter what the numbers look like when we clean up and go home. Right?"

And now the whole team answered, "Right!"

Side note: I really did say "shit," and Coach M, who was very strict about cussing, never said one thing about it to me. Also, I hadn't noticed, since I was actually looking at my feet—because I was afraid I might have drippy eyes—but while I was talking to the team (and my feet), another boy had come into the locker room. It was Nico Cosentino.

He stood behind the team, watching us and listening to me. When I looked at him, he nodded his chin in a silent, *hey, bro* kind of greeting that guys do sometimes.

So, yeah, even his chin *broed* me.

And he was dressed like a Pine Mountain kid—all done up in a full school uniform and tie. That was weird. I thought Nico withdrew from Pine Mountain. I looked at Coach and could see right away that he'd known Nico was coming to the game. It had to have been as big a thing—or bigger—to Coach M as it was for me. But I also could see that Nico didn't want to be pointed out to everyone. He wasn't that kind of guy. I knew that about Nico from the first time I'd ever said anything to him in Headmaster What-the-fuck's office. So before he could get noticed by the other twenty-two kids getting ready to play the game, Nico turned around and walked out of the locker room.

CHAPTER FIFTY-TWO

ANNIE WAS WAITING FOR ME. SHE stood beside the gate to the rugby pitch, just past the door where the guys came out of our locker room.

And I'll be honest—I felt a little guilty and ashamed because I was wearing Joey's jersey, and Annie knew it. Joey had been just as good a friend to Annie as he had been to me.

I grabbed her hand and squeezed while the team filed past us onto the field.

"Are you nervous?" she asked.

"Like always," I said.

"It should make you feel good to get out there again."

"Yeah. Hey, look—there's someone here that I want you to meet," I said.

"Oh? Who?"

"It's a surprise. Come on."

And I led Annie up into the bleachers, which were surprisingly full. There weren't a lot of things to do around Pine Mountain, so I was never sure if the kids and staff actually liked rugby or just came to the games to see who'd be carried off in a stretcher. I found Nico sitting near the top of the stands, all alone. It was kind of weird that I felt sorry about him being alone. What would I expect? Nobody here knew him—he was just this anonymous new kid who'd never been seen around before.

I said, "Nico Cosentino, I'd like you to meet Annie Altman."

Nico—as I would have expected of *anyone* who was related to Joey—stood up when I introduced Annie. And I watched her blush—*ugh!*—when he gently took her hand.

"Are you—" Annie began.

"Joey's brother," Nico said. "Joey told me about you. You're just as beautiful as he said you were."

I kind of choked a little. And then I said something really stupid.

"Annie's my girlfriend. We had sex last Sunday."

Okay. I'll admit it. The stupid thing I said did *not* include that second sentence, even if I wanted to say it. Because what made that entirely stupid was that I *knew* Joey would have told him Annie and I were boyfriend and girlfriend, but it was just that Nico was so goddamned good looking and nice, and I actually saw Annie blush.

"Bro. I know she's your girlfriend. Duh."

"Oh. Uh, I better get down on the field before someone says something. I just wanted you to have someone to hang out with during the game. Uh. Bro."

So there. I *broed* him back.

"Thanks, man."

This was interesting. Apparently, broing a bro promotes you to "man."

"Enjoy the game," I said. Then I gave Annie a quick ninja cheek-peck and clattered my metal cleats down the stands.

And as I was walking away from them, Nico said, "Hey, Ryan Dean. I like that jersey on you."

I stopped in my tracks. I turned around and locked eyes with Nico Cosentino. Neither of us said anything. We didn't have to.

It was a rough game, which as far as rugby is concerned made it a perfect game.

The team we hosted traveled down from Bellingham, Washington, where, apparently, there are a lot of really big teenage boys who play rugby, because all things considered, we were completely outsized. The opposing number ten was at least thirty pounds heavier than me. We hit each other a few times, and I definitely felt each and every one of those extra pounds.

Before the first half ended, Seanie Flaherty caught an elbow on the top of his head, which cut him pretty good. He had to come out of the game because he was a bloody mess, so T-Bag moved up to play scrum half, and a replacement winger came in. Seanie needed stitches. There was almost nothing our medic could do for a cut in the top of a kid's scalp except tell Seanie to keep it pinched shut, because Seanie refused to leave the sidelines until the game was over.

At halftime, when we were down 3–0, Seanie told me, "Hey, Ryan Dean, I'm going to get to see that hottie nurse after the game."

"Lucky you, dude," I said. I didn't have the heart to tell him that Nurse Hickey was out on maternity leave and that he'd most likely get the full-on once-over from Doctor No-gloves.

Poor Seanie.

Halftime in rugby lasts exactly five minutes, and during that time players are not allowed to step off the field of play. That's how the game is: brutal. We circled up so we could talk about what we needed to do to pull the win. And I glanced up in the stands and saw Nico Cosentino looking right at me, like he was saying, *Hey, bro, get your shit together*. He was sitting between Isabel and Annie, which, for whatever stupid laundry list of reasons, made me feel kind of jealous.

Coach M never said anything to us about how we were playing during games. He'd just stay on the sidelines, taking notes and watching. That was one of the things that made him such a great coach. He'd say that his time to tell us what we needed to do was at practice. During a game, he said, we were all on our own. The real game was our chance to show him what we had learned, what we could do, and all the grown-up talk in the world was not going to change what boys do out on the pitch.

"Nice job at scrummie, T-Bag," I said, and patted Timmy Bagnuolo's shoulder.

"Yeah. Nice job," Spotted John said.

"Look, we're going to have to ruck and post and run on these guys, even if we only get five meters at a time, because we're not busting through in open-field play," I said. "Let the forwards do their job."

JP looked mad. The open field was my responsibility, and I wasn't getting us anywhere today.

"Bullshit," JP argued. "Get the ball to me, Ryan Dean. I'll put it in goal."

I looked at JP. Another stare-down standoff.

I nodded. "I think you can do it, JP. Let's give it a try."

So there, asshole.

And I added, "If we can get a scrum deep in their end, let's wheel it and see if we can't get them tripping all over themselves and open up for us."

"That's dangerous, and against the laws," the Abernathy, who had carried water bottles onto the field and had also, apparently, been studying the International Rugby Board law book, said. (There are no rules in rugby—there are only "laws," which, like all laws, only have teeth if people get caught breaking them.)

"Shut up, Snack-Pack," Cotton Balls said. "We know what we're doing."

I'll admit it: Intentionally wheeling a scrum is dangerous and arguably illegal, but we'd been practicing plays with the forward pack where we'd wheel the scrum (which means causing the pack of bodies to rotate) just slightly—twenty-two-and-a-half degrees, to be precise—which could really block off the opposing scrum half and back line if we did it right, and if we also had them butted up against a touch line. ("Touch" is what Americans think of as "out of bounds.")

We tried, we tried, but almost nothing worked against those guys.

When seventy minutes had elapsed, our teams were tied at three points each. Almost unbelievably, and to both sides' forwards' credit, neither team had been able to get the ball into goal. Our scores were both penalty kicks. JP, who admittedly was Pine Mountain's best kicker, made ours for us to tie the match and save us from a preseason loss late in the game.

Usually, during preseason friendly matches, if the score is tied when time has expired, they'd usually let it stand as a tie, since there was little sense in getting players messed up over a game that didn't count for anything. But the coaches talked to the referee, and both sides agreed to play a sudden-death overtime so that the game would end with one team winning.

Which meant someone had to lose.

Our opportunity (to win, not to lose) came quickly. Overtime was our kickoff, and I was the guy who did kickoffs. I'd been working on high, deep hangers that gave our fastest backs the opportunity to get underneath them and actually receive our own kicks, and I nailed one. The Bellingham fullback took his eyes off the ball, which gave our inside center, Corn Dog (you really do not want to know how he got that name) a chance to get under it and take the ball for Pine Mountain.

JP came crashing up from the back, hollering for the ball. It was a very risky move, considering the fullback is the last line of defense and there was a hell of a lot of open pitch behind us.

Just as he got caught up in a crushing maul that was not going to move anywhere, Corn Dog popped the ball back to JP, who was busting through at full speed. JP made it over the goal line and—*whack!*—he got hit so hard by one of Bellingham's flankers, it sounded like a two-by-four breaking on a cinder-block wall.

Okay, so here's another rugby lesson for you if you don't know the game: In order to score a try (which is what a goal is called in rugby), the ball has to be touched down onto the grass in goal by the ball carrier. This is where the ridiculous term "touchdown" comes from in American football—where nothing at all gets *touched down* and there is most often silly dancing involved, which is absolutely against the law in rugby. If an opposing player can slip his hand (or any other body part—*ewww!*) between the ball and the grass, then the score does not count and the ball is called "held up in goal," which is what looked like was going to happen to JP.

Our guys piled onto JP from behind, trying to get him down to the grass, while the Bellingham guys plowed into JP from the opposite side, trying to keep him up on his feet. I stayed back, just off T-Bag's right shoulder, in case the ball got to our scrummie.

It didn't.

JP Tureau was monstrously strong. The muscles on his legs strained so hard, I swear it looked like he was about to snap his thigh bones like pencils. He drove forward and got the ball lower. And that's when just about the worst possible thing that could ever happen to a dude with a titanic ego like JP Tureau's happened to JP Tureau and his titanic ego.

The HMS *JP Tureau* hit the knock-on iceberg.

As JP got the ball down to grass level, a surging press from Bellingham twisted him around (it looked like JP nearly snapped in half), and—*plunk!*—the ball squirted forward from JP's fingers and bounced free. That, in rugby, is what is called a knock-on, which means the ball carrier somehow allowed his ball to drop free in front of his body, and it is not a good thing. When it happens in goal, the referee calls for a scrum (with the opposing team given the slight advantage of feeding the ball in) on the five-meter line.

So this was it: We were close to the goal, in a scrum, with Bellingham butted up against a line of touch—a perfect storm for our little wheel play.

In set plays, like scrums, I would call audibles to the team. The stand-off, number ten, is equivalent to quarterback in American football, so that was my responsibility. As the front- and second-row guys began lining up, Spotted John turned back to me and pointed his index finger at his left palm, which meant he wanted to try to sneak the ball out from the scrum. The only two players who are allowed to reach below the scrum's tangle of bodies and pull the ball out are the scrum half and the eight-man, and when the number eight did it—this was usually rare—it often caught the other team by complete surprise.

I shook my head, dismissing Spotted John's idea.

"Twenty-two point five!" I called, which was the signal for the tighthead prop to drive an extra step forward and the loosehead prop to ease back after engagement, which would angle the scrum, make it more difficult for the Bellingham scrum half to reach the ball, and paint their number ten into a corner.

The scrum was set. The teams hit. It sounded like a herd of bulls slamming into a herd of bigger bulls, and the twist worked perfectly. Cotton Balls, who was a natural lefty anyway, hooked the ball back toward Eli Koenig, Tarzan, our number seven flanker, and Eli kept the ball right at the edge of the scrum. The Bellingham scrum half couldn't even see the ball through the forest of legs below the pack.

Timmy Bagnuolo waited. He played the position perfectly—better than Seanie had done all last season. T-Bag glanced at me as I faded farther back to the center of the field. He knew what I was thinking, which, again, is what a good scrummie has to be able to do. Then he went for it. He reached in and grabbed the ball perfectly and sailed a diving pass back to me—as hard as the kid could throw.

The ball stung when it hit my hands. In my peripheral vision, I could see the Bellingham boys looking confused and disorganized— most of them hadn't realized the ball was out of the scrum. I took a step forward. I dropped the ball right in front of my left foot, then kicked.

The ball spun, end over end, and made a perfect rainbow, up between the posts.

That's what's called a drop goal in rugby. Not many teams—especially at the high school level—ever attempt drop goals, but it was something I (and Coach M) loved to see put into play, and it won the game for us.

Final score: 6–3.

The Bellingham boys were stunned. I heard a couple of them say "What the fuck?" and "No fucking way!" And it was such a tough game, most of them just sat down where they were in the grass and shook their heads while the Pine Mountain boys cheered and swarmed around and piled on top of me to the point where I actually thought I was going to be smothered and die beneath fourteen (well, thirteen, actually, because I'm sure JP Tureau wouldn't get involved in a Ryan Dean West dogpile) stinky, sweaty, gross boys.

The referee blew the whistle—a long continuous blast with his hand straight up in the air, followed by three more blasts, signaling a score and the end of play. And despite being crushed and dripped on by boy sweat and gasping in the disgusting gaseous vapors of an entire rugby team, it was probably the best feeling I'd ever had in more than a year (if you exclude what Annie and I did the previous Sunday, that is).

It turned out there really were fourteen guys on top of me, because the Abernathy piled on last. When they disassembled the pyramid of bodies, all the guys stood around rubbing the Abernathy's hair and tossing their soaked jerseys at him. That's when I saw JP down the field, in the same spot where he'd played to watch for a kick out of that last scrum.

He was lying on his back in the grass with one knee bent up and one leg turned over to the side, and he wasn't moving.

That last hit on him, when he was in goal, really did JP in.

I walked back to where JP was splayed out on the grass and stood over him.

"Are you okay?"

JP opened his eyes. "I'm wiped."

"So am I."

I held out my hand to help him up. JP took it, and I pulled him to his feet.

I said, "It was a great game, man."

JP nodded. That was about as nice as we'd ever be to each other.

CHAPTER FIFTY-THREE

"HEY."

I shook Dominic Cosentino's hand and sat down across the table from him at our postgame dinner.

"Hi, Nico. It is okay if I call you Nico, right?"

He nodded. "Sure."

"I'm glad you came. What'd you think?"

"You guys are really good. Nice drop goal, by the way."

"Thanks. Hey . . . I thought you weren't coming to school here."

I pointed at my necktie. As always after our match, we had to shower and get dressed back into our school ties so we could sit down to dinner in the basketball gym with the boys from Bellingham, who got to shower and put on their warm-ups. They were a club team—not a private school—and I'd bet that most of them had never even worn a necktie.

Nico said, "I'm not going here. Coach McAuliffe told me I should dress this way so I'd blend in if I wanted to hang out with you, since I can't get a bus back until tomorrow."

So Coach *did* know that Nico was coming to the game.

We sat at the end of a long banquet table that was pretty much vacant, away from the other players, most of whom were snaking through food lines and filling up plates with pizza and salad and cookies—a typical postmatch meal for us.

I took a bite and looked at Nico, who was watching me like I was supposed to do something, but I didn't know what it was.

"You should get some food," I said. Then I realized he probably felt awkward and out of place, so I added, "I'll go with you."

"That's okay. I'll get it."

Nico got up and went to the food line.

He looked so much like Joey that I honestly wanted to hug him, but that would have been too weird—especially in front of all the other Pine Mountain guys who had to have been wondering who the new kid was and why was he sitting with me, not to mention why I was hugging him. Also, Nico's eyes were very sad, unlike Joey's, and that made me feel especially sorry for him.

He came back with pizza and cookies. No salad. Good choice.

"By the way," he said, "thanks for introducing me to Annie. She's such an amazing person."

I blushed. Goddammit. "I know, right?"

"So, what are we supposed to talk about?" Nico said.

"Probably nothing," I said.

Nico shrugged. "Okay with me, bro."

"Well. What I meant was that we shouldn't worry about talking about anything specific. We should just be normal, right? I mean, it's not like a therapy session or anything."

"I go to therapy," Nico said.

I nodded. "So do I."

"Yeah."

"So you moved up here to Oregon?" I remembered how frequently Joey had flown down to San Francisco last year to spend time with his family.

"We actually came from here. We have a house on the beach in Pacific City. It's why Joey and me both wanted to go to Pine Mountain. Our dad went here. So, after, you know . . . we just wanted to come back."

"Oh. Pacific City. Nice."

Then Nico told me, "I thought I was going to die after Joey got killed."

I got a pizza-crust-corner throat slash and washed it down with a gulp of lukewarm soda. "Me too. Something happened inside me, and it's like I can't get it back."

"Losers, huh?"

I smiled. "I always think I'm a loser."

"Joey said that about you."

"Well, if Joey said it, then it must be true."

Nico shook his head. "No. Joey didn't think you were a loser. He told me you always called yourself a loser."

I thought about Joey's to-do list I'd found in O-Hall. I wondered if Nico knew anything about what Joey needed to tell me. But I decided I wasn't going to say anything else about Joey. It was too early in the evening, and I wanted to get to know his little brother—who seemed like an okay guy and also happened to be just about my age.

"I hope you like watching the Cooking Channel," I said.

Nico leaned in like he was sharing a secret that shouldn't be spoken out loud in the presence of all these rugby guys. "Dude. You watch the *Cooking Channel*?"

I shook my head. "My roommate does. He's like a savant when it comes to cooking."

Nico said, "I'd lock him in the closet or something."

"Can't," I said. "We don't even have closets, and the kid is so claustrophobic, he'd probably stop breathing."

"And you're rooming with him because why, exactly?"

"Because I am a total loser, Nico."

Nico smiled. It made me feel good.

Then I saw the Abernathy—all suited up in his perfectly creased Pine Mountain size extra-small boy suit (he must have thrown all the guys' clothes in the washers and then waited for everyone to leave the locker room before changing)—winding his way like a malnourished albino chipmunk through a redwood forest of rugby players, balancing a plate of food in his hands while everyone he passed smeared their fingers through his hair.

"There he is now," I said.

"That little guy?"

"Yep. That's my roomie, our team manager and laundry boy, Sam Abernathy. He's twelve."

Nico got this wide-eyed, understanding look on his face. "Oh! So *that's* why they put you guys together."

Apparently, Joey had told Nico pretty much everything he knew about me, which was pretty much everything I knew about myself.

"Hi, Ryan Dean!" The Abernathy, all excitement and wriggling joy, sat down right next to me.

No. Not now.

Then the little peach-assed puppy fired his glinting love-beam eyes at Nico, stuck his hand across the table, and said, "I'm Sam, Ryan Dean's roommate. Are you new here?"

And Nico, entirely not repulsed by Sam Abernathy's enthusiasm, shook the kid's hand and said, "Hi. I'm Nico. And I'm . . . No, I'm not new here. Ryan Dean and I have known each other for a while, and he invited me to the game."

"It was a great game!" the Abernathy burbled.

Nico took a bite of pizza and said, "You guys are a great team."

It looked like Sam Abernathy grew two inches on the spot, thinking how Nico had just confirmed he was part of the team.

No. Never.

And then, this:

RYAN DEAN WEST 2: Why do you have to be such an asshole?

RYAN DEAN WEST 1: I don't know what you're talking about.

RYAN DEAN WEST 2: Yes you do. You're being an asshole to the Aberna-
     thy. And after all the shit he's done for you in the last few weeks.

RYAN DEAN WEST 1: I just want to be left alone. I need to talk to Nico. Maybe he can help me sort things out.

RYAN DEAN WEST 2: Maybe he can help you stop being an asshole, too. The Abernathy saved your ass from drowning in a freezing lake. He stepped into the middle of things when JP was getting ready to kick the shit out of you.

RYAN DEAN WEST 1: Whatever.

RYAN DEAN WEST 2: Dude. He makes popcorn for you. He does your laundry and folds your clothes. He would do anything for you. You're his fucking hero, and his hero happens to be an asshole.

RYAN DEAN WEST 1: I don't want him to be my friend.

RYAN DEAN WEST 2: And that's exactly what's wrong with you. You think you lost your heart. But you threw it away. You don't give a shit about anyone. Not even Annie.

RYAN DEAN WEST 1: Shut the fuck up and leave me alone!

RYAN DEAN WEST 2: Asshole.

"Hey. Dude. Are you having a seizure or something?"

"Huh?"

When I snapped out of it, Spotted John was standing next to our table, holding a plate that looked like it had enough food on it to feed the population of Wyoming. "I said, who's your friend, and do you mind if I sit down with you guys, Ryan Dean?"

"Oh. Yeah. No. I'm sorry. I was thinking about something. Sure.

Sit down, Spotted John. This is . . . uh . . . my friend, Nico. Nico, this is Spotted John."

And the Abernathy half whispered, "But, dude, seriously, don't ask him where the name came from."

Nico grinned and whispered back, "I already know."

Yeah. Confirmed. Joey told his little brother everything.

I noticed something strange that evening at dinner. Naturally, there was no getting around the fact that Nico was Joey Cosentino's younger brother, and at least half the guys on the team had played alongside Joey last year. So once the word spread around, I could see how the guys all quietly glanced over at us and kind of stayed back, like there was an invisible force field repelling them from getting too close.

It was a nearly sacred thing, I thought—that not one of the boys could bring himself to touch a life which had been so closely touched by death.

Teenagers—teenage boys, especially—just don't have the words sometimes to say what they need to say to another boy who's had to deal with death.

It was weird to the point of creepy, and I decided that I'd ask Mrs. Dvorak about that next time we talked.

And speaking of weird to the point of creepy, there was definitely an armistice on the awkward silence around me and Nico that took effect when Seanie Flaherty showed up after his trip to the school clinic.

"Dude. Let's see it," I said.

Seanie sat across from me, next to Nico. I was sandwiched between the Abernathy and the ninja. I stood up so I could look at the top of Seanie's head.

Gross.

A picket line of black stitches pinched shut the bloodstained lips of Seanie Flaherty's head wound. But what made it particularly difficult to look at was that there was an inch-wide swath of iodine-stained naked, alabaster-white Seanie Flaherty cave-boy skin all around the gash that had been shaved completely bald.

"Oh," I said, which was a failed attempt at masking the I'm-completely-done-eating disgust I felt.

"I can't see it," Seanie said (*duh!*). "What's it look like?"

"A vagina," Spotted John said. Mrs. Blyleven would be proud. Then he added, "Dude. You have a vagina on your head."

Seanie, who undoubtedly never wanted to hear that he had a vagina on his head, slumped down in his seat, dejected, as guys came from all around to see.

"And the worst part," Seanie said, "was not only that your hot nurse wasn't there to give me a sponge bath, but it was just me and Doctor No-gloves, all alone in his creepy strip-down-to-your-underwear examination chamber. He gave me a tetanus shot. In my ass cheek. And then he wrote a note to Coach M. I have a fucking concussion. I'm out for at least a month, maybe more. He wouldn't have even let me come home if I didn't promise to have someone from the team keep an eye on me tonight."

Seanie put his face down in his hands and shook his head.

Everyone—except for Spotted John, who had both of his hands in Seanie's hair (*Wait . . . were they having "a moment"? No. No. It couldn't be—right?*)—at the table saw the thing (THE THING!) on the top of Seanie's scalp and said, "Gross!" and turned away.

Yeah.

Dinner was pretty much over.

CHAPTER FIFTY-FOUR

AS MUCH AS I HATE TO ADMIT IT,
Sam Abernathy knew what was up.

He's twelve years old! He's not supposed to know what's up with things like JP wanting to kick my ass or me needing to sort all this shit out with Joey's little brother! How can he know this stuff?

But the Abernathy left us alone when I told him Nico and I wanted to talk, and he went back to our soon-to-be-freezing claustrophobia-slash-popcorn Cooking Channel den, where Nico Cosentino would be spending the night on our floor.

Good luck! Just thinking about that made me feel even sorrier for the kid.

And maybe it was the concussion Seanie got during the game, but he deliriously offered to drive Nico home to Pacific City, which was not ridiculously far from Beaverton, since he would be taking Annie to the airport the next day. Of course, I told him I was coming too and that I would just catch a bus back to Pine Mountain from Beaverton. Because although I didn't say it, there was no way I was going to spend the weekend at Seanie Flaherty's house.

Gross.

"When I came back to school this year, I started getting really scared at night. I think it's like panic attacks. And it gets so bad, sometimes I think I'm actually going to die."

Nico and I walked on the trail beside the lake. We sat down at the bench by the jumping-off spot and tossed pebbles into the water.

"That happened to me," Nico said.

"What did you do about it?"

"Talked to people. Went to therapy. Thought about smoking weed and shit. Wondered if I was losing my mind."

"Me too. Well, not the smoking weed part," I said.

"It's kind of like a seed that you don't notice is sprouting, and all of a sudden when it shoots up you have no idea where it came from or how it grew into such a huge weed."

"You sound just like your brother. You know that?"

Nico threw another rock.

"Everyone likes you, Ryan Dean. You have lots of friends. You should have heard those two girls—Annie and Isabel—talking about you during the game."

This was important information.

"No, dude. Everyone does *not* like me. JP Tureau, our fullback, for example, hates my fucking guts."

"Wow. Joey always told me you never swore," Nico said.

"I don't. I just did because . . . I don't know . . . you're such a *guy*. Now I feel like a douche. That's not cussing, is it?"

Nico laughed. "You think I'm *such a guy?* Yeah. Well, 'douche' is probably safe in most states. But the girls talked about JP, too."

And this was *very* important information.

"What did they say about him?"

"Oh. It was girl stuff. You know. They talked like I wasn't even listening at all, even though I was getting it in stereo. They think JP's conceited."

Well, he is.

And Nico went on, "And I guess Isabel had sex with him over the summer, and she said it was the biggest letdown of her life."

THANK YOU, GOD.

"Nico?"

"What?"

"Can I high-five you? I really need to high-five a dude after that."

"You're really weird, Ryan Dean."

Weird or not, Nico was willing to honor my request. It was a blistering five out of five unattended boilerplates on the Ryan Dean West Things-That-Sting-the-Shit-Out-of-Your-Palms Scale. Nico slipped and buried his left foot in the mud. He nearly fell into the lake. That would have been bad.

I grabbed his hand and pulled him back up the bank.

"Thanks," Nico said. "I almost ate shit, bro."

"Come on," I said. "We should get back before we freeze to death. And while there's still so many guys going in and out, it will be easier to sneak you past Mr. Bream."

We walked back toward campus through the woods. It was

drizzling slightly, and we both had our hands in our pockets, just about up to our elbows. I noticed Nico was shivering a bit too.

"I'm really glad you decided to come," I said.

"What else was I going to do? It's not like I had any plans this weekend."

"Don't you go to school?"

"Nah," Nico said. "I do school online, from home."

"Is that fun?" I asked.

"No. It's terrible. I never get to talk to anyone. I don't have any friends. I never have a chance to get in trouble, or anything normal. And the dances? Pathetic."

"Why don't you go to a regular school, then?"

Nico sighed and shook his head. "In case you're wondering, I'm not gay."

I stopped walking. "Why would you even think I was wondering if you were gay?"

"Because the other guys I've known always do. It sucks when you're thirteen or fourteen and your older brother is out and everyone's okay with it and he's happy about who he is and you love him, but then all the dudes at school give you nothing but shit, and then I'm like, I wonder if my mom and dad are going, 'Why doesn't Nico have a girlfriend?' and sometimes I just get so sick of all the shit, you know?"

His voice got a little knotted up. I knew it was hard for Nico to say it, and I never thought about how tough it must be for a kid in junior high school—about to start high school—when the social trail through the underbrush of assholes and knuckleheads in front of him was cut by his older brother, who happened to be gay, and who happened to be my best friend, too.

"That really sucks. I'm sorry," I said.

Okay. So, you know how when sometimes a person who you think is an okay guy tells you something you know he's been holding inside for a long time and it makes you feel really bad for him and you try to think of a thousand things you could do or say to make him feel better, but there's just nothing you can do at all—which is why I now understood how none of the rugby boys at dinner wanted to talk to Nico—so you just feel awkward and sad and stupid because you really think the other guy (who you think is an okay guy) probably just needs a hug from a friend and to hear a friend tell him "none of this bullshit matters," but you don't think you can do anything like that, so you just keep your hands in your pockets and you say nothing and you feel like a massive pile of shit and you know he feels like shit and there's, like, this huge, incredible, growing shit supernova swallowing you up and making you both feel so terrible and you're not really looking where you're going because it's dark and you've just cut through the woods and your toe gets stuck beneath a goddamned tree root (screw you, goddamned tree) and you fall down in wet tree mulch and get a cigarette butt stuck to your forehead because your hands were in your pockets and this happened to be the—air quotes—assembly hall—end air quotes—for the Pine Mountain Nicotine Club and then the guy you think is an okay guy is laughing, and that makes you feel better, because of all the things you thought about that might make him not feel so shitty, gravity was not on that list?

Yeah. That's what happened.

And screw you, gravity.

"Dude! Are you okay?" Nico grabbed my arm and pulled me up.

I was wet, and partially camouflaged with forest detritus.

"I meant to do that," I said.

Nico smiled and shook his head.

I am, as always, such a loser.

I wiped the cigarette butt off my forehead. Now everything in my shit-supernova universe smelled like a goddamned ashtray. "So gross."

"Do you guys still have those poker games?" Nico asked.

"Nah. All those hardcore dudes graduated last year. I miss those guys, though. Even the assholes—excuse me for saying that, but there were some assholes who played in those against-the-rules poker games," I said.

"Too bad," Nico said. "I would kind of like to have a beer with you, Ryan Dean."

"That would emotionally scar the Abernathy. It would devastate the little whelp," I said. "But I just might be able to do something about that."

CHAPTER FIFTY-FIVE

LIVING IN UNIT 113 WAS KIND OF LIKE camping without a tent, in the middle of fucking winter, with strangers who wore soccer pajamas.

I explained all of this to Nico, who, like his brother, was one of those extremely rare human beings who seemed to be able to put up with anything wierdos like me or Sam Abernathy could dish out and still conduct himself with nothing but understanding and patience.

I know, right? What planet did the Cosentino boys come from?

We'd pushed our desks up against the TV-slash-microwave shelf, then stacked our chairs in the corner beside the bathroom door in order to make enough space on our floor for poor Nico to sleep. Naturally—and I shouldn't have wondered about this at all—the Abernathy had a complete spare set of blankets and sheets (they were Donkey Kong, which made me momentarily seethe with jealousy because Donkey Kong is way cooler than Princess Snugglewarm, and I could only imagine the Abernathy hatchling snatching up the last available set of Donkey Kong bedding at the one and only local store).

But there was going to be one big claustrophobic problem.

I said, "Look, Sam, we can't leave the door open because Nico is *not* a student here, and someone will see him. And, although you know I'm willing to put up with it, it would be cruel of us to force him to sleep on the floor below an open window. So we're going to have to brainstorm a solution to this whole claustrophobia situation."

When I said "brainstorm," I made air quotes.

And then Nico said this: "Oh. I totally don't mind, Ryan Dean. I understand, and it's okay with me."

For some reason, human evolutionary pressures had failed to eradicate the *compassion* gene, despite all the apparent evidence to the contrary.

The Abernathy squiggled like a chihuahua on a trampoline on his bed. In his soccer jammies.

He said, "Thanks, Nico! Sleepovers are the best!"

No. Just no.

Whatever.

I took off my tie and shirt and slipped on a hoodie and some sneakers. Then I tossed a clean sweatshirt to Nico.

"Here," I said. "You might as well put on something dry and warm, then."

"Thanks." Nico shook out the sweatshirt and sniffed it. Something all guys do, I think—just to make sure there's no gross boy-B.O. stuck to it.

And I added, "I'll be right back."

"Where are you going, Ryan Dean?" the Abernathy chirped.

"Up to Spotted John's."

The Abernathy's eyes widened. The last time I did this, things didn't work out as planned. Not that I ever—air quotes—made plans with the Abernathy.

"Don't worry," I said. "I'll be back in, like, two minutes."

CHAPTER FIFTY-SIX

THIS TIME, I SHOWED A LITTLE MERCY to Spotted John's door sock. I really did feel bad about burying his first door sock in the potted palm. Burying another one would make me like a serial killer. Of door socks.

I knocked.

Waited.

Nothing.

So I knocked again.

"Go the fuck away. Can't you see the sock?" came the choppy Danish-accented warning from the other side of the door.

"Spotted John, it's me, Ryan Dean. I need a favor."

"Dude. You still owe me for the last one. Go away."

"Please?"

I used my sad-puppy-in-the-pound-about-to-be-euthanized voice, something I only use on special occasions.

It always works.

"Oh, bloody hell."

I heard a groan. I imagined Spotted John getting up from his ninja-video-game love seat. Sometimes, and it usually happens a couple hours after a rugby game, the soreness starts setting in, and it becomes really hard to move.

He cracked the door and glanced around in the hallway behind me to make certain I was alone. Spotted John's eyes were red—half closed—and he was standing there in his boxers and shirtless. And there was a hickey the size of a half-dollar on his collarbone. You don't get hickeys playing rugby, by the way. In case you were wondering.

"Oh, you didn't need to get dressed up just for me, John," I said.

"Be quiet. Cotton's asleep," he whispered. "All right. Come in."

Okay. So the place smelled like pot. That was weird and made me feel awkward. But the weirdness and awkwardness I felt were guppies in a fish tank of tiger sharks compared with the weirdness and awkwardness I felt when I saw Seanie Flaherty sitting on Spotted John's love seat. Stoned. Shirtless. In his boxers. And there were socks and T-shirts and half-knotted neckties and Pine Mountain good-boy uniform slacks and shirts scattered around the floor like Spotted John's flat had been redecorated as the inside of a clothes dryer.

So freaking awkward.

Side note: Cancel those two questions I was going to ask Annie.

I cleared my throat and stood just inside the closed door while Spotted John went over and sat down on the love seat next to Seanie.

"Uh. Hi. Seanie," I said. "Um. How's your cuddle—er, concussion? Head? No! No, I mean your stitches? How are the stitches, Seanie?"

God! I am such an idiot sometimes.

But for the first time in his life, I think Seanie just didn't have anything to say to me to deflect my observation of what had obviously been going on here. In fact, he looked a bit sick.

Okay. So, we've all *heard* stories about teenage boys who get caught doing—air quotes—the thing that every teenage boy is an expert at, like maybe when his mom bursts unheralded into his room on some all-of-a-sudden, stealth "I just want to empty your trash can" urge, or maybe when a sibling trespasses through his closed door with a riveting story about something that happened at softball practice that just couldn't wait until some other time—like never—to be told, neither of which could have ever possibly happened to me since (1) we have a maid, so my mother wouldn't know *how* to empty a trash can, and (2) I am an only child (but let me state for the record that my parents have hired a new maid since last summer, so it doesn't technically count about what *the first maid* saw, and I hope she never remembers who I am anyway, and—*God!*—why couldn't that woman—Ursula was her name; I will never forget it—learn how to KNOCK ON MY FUCKING DOOR before walking into MY GODDAMNED bedroom), well, I can only imagine that the look on my face—no! I meant my hypothetical "his" face, not mine, people—would be exactly the expression Seanie Flaherty had when I said my extremely awkward "hi" to him as I came into Spotted John's pot-filled dorm room and found my friend Seanie Flaherty there, with Spotted John, stoned and sitting on a love seat (which was not so much a love seat as a chair wide enough for a fold-out single-size foam mattress bed), snuggled up together, stoned and wearing absolutely nothing but their boxers.

It was a beautifully touching moment that also made me feel really, really weird.

Seanie just moved his mouth, like a bloodless albino fish on a hot summer sidewalk.

Whatever. Like I cared about this stuff, anyway.

Spotted John put his hand on Seanie's bare thigh and said, "Ryan Dean's cool with me, Seanie."

So I wagged my finger at Seanie and made a joke. "This is exactly why I *never* play strip Battle Quest: Take No Prisoners with Spotted John. I'll bet the shirt off my back you're naked in, like, thirty seconds, Seanie."

Okay, given the scene, the shirt off my back was probably the wrong thing to wager.

"Whatever, Ryan Dean," Spotted John said. "What the fuck do you want?"

By the way, the TV—the video game—wasn't even turned on.

"Hmmm," I said, "I—I *can't remember* what I wanted."

What I actually wanted was to not EVER have walked in on Seanie and Spotted John Nygaard on a love seat together in their boxers.

But I seriously could not remember why I came to Spotted John's room for, like, the thirty most agonizing, staring-at-my-buddy-practically-naked-with-another-guy seconds (not that I've had multiple experiences with such a situation) of my life.

Oh yeah.

"Oh yeah," I said. "I came to ask you if I could borrow a couple cans of beer. Well, not borrow, since you undoubtedly won't want them back after we drink them, but *have*. Yeah. Um. Shit.[7] Can I have some beer, Spotted John?"

And now I was blushing, but I couldn't force myself to look away from Seanie and Spotted John. They were, to be perfectly honest, a cute couple.

"Stop staring at us, you weirdo," Spotted John said. "What? Are you and Snack-Pack going to get drunk tonight? Sounds like a wild time."

Stop looking at them. Stop looking at them. Stop looking at them.

"Um. No. No. It's for me. And Nico."

And Seanie said, "Dude. Don't say anything about this, okay?"

"Shut up, man. You guys are my friends. Why would I ever say anything?"

Stop looking at them. Stop looking at them. Stop looking at them.

I actually wanted to tell someone so bad, my head felt like it was about to burst. So I said, "Well, Spotted John? Can I?"

"Help yourself. They're in the minibar. And now you owe me again."

"Thanks, dude. You're the best," I said. I declined to add a sure-to-be-broken I.O.U. of *whatever you want.*

And, yes, Spotted John Nygaard had an actual minibar beneath his not-turned-on television. And it was filled with beer, those little

---

[7] Yep. Said it.

airplane-size bottles of liquor, and all kinds of other weird stuff.

"Wow! You have *cookie dough*, too?"

"You can't have my cookie dough," Spotted John said.

I slipped two cans of beer into the pouch on my hoodie. I looked like a deformed kangaroo.

"Huh! Big balls, Snack-Pack Senior," Spotted John said.

I grabbed the cans where they hung down in front of my hoodie and jiggled them. "It takes the better part of an hour for me to do my TSE on them."

Then I realized I really, really did not ever want to talk about grabbing my balls in front of Seanie Flaherty and Spotted John Nygaard while they were sitting together—I mean *really together*—in their boxers.

I felt myself nearly choking from embarrassment.

Such a loser.

"Um. Well. Thanks for letting me ride with you to Pacific City tomorrow, Seanie. I'll . . . um . . . see . . . See you then."

Seanie didn't say anything. He just lifted his fingers in a would-you-get-the-fuck-out-of-here-and-leave-me-alone insincere wave.

So I thanked the ninja again and took one more photographic glance at Seanie Flaherty and Spotted John Nygaard before ducking out the door.

So weird.

CHAPTER FIFTY-SEVEN

THE ABERNATHY SHOOK HIS HEAD and made a bookshelf with his lower lip. "No, no, no, Ryan Dean!"

I anticipated the grub's reaction would be something along these lines if he saw the cans of beer I smuggled down from Spotted John's penthouse.

"Look, Sam. It's part of *the code*, okay?"

Nobody—not even a twelve-year-old virgin with holy water for blood—can argue with *the code*.

Unit 113 smelled of popcorn. Nico, wearing my sweatshirt, sat cross-legged in his floor bed beneath the Donkey Kong blanket the Abernathy had given him, while the television played a program about sauteing white-perch roe with onions.

Gross.

The Abernathy, who was practically hyperventilating, drew a triangle with his pink little pointer finger in the air between the three of us. "We could get into so much trouble!"

"Relax, Sam. It's okay. Nobody's going to get in trouble. This is just for me and Nico."

"What if one of you goes crazy and jumps out the window or something?"

"Sam? Are you insane? Our window is two feet off the ground."

"Well, it could happen."

I handed Nico a beer and he opened it.

"I'll take my chances, Sam," I said.

And Nico said, "Will you guys be quiet? I'm trying to watch this show about cooking fish sperm."

He wasn't serious.

But the Abernathy corrected him. "Roe isn't sperm, Nico. It's eggs."

Nico took a swig of beer. "Well, it looks like sperm."

"Dude. That's totally gross." I opened my beer. "But you're right. It does look like sperm. And, by the way, although Mrs. Blyleven would be pleased we're using the word 'sperm,' I never want to talk to you boys about sperm again."

"I hate you guys," Sam Abernathy said.

Whatever.

"Cheers, Nico."

We clinked cans and drank.

By the time we were halfway through our beers, being the entirely unpracticed drinkers we were, Nico and I were both completely drunk.

I know. We are losers.

But at least we had Sam Abernathy there to keep us from doing anything stupid like jumping out the window.

Well, at least until he fell asleep.

"Awww . . . he snores," Nico said.

I hadn't noticed it before, but the Abernathy *did* snore—a tiny Pomeranian puppy kind of grunt-wheeze-snore that would have made me lactate if I was pregnant, and a woman, but since I wasn't, I kind of wanted to throw a shoe at him or put duct tape over his mouth or, just maybe, close the goddamned window.

Nico wobbled to his feet and grabbed the remote from the Abernathy's little moist hand, then turned off the television. "This is the grossest show I've ever seen. Was that supposed to make people *want* to eat fish sperm?"

Nico and I undressed and went to bed. And we both just lay there with our hands folded behind our heads, staring up at the blank darkness between us and the ceiling.

"Dude, I told you. The Cooking Channel is all the kid ever watches."

"You must be a really nice guy to put up with this shit, bro."

I shook my head. "If I was Catholic, they'd make me the patron saint of idiots and twelve-year-olds."

"And they would call you Saint Cuisinart," Nico said.

The Abernathy grunted and rolled over in his Mario bed.

"But the kid can cook," I whispered. "And I've never seen anyone who can pop every single kernel in a bag of microwave popcorn."

"I guess you have to give him credit for that," Nico said.

"If you want to, we can take our chances with closing the window, but he almost died last time I did it."

"It's okay," Nico said. "These blankets are kind of warm."

"Or we could do something really crazy, like jump out the window," I said.

"That doesn't exactly sound like fun, Ryan Dean."

"The dudes I got the beer from upstairs . . ."

Don't say it. Don't say it. Don't say it.

I didn't say it. You know, the thing I'd never tell anyone about Seanie Flaherty and Spotted John Nygaard, who, by the way, had a major hickey on his collarbone, which made him even more spotted. But I didn't say *that*, either.

"They were smoking pot," I said.

"You ever do that?" Nico asked.

"No. You?"

"Nah. Well, I did a couple times, but I'm not into it."

"I was thinking, between the Abernathy, me, and you, there's, like, three real nutcases in this one tiny room."

"The lunatics have taken over Pine Mountain," Nico said.

I laughed. "Can I ask you something?"

"Aren't you tired?"

I rubbed my eyes. "I am. I'm trying to stay awake, though."

"Oh. Yeah." Nico understood. "I still get scared at night once in a while."

"It's messed up," I said. "Sometimes I feel like there's this demon following me around and he's just waiting to drop the next terrible thing right in my lap."

"You can't live your life like that, bro," Nico said.

"I know that."

"Well? What did you want to ask me?"

"Was it tough, deciding not to come to PM?" I asked.

"Nah. Well, I wanted to come, but I think my mom really needs me to stick around her. She's scared. You know?" Nico said.

"You probably can't live your life like that, either."

"I kinda don't want to talk about this," Nico said.

"Sorry, man."

"No worries, bro."

I cleared my throat. "I'm all alone too. I mean, I don't have any brothers or sisters."

"You have lots of friends, though. And a girlfriend who's pretty amazing. And she's totally hot."

I pictured Annie blushing when she met Nico. I didn't think I liked him calling her hot, even if she was. And then I felt bad for all the times I thought so many women and girls were hot. Well, not bad, but weird and guilty, maybe.

Damn those Mrs. Blyleven consent/respect/Penis Commandment lectures!

So I said, "Thanks."

"I don't have any friends anymore. I just shut myself off from everyone. Decided I didn't need or want anyone to be close to me. My friends—they all pretty much stopped talking to me anyway, and I haven't been trying to talk to them, either."

I rolled over so I could see Nico on the floor. "Oh. I'm really sorry, man."

"It's all right. I figure I don't really want to be around anyone anyway."

"Yeah. Because what's the point, right?"

"Exactly."

I said, "Um, I'm your friend, Nico."

And I was glad it was pretty dark, because I felt myself getting embarrassed when I told him that. But Nico didn't say anything, so after a few seconds I reached my opened hand out, where he could see it hanging over his chest.

"No offense, bro. I really don't want any friends."

"Oh. Yeah. I get that, I guess." I pulled my hand back. "So, are you going to play on your rugby club this year?"

"I don't know."

"You should. You can't quit the game," I said.

"Sure I can."

"I have an idea. You should come to Pine Mountain," I said.

Nico turned over so he was facing away from me. He didn't say another word, and eventually we both fell asleep.

CHAPTER FIFTY-EIGHT

NATE DIDN'T COME BACK THAT NIGHT, so I managed to sleep without scaring the crap out of Nico by screaming or crying in the middle of the night.

So I guess that was something.

But I felt stupid and awkward about trying to be *friends* with Nico, so we didn't really say anything to each other after the alarm clock woke us up. We got dressed in silence. Nico put his Pine Mountain disguise back on in order to blend in with all the other boys who looked exactly alike, so he could come to breakfast with me. Well, not *with* me, because it wasn't like we were friends or anything. Then we left Sam Abernathy alone so he could shower or poop, or do his TSE, all of which were things I never, ever wanted to think about the Abernathy doing ever again.

After we picked up our food in the cafeteria, I saw Annie and Isabel sitting together, so we joined them. For some reason, I couldn't keep my eyes off Isabel.

"Ryan Dean, are you blushing?" Annie asked.

"What? Uh. No?"

To be honest, just thinking about Isabel and that jerkoff JP Tureau having actual sex made me feel extremely flustered, so, yes, I was blushing. But I said, "It just feels really hot in here."

Then I slipped my finger inside my necktie and tugged it loose.

Nico said good morning to the girls, and I watched as they both cast big baby-seal love eyes at him. Damn. Why'd he have to be so good looking and perfect? And why couldn't we be friends? That really sucked.

"Did you guys have fun last night?" Isabel asked.

I realized that everything Isabel ever said to me from that moment on would *forever* sound like she was talking about having sex. I was burning with jealousy, because I liked Isabel, and also because Annie and I hadn't quite done it yet, and thinking about it was driving me crazy.

Nico shrugged. "Yeah. I had fun."

And I touched Annie's thigh and added, "Seanie's letting me ride with you to the airport today. Then I'm going to catch a bus back from Beaverton."

"Why don't you just stay at Seanie's?" Annie asked.

I shook my head. That would *never* happen. "His parents make me go to church. It could get ugly. I wouldn't want to spontaneously combust in the pews next to all those Christian folk."

Then—*score!*—Annie blushed. She must have thought I was talking about how we had fooled around together on our detour during the "run" and committed the Sin of Onan, for which we both should be smitten.

Nico nodded, "That's considerate of you."

"Yeah," I said. "No fifteen-year-old dude wants to be smitten."

Then Nico said, "But you really don't need to ride all that way to Pacific City with us just to see me off. It's cool of Seanie to offer the ride. I'll be fine, bro."

Ugh. Broed over breakfast. And Nico was kind of making it clear that we'd probably never even talk to each other again. I don't even know why he came out to Pine Mountain in the first place. Whatever. I hoped that maybe, somehow, he might have felt better about Joey and the school, and the people who loved his brother. So good for you, Nico.

Bro.

I noticed Spotted John and Seanie sitting together at an empty table. And I could tell by how Spotted John was looking at Seanie that something really *was* going on between those two. I was kind of happy for both of them, even if Seanie Flaherty had to be the highest-maintenance boyfriend on the planet.

I said, "Excuse me for a second. I need to go tell Seanie something."

And Seanie Flaherty looked awkwardly embarrassed and creeped out when I came over and sat down next to him at the table with Spotted John Nygaard. This was a new thing, in so many ways. First, Seanie was always the guy making everyone else feel creeped out; and, second, I could really, really tell there was something "new" going on between Seanie and Spotted John.

I put my arm around Seanie's shoulders.

So Seanie just dropped his eyes down and stared into his swirling bowl of Frosted Flakes as he stirred and stirred. It was gross, because when he did that, I could see the bald spot and the stitches in his scalp.

"Hey, Seanie. Hey, John," I said in my cheerful-and-everything-is-completely-normal voice, not that everything *wasn't* completely normal—it's just that Seanie Flaherty was always wound up so tight.

"Hi, Ryan Dean," Spotted John said.

"Hey, dude," Seanie said.

I looked at Spotted John, then I looked at Seanie. "Can I just say something? No. Can I say *two things*?"

"Counting what you just asked?" Seanie said.

"No. So, okay, maybe three or four things," I said. "Better yet, let's not count. I don't have a math class this year."

Spotted John said, "Go for it, Snack-Pack Senior."

"Okay. Look, I'm not the guy who goes around posting stuff like Internet pictures of my friends while they're passed out in their underwear. I'm not someone who gives up personal details or gossips about other dudes behind their backs. You guys know that about me."

"What does that have to do with anything?" Spotted John asked.

"Those pictures of you were kind of hot, Ryan Dean," Seanie said.

Now, that sounded like something the old Seanie would have said. And the new Seanie too, come to think of it.

"Yeah. Whatever. Well, what I mean is—I'm glad if you two have something going on. That's really cool."

Seanie brightened a bit and looked up from his cereal bowl. "Okay. Thanks, dude. So Annie never told you about me?"

I shook my head. "Annie's not like that either."

"She was the first straight person I came out to. Then I told JP, which is why you don't really see us hanging out together anymore."

"Yeah. JP. What a stud," I said.

"I thought it wouldn't matter. We've been friends for so long."

"Whatever," I said. "Just remember what Mrs. Blyleven would tell you guys."

"What?" Spotted John said. "About putting my penis in a vacuum cleaner?"

"Well, she would be proud of you for remembering Commandment Nine, John. And using the word 'penis' as opposed to 'something else.'" I made air quotes when I said "penis" and "something else." "But I was thinking more about her advice against hooking up, as opposed to building a healthy and equitable, consensual relationship."

"Ryan Dean?" Seanie asked.

"What?"

"Shut the fuck up."

"Um. Okay. That's probably a good idea. But I am happy for you guys, anyway."

"Whatever," Seanie said.

"Also, I don't think I should ride with you today when you drive Nico back to Pacific City. I don't think he likes me very much."

"How much did you *want* him to like you?" Spotted John asked.

I shook my head. "No. Just no, John."

Then Seanie said, "Dude, I don't really want to go either. I was thinking I'd really just like to stay here at PM this weekend."

Of course.

I got it. Cotton Balls would be leaving for home. Spotted John always stayed at Pine Mountain on the weekends. Seanie and Spotted John could do whatever they wanted to, which I kind of didn't really want to think about ever again. And then Immature and Selfish Ryan Dean West thought, *It really sucks how easy it is for two guys to fool around here, when me and Annie have to freeze our balls off in that goddamned creek. Well, not Annie's balls. But . . . um . . . you know.*

"Well, what about Annie? She's counting on you to drive her to the airport."

Seanie sighed and looked at Spotted John. Yeah, they definitely had A THING going on, and I was a little jealous. Not of Seanie or Spotted John, but I was jealous. Again.

Bastards.

"Why don't *you* drive?" Seanie said.

"What?"

"Take my car. You know how to drive, right?"

Immature and Selfish Ryan Dean West made certain I didn't

hesitate before answering. "Yeah, of course I can drive, Seanie."

It wasn't a total lie. Well, to be honest, it pretty much *was* a total lie. But I'd been in cars lots of times and I'd *watched* people—people who actually *knew* how to drive—drive. So, how hard could it be?

"Just don't fuck up my car," Seanie said.

I was already starting to get scared thinking about driving, and thinking about fucking up Seanie's very expensive car. But Immature and Selfish Ryan Dean West was thinking about tricking Nico into drinking lots and lots of water and coffee, then ditching Nico at a pee stop so Immature and Selfish Ryan Dean West could have actual sex with Annie in the backseat of Seanie's Land Rover. Immature and Selfish Ryan Dean West was already crafting his hey-Annie-I-think-you-should-bring-those-condoms-your-mom-gave-you-to-the-airport speech.

"Dude, I'm a really good driver."

Immature and Selfish Ryan Dean West, who only took his flight plans from Copilot Two, was in total control of everything now.

Seanie dug around in his pocket and then pulled out the key fob for his car. My hand shook slightly when I took it from him. That nervousness must have been the last shred of Mature and Responsible Ryan Dean West surrendering to the inevitable and deplaning Ryan Dean West Airlines before departure.

"Thanks, dude. I'll see you when I get back."

I wished I could just ditch classes and leave on the spot.

And Seanie said, "Just tell Annie and Nico that I feel dizzy from the concussion and I better stay in bed this weekend."

Did he *really* just say he wanted to spend the weekend in bed?

"Um," I said.

Seanie turned pale and put his face in his hands. "Just please forget I ever said that, Ryan Dean."

I snatched up the key and stood up. "Said what, Seanie?"

And then I high-fived Spotted John, who immediately added, "This counts as only *one* of the favors you owe me, Snack-Pack Senior."

"Deal," I said.

Now, how the fuck was I supposed to drive halfway across the state of Oregon?

Oh well; I could figure that small detail out when I needed to.

CHAPTER FIFTY-NINE

"I DON'T GET IT, RYAN DEAN. WHY, exactly, do I need to take condoms with me to the airport?" Annie asked.

It was a fair question.

To be honest, I hadn't quite gotten around to telling her that I was going to be the one who'd be driving (or attempting to drive) her to PDX and that Seanie was staying at Pine Mountain to take care of his—air quotes—concussion.

I had all kinds of work cut out for me.

Nico, who'd gone to Conditioning class with me—well, not *with me*, since we were not friends—had been hanging out with Coach M in the gym, waiting for us to get out for lunch. I'd loaned him some of my gym clothes that morning, and he worked out with us. It was kind of sad, to be honest, because running with Nico along the lake trail felt so much like running with his brother, Joey. Except unlike Joey, we didn't really talk much on the run. Nico was an athlete too. You can just see that in guys sometimes. *He must be a hell of a rugby player,* I thought.

So my persuasive speech to Annie Altman about having sex with me went something like this: "What if Seanie's car breaks down and the only option the four of us have is to stay in a motel room

together, and the motel is supercreepy and you can tell by looking at it that it is totally haunted, but the haunted motel only has
rooms with king-size beds in them, and there are only two rooms
available, and there's no way you'd stay in one by yourself, but you'd
never share a room with Nico, who is a stranger, or Seanie, who is
gross and has a head wound, and so we finally have our opportunity
to be somewhere where we can have the right kind of consensual
sex, but we can't decide on names for the baby even if it is nine
months from now, but you know how we promised—and not just
because Mrs. Blyleven made all us boys sign a Condom Promise—
that we would use condoms the first time we do it, but mine are
still in that FedEx package my mom sent me last year, which is in
O-Hall, and I'm way too creeped out to break into O-Hall because
there are ravenous man-eating raccoons living in there? Have you
ever thought about that, Annie?" I asked.

"No, Ryan Dean, strangely enough, I have not ever thought
about that. And besides, Seanie's car is brand new. I don't think
you should count on it breaking down next to a haunted motel."

We were whispering in the hallway before Foods—er, Culinary
Arts—class.

"Still, it *could* happen."

Annie laughed. And I'll admit it, between my having-sex-in-a-
haunted-motel plot synopsis and her laugh, I was getting a bit . . .
well, worked up. So I said, "Trust me, Annie. I have a plan."

Just then, sadly enough, the Abernathy, weighed down with a school backpack as big as a fourth grader, all shiny shoed and perfectly parted hair, swallowed up in a necktie and impeccably creased dress shirt, came marching excitedly down the hallway.

"Hi, Ryan Dean! Hi, Annie! Happy Friday!" he yipped.

I held up my flattened traffic-cop palm. "No. Do not talk to my girlfriend."

Annie pushed my chest, which made Copilot Two even more determined to taxi onto the runway. I had to nonchalantly adjust myself, which is ridiculously impossible to be nonchalant about in a high school hallway standing in front of a twelve-year-old Cub Scout.

Annie smiled and said, "Stop it, Ryan Dean."

Which made me even more insane.

"Hey, Nico, there are some bottles of water back there for you if you're thirsty," I said.

"Thanks, bro. I'm not thirsty," Nico said.

"I really think you should drink a few bottles. I heard that hydration is superimportant when you're riding in the backseat of a Land Rover."

"That's the dumbest thing I've ever heard," Nico said.

Damn. I really wanted Nico to make me pull over so he could pee and so I could then abandon him. Well, I'd come back for him eventually.

"How about we stop for some coffee?" I said.

"Ryan Dean, how can we possibly *stop*? You haven't even started the car yet," Annie pointed out.

It was a valid point.

And she added, "Are you *sure* you're okay with driving Seanie's car?"

"Seanie's car and I have honestly and openly discussed the matter, and we both enthusiastically granted our consent," I said. "The only thing is, I'm not really sure how to turn her on."

Annie shook her head and groaned.

Nico was either relatively clueless or ignoring me, or maybe both.

"No. Really. I have never been in a car that doesn't have one of those things you stick a key in," I said. "In fact, Seanie's car doesn't even *have* a key."

"Why don't you try pushing that button there?" Nico, who was sitting in the backseat—which made me jealous in an embarrassed kind of way—reached between us and pointed to an illuminated red button in the dashboard:

Magic.

The engine came to life, and I sat there momentarily constructing a diagram of all the reasons why I should hate Nico Cosentino.

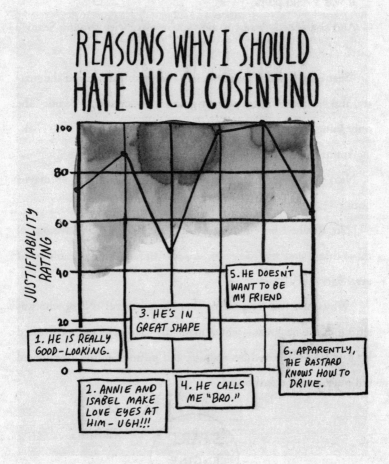

REASONS WHY I SHOULD HATE NICO COSENTINO

JUSTIFIABILITY RATING

1. HE IS REALLY GOOD-LOOKING.

2. ANNIE AND ISABEL MAKE LOVE EYES AT HIM – UGH!!!

3. HE'S IN GREAT SHAPE

4. HE CALLS ME "BRO."

5. HE DOESN'T WANT TO BE MY FRIEND

6. APPARENTLY, THE BASTARD KNOWS HOW TO DRIVE.

CHAPTER SIXTY

BUT I COULDN'T HATE HIM. I JUST FELT like such a loser.

Well. Thank God for GPS navigation.

When you don't actually drive, you just kind of take it for granted that you're going to end up where you're supposed to be. In my case, I didn't even know how to get out of the goddamned parking lot at Pine Mountain Academy, which meant finding something like an airport or the Pacific Fucking Ocean might prove to be impossible.

I also didn't know how to use the GPS in Seanie's dashboard.

So thank God for Annie Altman for so many reasons. She programmed in the address for the departures terminals at PDX.

After two trips around the parking lot—and confusing the living hell out of the seductive and friendly female voice coming from Seanie's GPS—I found the way out of the parking lot. It made me feel virile and manly.

That damned Nico Cosentino better start drinking soon or I was going to have to resort to extreme measures. Not that I had any extreme measures on my mind. But, what the hell? Come on, Nico!

Maybe I could subliminally get him to be thirsty, I thought.

I reached my hand back into the gap between the front seats. I also drove two wheels into the soft shoulder of the road.

Driving sucks.

"Ryan Dean!" Annie said.

"No worries, Annie. I just wanted Nico to pass me a bottle of water. I'm thirsty!"

"What is *wrong* with you?" Annie asked.

"I just want to pull over and have sex and still make it to the airport in time for your flight, but Nico doesn't seem to be—air quotes—getting the message," I answered.

Okay, to be honest, I didn't actually say that. What I did say was this: "I'm just thirsty is all. Lighten up, Annie."

Annie grabbed the bottle when Nico handed one forward, saying, "Here. I'll open it for you, Mario Andretti."

"Are you making fun of my middle name, Annie?" I said. (My middle name—one that I can't bear to confront—happens to be Mario).

Annie laughed and put her hand on my shoulder.

Damn, that was hot.

And the car, which kind of had a mind of its own, swerved into the opposite lane of the road leading away from Pine Mountain. I tried to get a grip on myself, but I was an overheated, gooey, gelatinous mess of driver's anxiety and sexual frustration, mixed in with an unhealthy dose of how-to-get-rid-of-the-body-in-the-backseat.

"Be careful, Ryan Dean," Annie said. "You could get in a lot of trouble for driving without a license."

"Nonsense." I lied, "I have a Massachusetts learner's permit. And Massachusetts was a state way before Oregon was. That makes me, like, a hundred years old in driver's years."

"What the hell is that supposed to mean?" Nico, the unthirsty, asked.

"Prepare to enter highway in eight-hundred feet," the sexy GPS woman told me.

Now everything the GPS said sounded like *having sex*. I felt a bead of sweat trickle down the edge of my jaw.

I entered the highway. And I drained the bottle of water as Copilot Two strained to come up with a Plan B for the kid in the backseat. And every mile that clicked off on the Miles to Destination box, every minute that disappeared from the ETA panel, made me more and more despondent that my first great opportunity with Annie was withering away.

"So. You talked to Seanie this morning. He seemed a little weird to me," Annie said. "He looked *different*."

She must have noticed the same post-having-sex look on Seanie Flaherty as I'd noticed on Isabel Reyes.

"First of all, *seemed weird*? Seanie Flaherty? Preposterous! And of course he looks different," I said. "He has a bald spot, a concussion, and eleven extremely gross stitches in the center of his scalp."

"It wasn't that," Annie said.

"Prepare to turn left in a quarter mile," Sexy GPS woman told me.

Damn! We kept getting closer and closer to failure. I took another gulp of water and glanced at the camel in the backseat.

"I am prepared," I said. And then I added, "Seanie came out to me last night, you know? I'm only saying that because he said he told you."

"Oh. Maybe it's that, then. It's about time, though. Poor Seanie. He's been so tensed up for so long about it," Annie said.

"Well, I'm happy for him. Finally," I said.

"He told me, too," Nico said.

I looked at him in the rearview mirror. Still no water. "That's kind of weird."

"I think it was because of Joey. He wanted me to know how bad he felt for all the shitty stuff he'd ever said about my brother—just because he was afraid of his own feelings. I think a lot of guys are like that in high school, you know?"

I nodded. "Yeah. You're probably right, Nico. But it's good if Seanie feels better about himself, though. I can't help but wonder how his douche-bag roommate is handling the news."

"Seanie told JP, too," Annie said. "And JP wants to move out now."

"What a total douche," I said. "I wonder if JP would like to live with a superstraight dude who's a really good cook and appreciates fresh air? We could make a roomie swap work."

Annie smiled and put her hand on my leg.

Ugh.

Then the worst imaginable thing happened. Somewhere after my second bottle of water (which failed to subliminally trigger a thirst response in *the alternate form of life in the backseat that is not dependent upon water*), Ryan Dean West, who had accumulated a sum total of twenty-seven miles of driving experience in his fifteen years of life, needed to pee.

And I needed to pee really, really bad.

Okay. So you know how sometimes, if you're a guy, because I'd have no idea if it's anything remotely similar for girls, you can be going along, not necessarily paying attention to anything because you're so consumed with thinking about having sex, and how everyone you know is apparently having sex whenever they want to with people who are probably not matches made in heaven for them, and then all of a sudden Copilot Two sends up a *Mayday! Mayday!* signal because the tanks are about to rupture and you need to find someplace—anyplace—to pee, like, ten seconds ago, and you're going, *How the hell did this creep up and blindside me all of a sudden?* but there's no possible way of getting around it and suppressing the urge, and—*God!*—for all the times my parents or grown-ups would say to me, "Just hold it, Ryan Dean," like they were telling me something as la-dee-dah as "I like those shoes you're wearing," because there is no "just" when it comes to *holding it*, and you know how when you're a little boy—let's say, like, Sam Abernathy's size on down—and you actually *do* hold it—literally—with your hand—those same grown-ups will scowl at you and tell you not to touch your pee pee in public, or actually not to touch it *ever*, for that matter?

Yep.

"Oh my God!" I grabbed myself.

Annie apparently thought something else happened. She jerked her hand away from my leg and said, "Oh!"

No. No. No.

"No! I need to pee so bad!"

"Dude, you drank three bottles of water," Nico pointed out.

Three? I'd lost count.

I really *should* hate Nico Cosentino.

I looked at the GPS and realized this was going to be one of the most disappointing days of my senior year. We were about twenty minutes away from PDX, in one of the last stretches of forested highway before reaching the endless housing developments of South Portland. My dreams were crushed. Well, maybe not the dream of finding a place to pee.

I pulled off the road and onto a dirt driveway that disappeared into the woods.

"Route recalculation," Sexy GPS woman said. "Prepare to turn around in two hundred feet."

"I just need to pee. I'll turn around after," I told her.

"She's not real, bro," Nico said from the backseat.

I put the Land Rover in park and barely managed to unhook my seat belt. And when I got out of the car and scanned the woods for just the right tree, Nico said, "I'll go with you. I need to pee too."

And Annie said, "Boys are so gross. Will you two just please hurry up?"

"Turn back in two hundred feet," Sexy GPS woman said.

Go to hell, Nico Cosentino. Just go to hell.

CHAPTER SIXTY-ONE

MISERABLE.

I dropped Annie off at her terminal and managed to get in about thirty seconds of frustrating tongue-in-mouth making out in front of one of those uniformed dudes on the curb who check in bags at the door and a drug-sniffing dog who paused to catch a whiff of the scent of my pee on my sneakers.

Whatever.

"I still don't understand the whole bring-the-condoms-to-the-airport thing, Ryan Dean."

I felt myself turning red. "I was trying—hoping—to ditch Nico somewhere, so we could . . . you know, break in Seanie's backseat. It didn't work, quite obviously."

"You were going to *abandon* Nico?"

"I would have come back for him. Eventually," I said.

Annie smiled and blushed. "You'll have to plan more deviously in the future."

I nodded. "Maybe Seanie will let me pick you up on Sunday. I can wear a disguise. That would be devious, right?"

Annie grabbed her bag and kissed me once more. "Too late for that. I already paid for a shuttle pickup before we left school. But seeing you in a disguise would be hot. You can wear it on Sunday, when I get back. I love you, Ryan Dean."

Nico got out of the back and moved up into the front seat.

I sighed. "I love you, Annie Altman."

So yeah, like I said: miserable. And Sexy GPS woman informed me after Nico punched in his home address that Pacific City, an unincorporated beach community in Tillamook County, was more than two hours away, which meant I probably wouldn't get back to Pine Mountain until about midnight. I'd been driving really slow all day, and not just because I was trying to get Nico out of the goddamned car, but because I was pretty much terrified of driving.

So it was going to be a very rough, very long, and very sad day for me, riding alone in a car all the way to the Oregon Coast with a kid who didn't even like me.

We didn't talk at all for the first hour of the drive.

So when Nico finally said something, it startled me and the damned car swerved again.

"Sorry to disappoint you," he said. "I'm really not very much like him, am I?"

"Who? Joey?" I asked.

"Yeah."

I shook my head. "I think you're so much like him, it's . . . kind of weird."

"I don't see it."

I chewed my lip. I'll admit it: I was pissed off at Nico, and it had nothing to do with my plans with Annie.

"You know, I bet a lot of people tell you how much you remind them of Joey. That must really suck, and I'm sorry. And you might think I'm an ass—and that's not cussing—for saying this, but it doesn't really matter in the long run because it's not like we're friends or anything, but I just wonder how long a guy can go through life trying to be such an asshole to people and pushing everyone away—and that probably is cussing."

No answer.

What could I expect, after all?

And then in the awkward silence that followed, I imagined Sam Abernathy—something that I never wanted to imagine again—saying pretty much the same exact thing to me.

And then I felt like shit.

"I'm sorry, Nico. I really wish I hadn't said that. It's not even any of my business what you decide to do."

Nico didn't say anything. I looked/tried not to look at him in my peripheral vision and noticed he'd turned his chin toward the passenger window. And I looked/tried not to look at him as he wiped at his eye.

Okay. So you know how sometimes when someone drops a bomb on you and it makes you feel like absolute horseshit and you can tell the other person is thinking, *Hey, is that dude actually going to CRY because of what I just said to him?* and then you get this terrible and sudden itch in your eye, so you rub it, and then you think, *Oh my God, I was only scratching my eye—please tell me the other person who just dropped a shit bomb on me does NOT think I am crying.*

But I saw Nico's hand, and it was streaked a bit with wetness.

I also swerved onto the shoulder of the highway (goddammit!) and almost ran Seanie Flaherty's Land Rover into a roadside cheese stand. God! I felt so terrible!

"What the fuck?" Nico said. "Dude. You are really the shittiest driver I've ever seen."

I put the car in park and sighed. "I've never driven once in my life until today."

"You trying to kill me?"

"No. I . . . um . . . wanted to get some cheese."

No response.

Who doesn't like cheese?

And then I said, "And I just want you to know, I'm really sorry, Nico. About everything that's happened in this past year. And I don't know what either of us can do to start to feel better, so getting some cheese is probably as good an idea as any. Right?"

Then I stuck my hand out for him again, thinking I was a dumbass for trying to shake hands with Dominic Cosentino no less than twice in the past twenty-four hours.

I watched Nico's Adam's apple piston-pump a swallow. And he rubbed his eyes again with the back of his hand. But he wouldn't look at me or take my hand.

So I said, "I don't know what the hell kind of rugger you are, Nico, but I'm holding my hand out, and we're not going to go anywhere, much less get some cheese, until you accept my apology."

Nico looked at me. I could see his eyes were wet, which made me feel like I was going to cry too, but that would be impossible to live with: two teenage boys sitting here on the side of the road by a cheese stand, crying together.

"Dude. You never give up, do you?" Nico said.

I shook my head. "I've given up before. Who hasn't? I hate it, though, so I am definitely not going to give up now."

I kept my hand open.

"Let's get some cheese, bro."

Nico took my hand and squeezed it hard—a real, good, rugger's handshake.

But, God! I needed to get out of that car fast because of two things: One—I actually was about to start crying, and two—goddammit, I needed to pee again.

Stupid devious plan.

Okay, maybe three things: I also really wanted some cheese.

CHAPTER SIXTY-TWO

"HANG ON A SECOND," I SAID. "IT doesn't look like there's a place to pee here. I need to pee really bad. I'm going in the trees."

"Dude, what is it with you and all that water?"

"I was trying to have sex with Annie," I said.

Nico followed me through a barbed-wire fence and into the woods beside the road. Naturally, he stood one full tree's length away. You know, when you're a guy and you're peeing, it's all about location.

"Watching you drink three quarts of water turns her on?" Nico asked.

Okay. Actual tears did leak from the corners of my eyes when I opened the pee floodgates.

"Dude. No. It was supposed to be for you. There. *Ahhhh.*"

I zipped up.

"Sorry. Watching a dude drink water does nothing for me, bro," Nico said.

So I explained the whole ridiculous scheme to Nico as we walked back through the damp and mossy woods. I was careful to explain the guidelines of consent and Mrs. Blyleven's Condom Promise, and how Annie and I were both totally okay with that stuff. You know, just in case Nico, who was fourteen, needed some serious life advice from a senior boy. Who was fifteen.

Whatever.

And then Nico said, "Dude. I never go anywhere without condoms."

"Even rugby practice?"

"Don't be dumb."

"You're only fourteen."

"What's that supposed to mean? My mom and I had the Talk and she gave some to me starting in eighth grade."

"Wow. Talking to your mom about stuff like using condoms is brutal."

"It wasn't so bad. But why didn't you just ask me to leave you and Annie alone for a while?"

I pried apart the strands of barbed wire, and Nico wormed his way through.

"Because I'm a loser?" I said.

Nico held the wires for me.

"Well, sorry. It must be impossible to have sex at Pine Mountain."

"Dude. I never want to think about having sex at Pine Mountain ever again," I said.

"I guess you're right. Besides, I'm hungry, bro, and cheese does sound pretty good right now."

The stand was a small plywood shell with an electric generator and a sign over the flap-board front opening:

"Do you think it's actual *boob cheese*?" Nico asked.

I shrugged. "All cheese comes from boobs, if you think about it."

"That's kind of gross."

"Dude. This guy's actual name is Jack Boob," I said.

Nico nodded. "I'm more interested in seeing if he only has one eye."

Jack Boob, the man who owned the cheese stand, did, in fact, only have one eye. Well, at least as far as I could tell he only had one eye, because he wore a green leather patch over the right one. And the most disconcerting thing about Jack Boob's green eye patch was that it had been implanted with one of those big, fake, plastic doll's eyes—with curly eyelashes and everything—and when he turned his head, the plastic eye would blink.

Super, super creepy.

Who would ever buy cheese from a dude who looked like Jack Boob?

Teenage boys who were very hungry would, I thought. The fact is, the best way to lure teenage boys to their death is to leave out plates of food. And, on the stand's counter, there were samples of perfectly cut little cubes of One-Eyed Jack's Boob Cheese lying out under spotless glass domes.

When we walked up to One-Eyed Jack's Boob Cheese stand, Jack Boob (who kind of looked like a flounder) eyed us (which is a totally gross thing to say) with a look (which is another gross and awkward thing to say) that said he'd been expecting Nico and me. Of course, there was no way Jack Boob would have known us—well, unless maybe this was Nico's favorite roadside destination in Tillamook County—because we were dressed as anonymous Oregonian teenagers. I wore my Pine Mountain Rugby Football Club warm-up jacket over a stretched-out, dingy, used-to-be-white Boston Red Sox T-shirt, and Nico still had on the hoodie I'd loaned him to sleep in.

"Are you two the Connelly boys?" Jack Boob asked.

I had to look away. The plastic eye bobbled up and down lustily.

"Yes," Nico said. "That's us!"

What the fuck?

I stopped in my tracks. "Dude. What the heck?" I whispered. "I don't want to be one of the Connelly boys."

Nico shook his head. "Bro. You are so uptight. I'm just messing around. Just relax for once and let's get some Boob cheese from this guy. He has free samples."

"But what if he's been hired to murder the Connelly boys? What if the Connelly boys are supposed to do something gross, like give him a pedicure or something? Have you ever thought about that?"

"No. I haven't. Not until just now, and I don't ever want to think about that again either."

Between the two of us, there were lots of things Nico Cosentino and I never wanted to think about again, including giving One-Eyed Jack Boob a pedicure in his cheese stand along the side of Old Woods Road.

One-Eyed Jack Boob squinted his one nonplastic eye at us as we got closer to the stand. The other eye half closed seductively.

Gross.

"You don't look like Connelly boys," he said. "Those Connelly boys have red hair."

"Oh! Did you say 'Connelly'?" I asked. "I thought you said *hungry*. Didn't it sound like he said 'hungry,' NICO COSENTINO, whose name is not Connelly, so you don't have to murder us, and neither one of us does pedicures, besides?"

Nico looked at me. "You're insane." Then he turned to Jack Boob and said, "So, is this actual *boob cheese*?"

"That's my name. Jack Boob. So of course it's Boob cheese. I also have Boob jerky and Boob juice for sale."

No. No. No. No. No.

"Good thing his last name's not Dick," Nico said.

"Who would ever name a kid Jack Dick?" I asked.

Nico nodded thoughtfully.

"Do you two know the Connelly boys? They were supposed to be here three hours ago," Jack Boob said.

Why would we possibly know the Connelly boys?

"We just came for the cheese, weird old man," I said. "So please stop talking to us and let us fucking eat."

Okay, to be honest, I did not actually say that to Jack Boob. What I did say was this: "Well, I think I can speak for Nico when I say that we are both elated to not be the Connelly boys and also to not have red hair, but we really just stopped by here because I needed to pee and we're both kind of hungry. For cheese."

"Imagine that. Those Connelly boys are going to get fired before they start their first day on the job. Are you boys looking for work?" Jack Boob asked. "I've got openings for a coagulation-vat tender and a curd cutter. I pay eight-fifty an hour."

"Well, as much as we both enjoy tending vats of stuff undergoing coagulation, we actually just stopped for some cheese," Nico said.

"And a pee," I added. "And maybe some Boob jerky."

Jack Boob shook his head. "I just don't understand kids these days. With all the opportunities there are in the cheese industry, nowadays all you boys just want to get into computer programming and video games. Where is *that* going to get us when the asteroids rain down from the skies or the supervolcanoes blow their tops? I'll tell you where: nowhere. Then you'll be wishing you knew how to make a decent wheel of cheese."

"Or a spaceship to get us the heck out of here," I said.

"What are you going to eat in space?" Jack Boob asked.

He was apparently a very lonely one-eyed man.

Nico pointed at one of the glass domes of cheese. "I'd be willing to eat this in outer space," he said.

There was a little flag on a wooden skewer sticking up from the cheese under the dome. It said FREAKING GREAT FARMSTEAD GOAT.

And it *was* good goat cheese.

After we tried a few of Jack Boob's samples, Nico and I purchased some Oregonian Kick-Your-Grandma's-Ass Gruyère, White-Is-the-New-Orange Cheddar, and Freaking Great Farmstead Goat, along with some rounds of toasted bread and Boob Jerky, which, Jack Boob promised, was actually made from a cow.

"This is going to make me thirsty," I said.

"Dude. Really? You're not going to drink some more, are you?" Nico asked.

"What, exactly, is in Boob Juice?"

Jack Boob leaned over the counter and squinted conspiratorially while his plastic doll's eye bobbed lazily. He whispered, "Don't you know what Boob Juice is, sonny? HA HA HA HA!!!"

Good one, Mr. Boob.

Then he slapped the counter and said, "I'm just kidding, son. My Boob Juice is fresh-pressed unfiltered Oregon apple juice."

"In that case, we'll take two boobs. Uh. Boob Juices. Please."

I paid One-Eyed Jack Boob for the things we bought, and Nico and I headed back to Seanie's Land Rover. That's when I noticed that an old Chevrolet Apache pickup had parked behind us, and two beefy teenagers with red hair were standing there, alternately looking at Seanie's car and at me and Nico.

The Connelly boys had shown up for their Boob job.

CHAPTER SIXTY-THREE

THEY MUST HAVE BEEN TWINS. IF THEY
weren't, it would mean that one of the Connelly boys actually *tried*
to look like the other. I would have at least shaved a gap between my
eyebrows. And they were hairy. They looked like they were maybe sixteen, but they already had gross wispy beards and probably weighed a
quarter-ton combined.

I could tell just by looking at them they were football players.

I hate football players.

Also—and all teenage guys know this—there is an unspoken message you get from other boys sometimes, and it rings as loud as a sonar
ping in a blind bat's ears, when another dude is preparing to start shit
with you. I've gotten that vibe before from maybe a half mile away,
and it's always been spot-on accurate.

So Nico held up too when he saw the Connelly boys standing
beside Seanie's car.

"Shoulda known some Pine Mountain rich-boy piece of shit not
even old enough to grow pubes would be driving a car like this,"
said Connelly on the left, who I only imagined was the coagulation-
vat twin.

And for a moment, I pictured hairless and peach-assed Sam
Abernathy driving Seanie's Land Rover, and then, for so very many

reasons, I decided to add that to my Things-I-Never-Want-to-Think-About-Again List.

I also made a mental note to myself to never wear my Pine Mountain sweats when driving a borrowed Land Rover through the untamed wilds of western Oregon.

Curd Cutter Connelly nodded and scratched his balls.

What nice boys, entering the dignified cheese-making profession.

"Look, we don't have any problems with you guys. We were just leaving," I said.

Coagulation Vat Connelly looked at his brother and then spit on the driver's door of Seanie's car. "I'd sure like to sit in that. I never sat in one of those things before. I'm just wondering—did the car turn you gay, or were you already like that before your daddy bought it for you?"

Nico grabbed a bottle of Boob Juice from my hands, opened it, and took a long drink.

"This is good shit," he said.

Then Curd Cutter Connelly said, "Yeah. I feel like sitting inside it too. And maybe taking a shit in the driver's seat."

Then both future cheese masters laughed. Coagulation Vat Connelly nodded enthusiastically. And I was terrified that I was, indeed, going to "fuck up" Seanie's car, that Nico and I were about to get into a dreadfully mismatched fight, and that Curd Cutter Connelly really *was* determined to make poo on the driver's seat.

Shit.

Nico calmly drank the entire bottle of Boob Juice. Then he wiped his mouth with the back of his (my) hoodie sleeve and stepped onto the macadam of the highway and yelled, "FUCK!" as he smashed the bottom half of the bottle onto the road.

It startled the Connelly boys, but not as much as what happened next. Nico stomped up to the nearest twin (Curd Cutter) and grabbed the bigger boy's shirt at the collar, pushing him back against Seanie's car.

Don't dent it. Don't dent it. Don't dent it. For Christ's sake DO NOT dent Seanie's car!

Nico held the broken neck of the bottle in front of Curd Cutter's face. He said, "I will dig your fucking eyeballs out and carry them home from here inside my underwear if you don't back the fuck off right now."

Coagulation Vat Connelly was stunned.

I was stunned.

Also, I fucking needed to pee again.

Coagulation Vat Connelly ran back to the pickup, and I thought, oh, God, he's going to get a gun; he's going to get a gun and kill us, and I totally blew my opportunity to have sex with Annie Altman on my final day with a pulse. But he didn't get a gun. He started the truck and drove away.

"Wait! Wait, fucker! Wait!" Curd-Cutter-Who-Needed-to-Poo Connelly was practically in tears. I actually started to almost feel sorry for him.

Almost.

Nico let go of him, and the big redhead took off down the road after his brother.

So much for the teen unemployment rate in Oregon.

CHAPTER SIXTY-FOUR

"I THINK I ACTUALLY MAY HAVE SHIT my pants," Nico said.

"Dude. Put his eyeballs *inside your underwear*? That is so gross. I could have thought of a lot of places to put a dude's eyeballs besides inside my underwear."

We were back on the road, eating Boob cheese and Boob jerky, and sharing the only nonlethal remaining bottle of Boob Juice, which was really good. The GPS estimated we were fifteen minutes away from Nico's house.

Nico said, "It was the first place besides my pocket I could think of. I didn't want to put his eyeballs in my pocket, because it didn't seem insane enough, so, you know . . . my underwear."

"I just want to say one thing, Nico: Back there at the Boob stand, you said *I* was insane. Me. Ryan Dean West. But that was the most insane thing I've ever seen in my life. I seriously thought you were going to stab that jerk in the eyeball."

Nico smiled and nodded. "So did I."

"Well, thanks for not stabbing him in the eye, and also thanks for getting us out of there with no scratches on us or on Seanie's car."

"No prob, bro."

Then Nico did something that really surprised me. Well, not as much as breaking a bottle and digging out eyeballs and sticking them inside his underwear would surprise me, but surprising in any event. He stuck his hand out and we shook. I also swerved the goddamned car again.

"You're a shitty driver," he said.

"I got us here, didn't I?"

"Well, this doesn't mean I want to be friends, because I don't. I just thought that was fun shit back there. And great cheese."

"Whatever."

Nico Cosentino could be such a jerk. And I decided that when I got back to Pine Mountain, I would start being nicer to Sam Abernathy, and that he was a good friend, which was something I needed. Gross. I was finally admitting to myself that I liked the little grub.

Nico pressed commands into the navigation unit, and Sexy GPS woman asked, "Are you certain you want to cancel my guidance?"

"What are you doing?" I said.

"I live here. I know where we are now," Nico said.

I felt sad for Sexy GPS woman. I could really use some guidance. We both could.

Then Nico added, "Turn right up there, where that sign is."

The sign said CAPE KIWANDA STATE NATURAL AREA.

I said, "We're going to the beach?"

Nico answered, "Yeah. Kind of."

Damn. It was getting late. I was already feeling anxious and scared about driving all the way back to Pine Mountain by myself and in the dark. I could already sense that icy and empty mood—the certainty that Nate was lurking around, just waiting for me to be alone and thinking about what a loser I was and how terrible Nico Cosentino made me feel about things.

Whatever. Once I got this over with and deposited Nico back at his parents' home, I'd never have to see or think about him again.

Yeah, right.

We left our shoes and socks at the end of a long trail we followed over dunes of wet grass that ended at the expanse of sand connecting the land to the sea. It was cold, and the wind howled like an animal. We kept our hands deep inside our pockets.

I walked beside Nico right up to the water's edge, and we both pulled our pant legs up when the first frothy wave spilled over our feet. Then we walked back to the base of a sea cliff and sat down in the sand. We stared out at the waves and the rocks that stuck up above the sea along the cape.

It was an incredible place.

Nico said, "I thought you'd want to see this spot."

"It's nice," I said, shivering. That water stung like needles.

"Well, the place where we stood in the water—after Joey died, we came here. We put his ashes right in that spot and we sat here and watched the tide come in and take him away. I thought you . . . I thought Joey would want me to let you know."

Oh.

My stomach knotted up.

I pulled my knees into my chest and closed my eyes, imagining what that must have been like for Nico to see his brother—for his parents to watch their boy—disappearing away from them like that, into the ocean.

"I'm really sorry," I said. "None of this was ever fair. Thank you for bringing me here, Nico."

"I come here a lot. If you walk down the beach that way a couple miles or so, you'll get to my house," Nico said.

I looked south, in the direction Nico pointed. This place was huge and wild and quiet. It was a perfect place to let Joey go.

"Can I ask you something?" I said.

"Go for it."

"Well, maybe two things."

"Ask whatever you want," Nico said.

"Do you really not like me? Because, I mean, I think we should be friends, Nico. I think we need that."

Nico shook his head. "It's not a matter of liking you or not. You're a good guy, Ryan Dean. It's just . . . I don't know."

"Yeah. I don't know either," I said. "Because I thought what you did back there to the Cheese Brothers was fucking awesome. And having a beer together last night, and the stuff we talked about. Friends do that kind of shit together."

"Joey wants me to tell you to stop fucking cussing, Ryan Dean," Nico said.

"Yeah. I kind of heard him saying that too. But the other thing—you know, I went back inside O-Hall by myself. It was creepier than anything, and I don't think I'll *ever* do that again. But I found a list of things Joey wanted to do. Did you know Joey made lists, like, every day, of things he had to do?"

"Yeah. He always did that."

"And the last thing on his list said, in capital letters, 'TELL RYAN DEAN.' And I don't know what it means, or if Joey ever did tell me what he wanted to tell me. And that's been messing with my head. But I never had the guts to ask you about it, so I figured that since we're not going to be friends and everything that I'd just ask you if you knew what it meant before I leave."

Nico looked at me like he couldn't understand what I was saying. Then he faced the water again and was quiet for a painfully long time before he said, "I know what Joey wanted to tell you. He talked to me about it every time he'd come home. It was that he was totally in love with you, Ryan Dean. And he was too afraid to tell you."

No.

What?

I felt like I'd been punched in the gut and had my eyes gouged out with a broken bottle. Of course Joey loved me. I loved Joey too. We were best friends. But the way Nico said it meant something else entirely.

"No way, dude. Joey had a boyfriend. We were best friends. Nothing could ever change that."

"No, bro. Joey did *not* have a boyfriend. It was kind of funny how much he was in love with you. And he was so messed up about it because he always told me how superstraight you are, and how much he liked Annie, too, so he didn't want to do anything that would make you not be his friend."

I put my face down in my knees again. Shit. I actually felt something leaking from my eyelids. I also felt kind of rugged because Joey and Nico both thought I was "superstraight."

Nico went on, "I kept teasing him about it, telling him how could a fly half in rugby be afraid of anything?"

"I'm afraid of a lot of things," I said. "But I kind of wished Joey would have told me."

"I wish he would have done that too," Nico said.

CHAPTER SIXTY-FIVE

I THINK THE COSENTINOS MUST HAVE been genetically predisposed to scolding Ryan Dean Wests about doing the right thing.

Ugh.

Because in the span of about fifteen minutes after arriving home with Nico, these were the lists of violations I had committed that now needed to be made right:

1. Laundry. Yes, laundry. Mr. and Mrs. Cosentino insisted that Nico wash and dry the hoodie I loaned him before letting me go back to school.

2. Dinner. They also said that I needed to stay for dinner, which was pretty awkward because I knew Nico didn't like me.

3. THE BIG ONE: driving without a license. If Mr. and Mrs. Cosentino were as volatile as Nico with a broken bottle, they might have threatened to gouge my eyes out over this matter, which led to Terms of Correction item number four.

4. Sleepover. I had to give up Seanie's key fob (and just when I was getting used to not swerving so much) and spend the night, so that Mr. Cosentino could drive Seanie's car back to Pine Mountain in the morning while Mrs. Cosentino followed in the family minivan, which turned out *not* to be rented (and I silently

prayed that I could ride in Seanie's car so that nobody I knew would ever see me in a minivan).

5. Buttermilk. Yes, *buttermilk*. By dinnertime, I was so terrified of Mr. and Mrs. Cosentino that when they poured me a glass of buttermilk (without asking, I might add—who *ever* gives someone a glass of buttermilk without asking, unless it was some form of punishment?) at dinner, I felt compelled by shame to drink it. I had never had buttermilk before, but if you blindfolded me and told me I was participating in a taste test of milk with piss in it, that's what buttermilk tastes like.

Nico watched me drink it with an amused look on his face. And that fucker had ice water. He knew what was going on. In the unspoken, wordless telepathy of teenage boys (who are all naturally and deeply disgusted by buttermilk) we had quite a cuss-out session over that goddamned buttermilk.

I nearly cried with joy when I finished the glass. And then I barfed a little in the back of my throat when Mr. Cosentino asked me if I wanted some more.

After dinner, Nico showed me the guest room where I'd spend the night. It was a far cry from Unit 113, but I actually missed being home, freezing my ass off with the Abernathy. The room was five times the size of my dorm room at Pine Mountain, with its own bathroom—a real bathroom too, not a closet with a shower in it—and a sliding door onto a balcony deck that looked out on the beach.

"Do you think I could borrow your phone, so I can call Seanie and let him know everything's okay and I'll be back tomorrow?" I asked.

"Seanie has a phone at Pine Mountain? Has that place gone entirely to hell?"

"No. The ninja dude. Spotted John. He and Seanie . . . well, he'll let Seanie know."

Nico passed his phone to me, and I scrolled through his recent calls until I found Spotted John's number. And Nico asked if I wanted him to leave me alone, but I told him no, that he could stay. Besides, I said, I needed him to show me how to work the TV.

I called Spotted John.

SPOTTED JOHN: Hello?

RYAN DEAN WEST: Hey, John. It's me, Ryan Dean West. Is Seanie around?

I'll admit, when I glanced at the clock and saw it was nearly ten o'clock at night, I felt embarrassed and guilty for asking that.

SPOTTED JOHN: What's wrong? Did you fuck up his car? (*Rustling noises and the sound of Seanie saying something I couldn't understand.*)

RYAN DEAN WEST: No, dude, I just wanted to talk to Seanie for a minute.

SPOTTED JOHN: Okay, bud. Hang on.

SEANIE FLAHERTY: Ryan Dean? Did you fuck my car up?

RYAN DEAN WEST: No, dude. Seriously. I just wanted to tell you the Cosentinos are making me spend the night here, then Mr. Cosentino is going to drive your car back to PM in the morning.

SEANIE FLAHERTY: Oh. Okay, Ryan Dean. They're not letting you drive back?

RYAN DEAN WEST: Nah, man. They're all responsible and stuff.

SEANIE FLAHERTY: Oh, man. Don't you hate that?

RYAN DEAN WEST: I don't know. It's all okay. But they made me drink buttermilk. (*Nico falls back on the bed, laughing at me.*)

SEANIE FLAHERTY: Gross. Ryan Dean, is everything okay? You sound kind of bummed.

RYAN DEAN WEST: About the buttermilk? No. Everything's all right. And how about you and John?

SEANIE FLAHERTY: Really good, man. Thanks.

RYAN DEAN WEST: Oh. Hey. Would you do me a favor?

SEANIE FLAHERTY: Sure. What do you want?

RYAN DEAN WEST: Would you check in on Snack-Pack before you go to bed. Shit! No. I mean, uh . . . before you go to sleep. When you sleep. Um. And let him know I'm okay and I'll see him tomorrow?

SEANIE FLAHERTY: Dude. You are soooo Ryan Dean.

RYAN DEAN WEST: I know. Sorry.

SEANIE FLAHERTY: I'll go down and see the kid and tell him.

RYAN DEAN WEST: Thanks, Seanie. And, Seanie?

SEANIE FLAHERTY: What?

RYAN DEAN WEST: I just want you to know, you're my friend, and I love you, dude.

SEANIE FLAHERTY: That's a weird thing to say, Ryan Dean. Why are you telling me that?

RYAN DEAN WEST: I don't know. You never know when you might regret not telling that to someone.

SEANIE FLAHERTY: I guess you're right. No regrets. I love you too, man. But you better not have fucked up my car.

RYAN DEAN WEST: Good night. And don't forget to tell Sam.

And when I handed Nico his phone, he said, "You've got plenty of good friends, Ryan Dean."

"Whatever."

"Do you want to play some video games or something?" Nico asked.

"To be honest, I'm really sleepy. There must have been something in the buttermilk besides piss and barf. And I suck at video games, besides."

"Okay, bro. Well, my room is the next one over. I mean, if something happens, like, you know . . . if you get scared or shit. You know, I know how it is, and I'm just right there."

"Hey, thanks, Nico. I'll be okay. But thanks for showing me where Joey is."

"He's not there anymore."

"Yeah he is. I could tell."

"Okay. You're welcome, then."

I said, "You got anything I can borrow to go for a run in the morning? I feel weird all day if I don't get a run in in the morning, and the beach would be nice."

Nico nodded. "Sure. I got extra running stuff. Maybe I'll tag along."

"If you want to."

After Nico said good night and left, I lay in a bed that was actually big enough that my feet didn't overhang the end. I watched a television program about poaching flounder filets in milk and banana leaves.

Goddamn that Sam Abernathy.

What the fuck had happened to me?

CHAPTER SIXTY-SIX

NICO AND I RAN UP THE BEACH ON the hard-packed sand left behind by a very low tide.

We didn't say much at all, but that was fine with me because whenever I ran I had enough voices arguing with each other in my head. It's probably why I needed running so much: It was really the only time when I could just forget about everything else and let things sort themselves out in my mind.

And I was sure Nico knew that I intended to go back to the place he'd taken me the day before, just so I could dip my feet into the icy water at that one exact spot a final time before I'd leave and never come back.

But Nico was wrong, or maybe he was just being a jerk or didn't want to admit it, but there was no doubt that I could feel Joey there. Nico knew it too; it was why he came there all the time, like he told me.

The run was windy and long and brutal; and I loved it.

When we got back, the house smelled like bacon and maple syrup. I hoped to God the Cosentinos had run out of buttermilk, though. I thanked Nico for loaning me some shoes and running clothes, and when I asked if he thought I should stay and do laundry in exchange, he told me not to be an ass, but that I did smell pretty bad, so maybe I should consider taking a shower before having breakfast with his family.

They were nice people, and as I sat at their table eating with them I felt kind of sad about not seeing the Cosentinos again.

Mrs. Cosentino smiled and looked at us and said, "We never asked about the rugby game. How was it?"

I glanced at Nico to see whether or not he was going to answer. Boy telepathy told me no.

So I said, "It was good. We won. Barely."

"Ryan Dean scored a bitchin' drop goal," Nico added.

I felt myself turning red.

Mr. Cosentino said, "I love seeing a drop goal. Freaks the shit out of the other team, doesn't it?"

I smiled and nodded.

Mrs. Cosentino said, "Did you have fun up there at Pine Mountain with Ryan Dean?"

I answered before the silence could get too awkward. I knew Nico wasn't going to say anything. Well, I thought he wouldn't, at least. "We had a lot of fun together," I said.

And Nico said, "There are some good guys who go to school there."

He put his fork and knife down on his plate and took a drink of orange juice (thank God), then Nico said, "Mom, Dad, I think I want to go to school at Pine Mountain. I talked to Coach McAuliffe about it yesterday. He needs a winger, so I thought I should give it a try. Do you think you could call Headmaster Lavoie and tell him I'd like to start on Monday?"

Mrs. Cosentino coughed a little bit.

Mr. Cosentino looked as happy as a dude who was just told he'd never have to be seen driving in a minivan again.

And I was stunned.

NICO COSENTINO ACTUALLY PRONOUNCED THAT ASSHOLE'S NAME.

Luh. Voy.

Duh!

I felt the rush of a truly religious epiphany. I wanted to stand up and sing!

But wait. What the fuck did he actually just tell his parents?

Mrs. Cosentino said, "What?"

And Mr. Cosentino added, "I am so happy about this, son. What made you change your mind?"

Nico stared at the leftover scraps of pancake on his plate and, without looking at any of us, shrugged and said, "A friend of mine goes there. I was thinking I'd like to play rugby with him this season. You know, before he graduates and goes away to college."

I was stunned. I wanted to jump up and high-five Nico so hard, and hug him and swing him around and cry, but I completely maintained my composure, kicked my feet beneath my chair, did a quick little excited-Sam-Abernathy TSE, and just said, "Lavoie. Lavoie. Lavoie."

But I did worry that saying his name three times aloud might have accidentally summoned Beelzebub.

CHAPTER SIXTY-SEVEN

SO WE WENT BACK TO PINE Mountain Academy.

Nico's stuff was still packed up in tidy plastic totes for the start of school—his Pine Mountain uniforms, rugby equipment, school stuff, a small television, coffee maker, and sets of sheets that weren't designed for a third grader. We loaded it all up in the minivan (gross), and Mrs. Cosentino followed behind us while Nico's dad (who, remarkably, never swerved even one time) drove Seanie's Land Rover.

For some reason, the drive back didn't take nearly as long as the drive out to Pacific City had taken us the day before, but then again, we didn't stop to nearly get murdered at Jack Boob's cheese stand that day. I did see Nico looking at the Boob cheese shed as we passed it, though. We both wanted to see if those Connelly boys had come back to work.

They hadn't.

But on the ride back, I couldn't help but feel a kind of lingering smile on my face. Something was fixing itself inside me finally, and although I knew I'd still have to do some work with Mrs. Dvorak, Annie, and even the Abernathy to make that dark guy Nate disappear forever, I was finally beginning to believe I would be able to do it.

So when we got back to Pine Mountain, the Cosentinos took

Nico in to see Headmaster Dude-whose-name-I-now-knew-how-to-pronounce-which-made-me-feel-like-I-was-a-member-of-the-fucking-Illuminati. Mr. Cosentino obviously had plenty of clout with Pine Mountain's headmaster, because normally such things as enrollments and housing assignments would never be attended to on Saturdays.

And while they were in the office, I took Seanie's key fob and ran back to the boys' dorm. There were things I needed to do.

First stop: Unit 113, and not just because I needed to pee really bad.

When I opened the door, Sam Abernathy was sitting at his desk in his little soccer pajamas (even though it was afternoon), wearing eyeglasses and working on his Calculus homework while the television played a program about making persimmon and raw pistachio salad.

"Hi, Ryan Dean!" he gurgled.

I held up my hand in a stop-in-the-name-of-the-law gesture. "Wait. I really need to pee. Oh my God. You wear glasses?"

Something about seeing the Abernathy in his jammies with glasses on made me want to tuck him in and sing him a lullaby, but I desperately needed to pee first.

And the Abernathy turned all kinds of red and swiped the eyeglasses away from his little face.

"I'm supposed to wear my glasses when I read, but I hate them. They're dorky."

Wait. The Abernathy has dork awareness?

Who knew?

"Don't talk to me. I'm about to pee my pants."

I squeezed myself and my bladder into our toilet coffin. When I came out, the Abernathy had hidden his glasses.

"Stand up," I said.

"Why?" the Abernathy asked.

"I want to do something."

"What?"

"I want to give you a hug," I said.

"Did you wash your hands?"

Shit.

"Hang on."

I went back into the toilet coffin and washed up.

I said, "Okay. I've washed my hands. Take two. Stand up. I want to give you a hug."

"Why?"

"Because I missed you, and you're really a good friend, Sam. And I've been a total ass to you all this time."

"Don't swear, Ryan Dean."

"'Ass' isn't swearing."

"Yes it is," the Abernathy argued.

"Look. I'm just trying to do something nice for once," I said.

"Well. Okay. As long as you washed your hands. But no swearing."

The Abernathy stood up. I took a breath. And then I tripped on the leg of my fucking desk and fell into the Abernathy and nearly ended up tangled up with him on his bed. That would have been really awkward. But I managed to stay on my feet, and I gave the kid a solid dude hug.

"Ryan Dean?"

"What?"

"Is something wrong? You're squeezing me really hard."

"Oh. Sorry, man." I let go of Sam Abernathy. "I just, well . . . I realized how big of an . . . uh . . . jerk I've been to you this year, Sam. And I also realized that you are really, like, my best dude friend I have here at Pine Mountain, so I wanted to say I'm sorry for how mean I've been. And I won't ever do it again."

The Abernathy said, "Wow. Just driving to the beach made you think all that up?"

I nodded. "I guess so."

"Well you're my best friend too, Ryan Dean. But I always knew that, anyway."

"Yeah, well. What can I say? You're smarter than me, Sam."

"You want to go outside and do something?"

I smiled. "Sure. Just let me get Seanie's key back to him, and I'll be right down."

The Abernathy wriggled in excitement. "I'll get dressed in outside clothes!"

Unbelievable.

What the hell has happened to me?

CHAPTER SIXTY-EIGHT

The Abernathy and I lifted weights with Spotted John Nygaard that afternoon.

Rugged.

Seanie came along, but he only watched. Creepy. He said he needed to take care of his—air quotes—concussion.

And while we were gone, a school custodial crew moved a bunk bed into Unit 113. Nico Cosentino was going to be the third sardine in our can. Of course we didn't have to agree to it, but Sam and I didn't mind, and Nico felt really anxious about moving in with someone he didn't even know.

I could empathize with that.

There were only two problems with having the three of us in that one tiny room. Well, maybe three. First, there were only two closets, so Nico had to squeeze half his stuff in with mine and the other half in with the Abernathy's. And although Nico was willing to put up with Sam's claustrophobia, the Abernathy was just going to have to deal with not kicking us out when he wanted to undress or poop, or take a shower, and why am I even thinking about that again?

It was two against one, and Sam sadly admitted that he'd have to resign himself to growing up, even if his body wasn't very cooperative in the physical maturation department.

So gross.

And the third thing, speaking of claustrophobia, was that the crew who'd moved Nico's bunk bed into Unit 113 stacked it on top of Sam Abernathy's bed. Sam didn't have to say anything. When we got back from weight lifting and met up with our new roommate, I could plainly see the look of terror on the Abernathy's little face when he saw the small and dark space beneath Nico's top bunk that used to be his bed.

So it was awkward and straining, and we almost broke stuff doing it, but Nico and I managed to lift his bed across the barrier of desks so we could stack it on top of mine. It was worse than grown-up prison, but we were all going to get along just fine.

And that night, we all stayed up late eating popcorn and watching a program about quinoa with broccoli and prosciutto, laughing together and talking about cooking and rugby, and all the secret details of THE CODE.

It was the best night ever.

CHAPTER SIXTY-NINE

SENIOR PROM

OKAY. SO, YOU KNOW HOW SOMETIMES you can be so stubborn about adapting to the way things are that you fail to appreciate the simple fact that *the way things are* is actually not only not bad, but—to be honest—pretty good, but you insist on getting all hung up on imagining all the failures and negative qualities of Joe Randomkid a.k.a. Sam Abernathy a.k.a. Stan Abercrombie a.k.a. Snack-Pack a.k.a. one of the best friends you ever had, but instead of appreciating that stuff—like how cool it is (like, literally *freezing* at times) living in Unit 113, even if it is smaller than most hamster cages I've seen before—you keep imagining this dark dude following you everywhere, just waiting for an opportunity to drop some horrible thing on your life and ruin everything, so you make him all big and real, and then you even give him a name—Nate (Next Accidental Terrible Experience)—and all the while you miss stuff, like how much people care about you, or how much you love rugby, your family, your girlfriend, and even (gross) your school, and how it might not be easy to let go of things that dragged you down in the past, even if it is possible to move on and, by doing so, let those things get more and more distant, and it only requires your willingness to allow those things to recede, but you're too stubborn, thinking about how horrible everything is, painting every wall in the house of your life the most terrible colors, even if all the good stuff that needs—deserves—your appreciation goes unnoticed?

Yeah. All that and more.

So in his senior year at Pine Mountain Academy, Ryan Dean West came to appreciate things that he'd tried to resist, and one of those things was *change*.

I couldn't remember ever sleeping as good as I slept that first night when Nico Cosentino moved into our dorm and Sam and I stayed up way too late with him watching TV and laughing about all kinds of ridiculous things. And the next day, which was a Sunday, I really appreciated the code and that Unit 113 was a ground-floor dorm room, because Nico took the Abernathy away for a couple hours (I asked him to do this) after Annie Altman came back from her trip home, and then Annie snuck in to my room through our permanently opened window, which I then promptly closed and covered.

Let me tell you how much I appreciated that. Well, to be honest, how much both of us—Annie and I—did.

Afterward, we lay together in my Princess Snugglewarm sheets and blankets, in a rickety bunk bed that was not long enough to contain my feet, and it was one of those warm and close moments between Annie and me that I wished would never end. But that wouldn't be a good thing, right? Because eventually we'd need to get up and go places and do more good things.

"I really appreciate this," I said.

Annie laughed. "I love you, Ryan Dean."

And I said, "I think things are going to be okay, Annie."

I started my senior year at Pine Mountain assuming that everything would be easy. It took me a long time to learn that the only reason things weren't easy for me was because of *me*—Ryan Dean West. Mrs. Dvorak helped me see that, but I would never have had the guts to talk to her in the first place if I didn't have friends like Sam Abernathy, Nico Cosentino, and, especially, Annie Altman.

I'm going to Berkeley next year. I checked, and there are other sixteen-year-old kids who'll be at Cal too. Imagine that—for the first time in my life I won't be an "only." Not that I care about that stuff anymore. In the long run, a guy has to grow up, right? And Annie got into Cal too. That guarantees we're going to be late more than a few times on turning in assignments, not that I even know if they make kids do actual *assignments* at Berkeley.

Sam Abernathy gets to be the "only" now. I'll miss living in the same refrigerator box with him and Nico, but I know that we'll always be friends, no matter how grown-up we all get, which is kind of gross and also something I never want to think about again—being bald and being used to everything, and not thinking anything at all is such a big deal. Who wants to be like that?

I know I'm not ready for it.

Rugby season ended in April. Pine Mountain came in second

place in the Pacific Northwest Rugby Football Union. So, rugby is all over for me. I can't imagine I'd ever be able to play at Cal. Have you ever seen their team? Huge and scary. So unless they're in the market for a winger who's a small and fast guy who's pretty much not afraid of getting smashed, my future in rugby is going to be sitting in the stands. To be honest, I was kind of happy that we came in second, because if we'd won the union, we would have had to go on to nationals, which meant I would have missed going to Pine Mountain's senior prom with Annie Altman.

The prom is tonight.

It's a kind of ridiculous affair, because our entire senior class has ninety-six kids in it, and I found out that there are only about thirty couples going to the prom. And no, we're not all girl-boy couples either. We may make a lot of cheese in Oregon, but we're pretty much above the bar when it comes to not paying too much attention to stuff that doesn't matter. But—*God!*—that could have been the thesis statement for my entire senior year, right?

"How do you even *know* how to tie a bow tie?" I ask.

All day, Nico and the Abernathy have been hovering around me, just watching me get ready. What else could they do, anyway? If one of us stands up in Unit 113, the other two can't even watch TV.

"I've been tying bow ties by myself since I was, like, seven," the Abernathy says.

"Which was what? Last month?"

"Do you want me to make it look nice or what, Ryan Dean?"

"Sorry, Sam. Don't choke me, dude."

"If you do choke him, I'll steal the tuxedo and take Annie to the prom," Nico says.

"Nice try, but you're a freshman," I say.

"Good point. But you're only four months older than me."

And the Abernathy brushes something away from my collar and says, "There. Done."

Nico peers down from his spot on the top bunk. "High five, bro."

I slap his hand, and then the Abernathy's little pink palm too.

"Thanks, Sam," I say.

"You're going to be late. Annie's probably already waiting, alone, by the door," Sam says.

The prom is in the sports complex.

Fancy.

"Never talk about my girlfriend again," I say, and Nico and Sam both laugh because they know all about what an ass I'd been. That's not cussing, right?

But the little tadpole is right: Annie probably *is* waiting, and I can't even begin to appreciate how grateful I am for all the waiting Annie Altman has invested in me.

At the door, I pause and look back at my friends. "In about six weeks, I'll be graduating." I shake my head. "What am I going to do without you guys?"

"One thing," Nico says, and then, making fun of me, adds, "Well, maybe two. First, you're not going to be *without us*, bro. And, second, dude, Annie Altman."

"Okay. Just don't eat all the popcorn before I come home tonight."

Because Sam is right, and Annie is waiting.

ANDREW SMITH

WINGER

'smart, poignant and entertaining . . . Smith's
funniest book by far' – *The New York Times*

He just wanted a decent book to read ...

Not too much to ask, is it? It was in 1935 when Allen Lane, Managing Director of Bodley Head Publishers, stood on a platform at Exeter railway station looking for something good to read on his journey back to London. His choice was limited to popular magazines and poor-quality paperbacks – the same choice faced every day by the vast majority of readers, few of whom could afford hardbacks. Lane's disappointment and subsequent anger at the range of books generally available led him to found a company – and change the world.

'We believed in the existence in this country of a vast reading public for intelligent books at a low price, and staked everything on it'
Sir Allen Lane, 1902–1970, founder of Penguin Books

The quality paperback had arrived – and not just in bookshops. Lane was adamant that his Penguins should appear in chain stores and tobacconists, and should cost no more than a packet of cigarettes.

Reading habits (and cigarette prices) have changed since 1935, but Penguin still believes in publishing the best books for everybody to enjoy. We still believe that good design costs no more than bad design, and we still believe that quality books published passionately and responsibly make the world a better place.

So wherever you see the little bird – whether it's on a piece of prize-winning literary fiction or a celebrity autobiography, political tour de force or historical masterpiece, a serial-killer thriller, reference book, world classic or a piece of pure escapism – you can bet that it represents the very best that the genre has to offer.

Whatever you like to read – trust Penguin.